The S

of

Joe Foster

Phillip Strang

BOOKS BY PHILLIP STRANG

Copyright Page

Dedication

For Elli and Tais who both had the perseverance to
make me sit down and write.

Chapter 1

"'And to my son, Tom, a man who has achieved as much as a rat in the gutter, I bequeath nothing",' the solicitor, Gerald Braxton, a small and balding man in his late seventies, read out. He was not pleased to be in a room with the Foster clan, a notorious crime family that had been led by Joe Foster, the father and former patriarch and, thankfully to many, dead. It was the dead man's will that he was reading.

Braxton looked around at those in the room.

To one side of the large table sat the late man's first wife, Gladys, a woman in her sixties, wearing clothes that were more suitable for someone younger: a skirt that was too short, a too-tight blouse that was peppered with cigarette ash.

To her right, the children she had borne to Joe. First, Terry, the eldest at forty-five, a man who had seen the inside of a prison cell, and then, to his right, Samantha, forty-three, with a strong resemblance to her mother, and Tom, two years younger than Samantha, an unkempt and dissolute individual, who Braxton reckoned wasn't too bright.

Samantha sat quietly, listening to every word the solicitor spoke. She was, Braxton judged, an intelligent woman, not given to rash decisions, but considered in her actions.

Two more children completed Joe and Gladys's side of the family: Billy, who at thirty-six years of age made a good living stealing luxury cars, and then shipping them off overseas, and to his right, at the end of the table, Ben. He was, Braxton knew, the only one of the first family who had not embraced crime; a man who at the age of thirty-four preferred his own company, apart from his live-in girlfriend, and held down a good job as a stockbroker.

'He can't do that,' Tom said. 'Not after what I did for him.'

'Shut up and listen for Mr Braxton to finish,' Samantha said.

'He's going to cut us off, leave us on the street,' Tom, incensed beyond reason, shouted.

Terry, overt with his violence and quick to temper, got up from his seat and walked over to where Tom was continuing to disrupt proceedings. With one slap from his right hand, firmly planted on the left-hand side of Tom's face, the man went quiet.

Braxton feared for his safety. After all, he hadn't wanted to be there, preferring to leave it to a junior partner, but none had been willing.

'Carry on,' Samantha said to Braxton, briefly casting a condescending look across to the other side of the table, at Emily, her father's second wife, and what were, to Samantha, two children of dubious blood.

Emily, at forty-one, younger than Joe and Gladys's two eldest, with blonde peroxide hair and a figure that men lusted after, just smiled back at her.

After all, she was the prize of a successful man. Tired of his ageing wife and her coarse habits and excited at the promise of hidden delights and endless passion with a younger woman, Joe had married her twenty-one years previously. To Emily's left, her twenty-year-old, Gary, and nineteen-year-old Kate.

They were, Braxton could see, chalk to the cheese of the dead man's first family, although he knew appearances could be deceptive. Compared to the violence of Terry, the scheming of Samantha, the stupidity of Tom, the criminality of Billy and the smartness of Ben, very little was known about the second family.

Braxton continued to read the will, aware of the seething hatred that existed between the two families. "'To Billy, a man who knows the value of money, I bequeath my Mercedes.'"

'At least the man has done me right,' Billy said.

'What do you mean?' Terry said from the other end of the table. 'You steal them all the time.'

Emily Foster sat quietly, saying nothing, as did her two children. She had raised them well, Ben Foster knew, the only member of the first family to recognise that his father had chosen well. And whereas Emily had used her physical assets well, she hadn't squandered them since.

But then, to him, Emily, his widowed stepmother, was still attractive, and now free. Depending on how the cards played, he could see himself with the woman, from father to son.

"'To my son, Ben, a man to be proud of, I give him my best wishes and the proceeds of the sale of an apartment that was acquired legally, to dispose of in the same manner,'" Braxton said.

'Is that it? Best wishes?' Samantha said. 'And what about me?'

'In due course. Everyone is mentioned.'

Ben Foster sat with his arms folded. He had neither expected anything nor did he want it. After all, his father's wealth had come from crime.

"'To Terry, I bequeath the three pubs, for him to dispose of or to keep, or to drink himself into oblivion.'"

'Fair enough,' Terry said.

"'To my first wife, Gladys, a woman who has raised five of my children, making a poor job of it, apart from Ben and possibly Samantha, I give her the house in Notting Hill, and a cash amount of three hundred thousand pounds. Hopefully, she will use it wisely.'"

'He's forgotten me,' Samantha said, more agitated than before.

Braxton ignored her and continued to drone on. "'To my daughter, Samantha, a clever woman, I give my stocks and shares, a conservative value of four hundred thousand pounds.'"

Samantha leant back on her chair, pleased with the outcome.

Braxton looked over at Emily. "'To my second wife, Emily, knowing that she will ensure that our two children, Gary and Kate, will continue to make us both proud, I give three million pounds, as well as the house in Holland Park.'"

'That's not fair,' Samantha said.

'If you'll wait,' Braxton said, 'there's more.'

Gladys Foster took a cigarette out of a packet and put it into her mouth. She cast a steely glance over at Emily.

'He did right by us,' Gary Foster said to his mother, Emily.

Braxton continued. 'There is one condition of the will.'

'What's that? Terry asked.

'I'll read it *ad verbum*: "All those assembled have been treated fairly without prejudice. However, there is one condition."'

'That's Joe,' Gladys said as she blew a smoke ring over towards Emily.

'"The bastard who killed me gets nothing."'

'What?' Samantha, the first to speak.

'It seems, Miss Foster,' Braxton said, 'that your father foresaw his death at the hand of his family. How and why I'm not privy to, however, I must adhere to what he has stated. Someone in this room killed Joe Foster, and he has made it clear what will happen.'

'Is there any more?' Emily asked.

'There is.'

'Hurry up, we haven't got all day,' Samantha said.

'"Whereas Terry, by seniority of age, takes on the mantle of leadership of the Foster empire, he is there for as long as he can hold it. I, Joe Foster, maintained control through sheer determination, hard work and the appropriate use of violence. If he can maintain control, then it is his. If he can't, it will go to either Tom, although I believe he's too stupid, to Billy if he wants it, or to Ben, smart enough to do me proud, but too honest to be interested. In short, some of you may die; some will succeed.

'"As for Emily, Gary and Kate, there will be no animosity directed against them. Any digression and that person's inheritance is null and void."'

'Leave them alone,' Gladys said after Braxton had spoken an additional condition of his will. 'The bitch can have what Joe gave her.'

'I don't want a part of it,' Ben said.

'It's favouritism,' Samantha said. 'That man has turned us against each other.'

'Has he?' Gladys said. 'He knew what would happen after his death, and maybe one of us murdered him. Accept the will for what it is, and as for the bitch across from me, leave her alone. When her breasts are down around her waist, Ben won't be lusting after her.'

'I dispute that,' Ben said.

'Don't play the innocent with me. You're eyeing her up in here, wondering how long it is before she's flat on her back, you on top.'

'I believe that concludes our meeting here today,' Braxton said as he stood up, took hold of his briefcase and walked out of the door. For today, he had had enough of them.

Chapter 2

Thirty-six hours previously, the day had started routinely, with the team assembled in Homicide. Detective Chief Inspector Isaac Cook, who was fretting about his wife, and DI Larry Hill, anxious for a drink as it had been ten days since alcohol had passed his lips., and Sergeant Wendy Gladstone and Bridget Halloran, Homicide's internet and computer aficionado, two women unlike in many ways, but the best of friends. Wendy, widowed two years previously, her two sons married with children of their own, and Bridget, on her own, occasionally meeting up with an old boyfriend, or someone new. The two of them were always planning where their next holiday would be. They had already been to Greece and Italy, although no one had pinched Wendy's bottom, much to her dismay, although they had Bridget's.

Wendy favoured Croatia for the next vacation; Bridget had a hankering for Spain, although it wasn't an issue for either of them. Wherever they ended up, there would be a lot of laughing, a lot more drinking, and a great deal of fun.

It was early in the afternoon when the call came through, a shooting in Notting Hill, a man on the ground, an ambulance on its way, a crowd of onlookers with their smartphones. The man's body shown around the world before Isaac Cook and Larry Hill arrived. The man had been declared dead, two gunshots: one to the chest, the other to the head.

Whoever had shot the man had been thorough, Isaac and Larry could see. After all, Joe Foster was well known in the area by the police and by the villains. If he had lived or had had time to say who had shot him, then their lives would be forfeit soon enough.

Spanish John, a local gang leader, someone that Larry had shared more than a few pints of beer with and who Isaac knew from his school days, had sidled up alongside the two of them.

'What goes around, comes around,' the gangster, tall, black and eloquent, said.

'Not a sad day for you,' Larry said.

'Not for you either.'

The three men, united by crime, looked down at Joe Foster, remembered what he had been, the trouble he had caused, the deaths that had been attributed to him, not that he had ever wielded the knife or pulled the gun's trigger.

'What's the word on the street?' Larry asked.

'Early days, but it's tense. News travels fast, especially when Joe Foster is shot,' Spanish John said. 'A power play for control, scores to be settled.'

'A chance for you to wrest control of Foster's more dubious business ventures,' Isaac said.

'Not me. I prefer to stay on the right side of the police.'

Joe Foster, a devoted family man to both of his families, a vicious gangster to others, had two sides to him, as well as a case file six inches thick in Homicide, or if Bridget was doing the telling, five gigabytes of memory.

'He could have chosen a better place to get shot,' Gordon Windsor, the senior crime scene investigator, said as he stood up from the body and came out of the crime scene tent.

Isaac concurred. He was the son of Jamaican immigrants who had come to England in the sixties. His parent's home city, Kingston, the capital of Jamaica, luxury interspersed with soul-grinding poverty and despair, one of the murder capitals of the world, was worse than London for violent crime. However London, especially where he headed up Homicide at Challis Street Police Station, was getting worse. Certain corners of the city were areas of lawlessness where the police moved in groups of three or only drove. No-go zones, not mentioned by any politician, but they existed, and Notting Hill, in Holland Park, down through Paddington and Bayswater, over to the northern perimeter and then down into Kensington, not far from one of the royal palaces, were all experiencing an upsurge in wanton acts of crime and random stabbings.

The more optimistic would believe that Foster's death would lead to a less violent neighbourhood, but Isaac Cook, born in the area, did not believe it would. He was, after all, a realist, knowing full well that a vacant space does not remain empty for long. Someone would fill the void, and whether it was one of the man's family, or Spanish John making a play for the position, or another gangster, it would be violent. And whoever had committed the murder was marked. He would soon be dead, an act of retribution, a sacrificial lamb, or else in prison.

'Any ideas? Larry asked Spanish John.

'None at all, other than his family. You know Terry Foster, don't you?'

'I do. What about the others?'

'You better ask them.'

Windsor pulled Isaac off to one side. 'It was point-blank, the last shot. You must have witnesses,' he said.

Isaac knew there would be, but whether they would talk, that was another matter.

***

Wendy Gladstone busied herself with the door-to-door, although she didn't expect anyone to say much. After all, it wasn't Holland Park or Bayswater, but a street not far from Portobello Road, where the affluent and those in council-owned housing with subsidised rents kept apart, and both groups minded their own business for different reasons. The affluent, mainly because they were often not in the area, either at work or travelling; those at the lower end of the social divide had other issues to worry about: lack of jobs, underlying racial discrimination.

For Isaac, a concern that he should be at home with his wife, Jenny, who was struggling, needing her husband to spend time with her and the baby as he had promised, and now another murder, and the balance between his vocation and his wife was wreaking its havoc. He did not want to disappoint his wife, not again, but he knew he would.

Chief Superintendent Goddard had even told him to take time off, to leave the running of the department to Detective Inspector Larry Hill, or for another DCI to be brought in at short notice, but Isaac had known the man was only saying it for effect.

If it had been quiet, no murders to deal with, then, yes, Larry could have looked after Homicide, but with Joe Foster murdered, the situation would need his experience as a senior investigating officer, his knowledge of the area. And besides, someone from another police station, his feet underneath Isaac's desk, a successful conclusion to the murder investigation, and that person wouldn't be so easy to shift.

Given the opportunity, Isaac would savour a promotion out of Homicide to superintendent, and an increase in his salary, but his career had stalled. Once the golden boy of the London Metropolitan Police, the future of the organisation, the meteoric rise from constable to sergeant and then inspector, his face on promotions for applicants to join the diverse, equal opportunity employer, he was now largely ignored by those in senior management.

A commotion at the murder scene, the arrival of the grieving widow, caused Isaac to move from where he was standing.

'Mrs Foster, Detective Chief Inspector Isaac Cook, Challis Street Homicide,' Isaac said, interceding as the woman remonstrated with a flustered constable not sure how to respond to the dead man's second wife.

'It's my husband. I have a right to see him.'

'I would agree; however, I can't allow it, not here,' Isaac said.

'I just heard. Is it true what they're saying, that he has been shot?'

'Unfortunately, Mrs Foster, that's true.'

The natural reaction of the widowed or related, heard so many times. 'Why? He hadn't an enemy in the world.'

An involuntary response, Isaac knew, not dealing with the reality, not addressing the fact that Joe Foster had lived by violence, died by it.

Even the West Indian gangs had been careful to give him space when he had been alive, but then, Joe Foster was not just a local villain. He had been national, controlling as he did the distribution of drugs throughout the UK: importing cocaine from South America and heroin from Afghanistan, as well as the laboratory production of ice and ecstasy and their variants.

The case files on the dead man were extensive, the criminal convictions negligible. The man had moved with impunity, and always with a couple of heavies to protect him, yet that day he had died alone.

Intimidation had played a large part in Joe Foster's criminal activities, the reason he had never stood up in court to answer for his crimes, although his first-born had. Terry wasn't as shrewd as the father, a man who drank little, and he got drunk more often than he should. With his temper unchecked and his actions not considered, he had put a few men in hospital, seriously maiming one, finding himself in prison for grievous bodily harm.

Emily Foster sat down on the pavement, a young woman of nineteen with her. Isaac knew that she was Kate, Joe and Emily's daughter, an educated woman from a stable and loving family home, which seemed a contradiction given her father's reputation. She and her mother shed tears for a man who was more of a rogue than a saint.

But then, children and loved ones often don't see the reality, their lives tempered by love. However, now that the man was dead, a lot of the truths would be revealed. How that would affect the young woman and her brother was to be seen, although the family of the first wife would not suffer the conflict of divided loyalty between a loving father and a gangster. None of them had ever been under any illusion.

Chapter 3

In death, saint or sinner, they all looked the same to the pathologist.

The cause of death wasn't in dispute, the gunshot wound to the chest visible, the gunshot through the man's temple under a congealed mess of dried blood and hair.

'A heavy smoker?' the pathologist, a man known for his lack of humour, said as he commenced his autopsy.

'He was,' Wendy said. 'Do the gun wounds tell you anything?'

'The first shot would have killed him. The second one is more dramatic. Someone who's watched too many American blood and guts movies, probably.'

'Violent death is only too common these days.'

From the other room, a woman's voice, louder than it should have been. Wendy left and went to check, only to find Emily Foster arguing with one of the Pathology Department's staff.

'It's not possible,' Wendy said. 'And why are you here?'

'We cared for him, my children and I, and now *she's* saying that I don't have any rights.'

'By *she*, I assume you mean Gladys Foster?'

'Who else?'

'Is it her decision? You were married to him.'

'You know Joe, who he was, what he was?'

'I do, but it doesn't explain why you're here.'

'There was good in Joe,' Emily Foster said.

13

Wendy had seen enough of the autopsy; Joe Foster's wife was of more interest, especially as she was willing to talk about her life and her husband, and what she thought of the first wife, Gladys.

'Tell me about your husband,' Wendy said. A busy restaurant wasn't the ideal place to conduct an interview, but it was close by, and the hubbub of the other customers was loud enough for the two women to speak without being overheard.

'Devoted to the children, always treated me well. I know what they said about him, but he never once raised a hand to me, rarely got upset with the children, and Gary could be difficult. Nothing illegal, but he liked a drink, they all do when they're in their teens.'

'Your husband?'

A waitress came over, put two plates on the table. 'Your order,' she said. 'It's meant to be picked up at the counter, but seeing that you're busy.'

'Surly bitch,' Wendy said, which caused Emily to laugh.

'It looks okay,' Emily said as she looked at the pasta on the plate in front of her.

'Your husband had enemies,' Wendy said as she ate her meal.

'He's dead; there's not much you can do to him, so I suppose it's alright to admit that he did.'

'Why are you concerned that Gladys Foster will cheat you? And what did you hope to gain at the pathologist's?'

'I wasn't thinking. His second family cared for him, not the first, and as for Gladys, a nasty piece of work.'

'Emily, let me be frank,' Wendy said. 'Your husband had a terrifying reputation, and from what we know, his sons have inherited his traits, at least Terry has.'

'Don't forget Samantha.'

'For yourself and your children, what do you expect could happen?'

'Joe loved us more than he did the others. We were the aura of respectability, something he wanted to portray.'

'But failed to achieve. Everyone knew your husband for what he was.'

'I know, and now Gladys and her children will fight for Joe's wealth.'

'Do your children know the truth about their father?'

'Gary and Kate do to some extent, although they don't know the full story. Nor would I expect them to.'

'But you do?'

'I don't think anybody knows it all, and besides, it wasn't something Joe and I ever discussed. When he was with the children and me, no mention of where the money came from.'

'You married Joe when you were a lot younger.'

'I was ambitious, determined to better myself; easier than I should have been. But Joe, he was a good-looking man back then, made me change, and then with Gary and Kate, I forgot what I had been, never once unfaithful, never looked at another man.'

'Did you screw around in your teens, before you met Joe?'

'More than I should.'

The waitress came over, took hold of the two plates. 'A dessert?' she said.

Emily declined; Wendy chose cheesecake.

'Why were you at the pathologist's?' Wendy returned to her questioning.

'I'm frightened, not sure what to do. I suppose I wanted to see Joe for reassurance. I know that sounds silly, but with his death, there's a power vacuum, and Terry and Samantha frighten me.'

'But why? Why bother with you?'

'A chance to exact revenge. I took their father away from their mother. The two of them will use threats and coercion, force if they must.'

'Against you and your children?'

'Against anyone, against each other.'

'The others?'

'Tom's a hopeless case. He'll take whatever he can, waste it on alcohol and drugs, but he'll cause no trouble. Billy's not around much, up to no good, no doubt.'

'Ben, the youngest?'

'I'm not sure. Ben's more intelligent than the others. I've always believed him to be honest.'

'Any ideas?'

'Not really. Ben's a strange character, more charming than the others, but deep. You can never be sure with him, whether he's biding his time or not. With Joe alive, he wouldn't have stood a chance, and Terry's violent, not frightened to use it.'

'If Ben wants to be involved in the business, he'll have to deal with the others. Your children, interested in becoming part of the action?' Wendy asked.

'Not mine, but Ben could.'

'Someone shoots your husband in broad daylight, yet no one comes forward with any information. Doesn't that strike you as strange?'

'People are scared.'

'Of what could happen?'

'As I told you, I never discussed his business with Joe, but people speak. I learnt most of what I know from others, harmless gossip. Ben used to come around the house; the others didn't.'

'To see his father?'

'That's what he said, but he used to look me up and down.'

'Liked what he saw?'

'I expect him to make a play for me when the dust has settled.'

'Receptive?'

'I devoted myself to Joe and our children. No other man interests me, not now.'

***

Gladys Foster made her presence known at Challis Street two days after Joe Foster's death, a day after Wendy had spoken to Emily, six hours after the reading of Joe Foster's will. Compared to Emily, Gladys was a disappointing woman, lacking in the qualities that made the second wife endearing.

'Thanks for coming in,' Isaac said. 'This must be a distressing time.'

'He died as he had lived,' Gladys said, lighting up a cigarette, even if the rules in the police station forbade it. Isaac decided to ignore the violation.

'By violence?'

'Yes.'

'Why are you here?'

'You would get around to me soon enough. It's easier to preempt, ask you to leave us alone to grieve.'

Wendy, who sat to one side of Isaac, couldn't see any sign of grieving. Apart from dressing in black, Gladys

Foster looked the same as she always did: a sullen look on her face, bright-red lipstick, too much mascara, fingernails stained with nicotine.

Wendy didn't mean to be too critical; after all, she had been a heavy smoker in the past. But in the room, looking at Gladys, reflecting on the meeting with Emily, she could see that the choice for Joe would not have been difficult to make. And it was true what the second wife had said, the children of Joe and Gladys were a disparate lot, ranging from the hit-without-thinking Terry, through the calculating Samantha, and then Tom and Billy, down to the honest and hardworking Ben.

'Are you grieving, Mrs Foster?' Wendy said.

'Call me Gladys, everyone else does.'

'I met with Emily.'

'In her teens, when Joe met her; a man in his forties should have known better. But then you know men, fresh meat and the tongue's hanging out. If you want me to sit here and tell you what a good man he was, how he'll be sorely missed, you'll be waiting a long time.'

'We didn't expect that,' Wendy said.

'What are you doing to find out who killed him?'

'Statistically, his murderer is someone close to him,' Isaac said.

'It wasn't one of us; I know that. None of us is stupid enough, and besides, we've got control of his assets. Whoever shot him did us a favour.'

So much for the grieving, Wendy thought.

'Your eldest, Terry, is a violent man,' Isaac said.

'He's not stupid, even if he's got a temper. Not that he cared for his father, hated him.'

'Because of his upbringing?'

'After he took off with *her*, he made sure we had a roof over our heads, money in the bank.'

'Terry's hatred of his father?' Isaac said.

'Joe kept him out of the business, apart from letting him run one of the pubs, keeping an eye on the strip joints. Terry hated him for that, but Joe was tough, reckoned that Terry wasn't capable of more.'

'It's difficult juggling all the facets of a criminal empire.'

'He started with crime, legitimised his businesses.'

'Was his leaving you and taking up with Emily part of the process?' Wendy asked.

'He left me for a tight arse and a pretty face, nothing more.'

'Do you hate her?'

'What do you reckon?'

'It would be a normal reaction.'

'Hate, no. But I believe she cheated our children out of a father. At nineteen years of age, I would have given her a run for her money, a real beauty back then.'

Wendy studied the woman's features, agreed with Gladys. In her youth, she had been attractive, and so would have Gladys Foster, both fresh-faced, desirable to men, the bane of their parents with their wanton ways. However, Gladys still smoked, and maintained an unhealthy lifestyle to the detriment of her physical appearance. In contrast, five years without a cigarette had allowed Wendy to regain colour in her cheeks, a sprightlier step.

'Does Terry intend to take over Joe's interests?' Isaac asked.

'He's the oldest.'

'Samantha? What does she intend to do?'

'Consolidate what there is.'

'Joe's death has been fortuitous for the Fosters.'

'If that means, are we glad he's dead, then we aren't. Life goes on, and someone's got to pick up the pieces while you try to find his murderer.'

'Those people might be after whoever follows Joe.'

'Joe made enemies.'

Isaac wasn't sure what to make of the situation. 'Joe would have made more than most,' he said.

'We need to come to terms with his death, to get on with it.'

'And to agree to a truce with Emily?' Wendy said.

'If we meet, we'll be polite, nothing more. I'm sure you can understand that.'

'We can.'

'We'll need to interview your offspring,' Isaac said.

'Do what you must, but don't expect any more from them than you got from me,' Gladys said.

Chapter 4

The extent of Joe Foster's empire started to reveal itself. Apart from the three public houses, a couple of massage parlours and a gentlemen's club in Bayswater, there was a lot more to Foster's activities.

Bridget sat in the office researching the man, not only what was already known by the police, but what was suspected. Larry was out on the street or, in his case, in the pub.

'He scared me,' Harry Gibson, one of Larry's informers, said.

The two men had been drinking pals for a long time, although the information from Gibson had never proved to be of much worth.

'Why? What had he ever done to you? It's not as if you haven't enough villains around here,' Larry said.

'Villains you can see, but Joe Foster kept himself to himself, apart from when he came to the pub with his wife.'

'Emily?'

'The good-looking one.'

'You fancied her?'

'Who didn't around here, but Foster, he knew that. Make one wrong move, look at her sideways, or even smile at her, and you'd be in trouble.'

'Anyone we know?'

'No one in particular, but Foster was possessive of her, not that you can blame him.'

'He was a devoted family man, never involved Emily and her children in crime,' Larry said as he downed what remained of his second pint of beer.

'She would have known, and I'm not saying he wasn't what you said, but she wasn't stupid. She must have known what was going on.'

'Should she? After all, his pubs were bringing in good money, as were the massage parlours and the gentleman's club. None of them strictly illegal, although we have our suspicions.'

'Foster wouldn't have been so stupid.'

'What makes you so sure?'

'He wouldn't have risked anything with those businesses.'

'Those?' Larry said as he handed over another pint to Gibson. 'Are you intimating there are more?'

'I'll not tell you, not with Terry Foster making himself a nuisance.'

'Anything we should know about?'

'I'm not saying, not now. I'm rather partial to my life.'

Larry put a hand in his jacket pocket, withdrew an envelope and passed it over.

'Joe Foster was involved in drugs, but you'd know that,' Gibson said as he stuffed the envelope into his jacket's inside pocket.

'We did, but never proof, or not enough to charge him,' Larry said.

'Terry's not as smart as his father, and he's more visible.'

'He's the natural heir to Foster's empire.'

'Joe was a decent enough person, remembered his roots, but Terry, he's bad news.'

'Violent, a quick temper,' Larry said. 'It's got him into trouble a few times.'

'Joe had others involved in his businesses, but some of them aren't too keen on Terry, see him as a loose cannon.'

'Names?'

'I don't know, not them.'

Another envelope, another pint of beer and the tongue continued to loosen, more loudly than it should have, Gibson's voice carrying across the pub.

'Keep it down,' Larry said. He was on his fourth pint, an occupational hazard, although his wife didn't see it that way. But she was a conservative woman who was careful in her diet, and she exercised every day.

When they had first met, he used to run every day, but now, middle-age spread, a blotchy complexion, and out of breath after the slightest exertion. He had tried, even stopped drinking alcohol for two months at one stage, but as the beer went down his throat in the pub, it was heaven to him.

'Talk to Jacob Morgan,' Gibson said, his voice lower than before.

'I've not heard the name mentioned before,' Larry said.

'That's why you should talk to him. He's got an office down in Hammersmith, pretends to be an accountant, file your tax return for you.'

'But he was involved with Joe?'

'Financial adviser, supposedly, but Terry's been to see him.'

'Friendly?'

'With Terry? If Morgan's got the dirt on the Fosters, Terry wouldn't like it.'

'And Terry's arrogant enough to reckon he can go it alone.'

'Nobody can,' Gibson said as he pushed his empty glass forward.

'How do you know so much?' Larry asked.

'I keep my ear to the ground.'

It wasn't a satisfactory answer, but Larry knew that prying into how a man of little consequence, a street hustler, could know so much was not that important.

***

The fear, four days after the murder, was of a gang war, and not the usual, the West Indians fighting in dark alleys or on vacant blocks of land close to the canal. It would be more sophisticated, as the smarter villains vied for control, removing people who got in the way, threatening others.

Joe Foster had been a cut above the rest, and in Holland Park, where he had lived with Emily, those who did not know the man would have thought him to have been a successful businessman, a banker or a doctor.

Isaac stood outside the three-storied terrace house. A phone call from Emily had summoned him. Wendy was on her way, and he'd wait for her before knocking on the front door. He looked around the area, said hello to a woman walking by, a small dog on a lead. He reflected on the house he had bought with Jenny, a place befitting of a detective chief inspector. The suburb of Holland Park, and definitely Joe Foster's home, was too expensive for him, but he liked what he saw.

Inside the house, Wendy having arrived after five minutes, Isaac sat to one side of the living room, Wendy to the other, and Emily was standing up.

'Gladys has been here,' Emily said.

'Any reason for us to worry?' Isaac asked.

'I felt uneasy, as if she was prying.'

'Start from the beginning,' Wendy said.

'It was two hours ago. She knocked on the door, didn't wait for me to invite her in, just barged through.'

'She's not strong on etiquette,' Isaac said. 'Was it bad manners or hostile?'

'She wanted to talk, and as she said, to clear the air.'

'But you've got nothing on her, only that you want you and your children to be left alone, enough money to live.'

'She's worried that I might do something. That Joe had told me things she should know.'

'Terry's been making a nuisance of himself, starting to throw his weight around,' Isaac said.

'Joe didn't have a lot of time for him, reckoned the man didn't have the discipline for leadership. He thought Samantha was a better bet, his only concern was that she was crude, and one thing he believed in more than anything else was good manners, for a person to hold their head high, to dress well at all times.'

'Samantha?' Wendy said.

'I can't say I know her that well. None of his first family came to our wedding. I can understand that, although Joe thought they were wrong. He gave them all a good telling off a week later.'

'Why wouldn't they come?'

'Terry, out of anger, Samantha, just to be bloody-minded, moral support for her mother, not that Gladys had any reason to be upset.'

'Why?' Isaac asked.

'Their marriage was over when I hooked up with Joe. I wasn't a bit of fluff on the side, a mistress. When I met him, they were separated, and Joe was living on his own in this house, but no doubt, Gladys will tell you a different story.'

'So far, we've credited you with telling us the truth,' Wendy said. 'If you've been feeding us lies, it'll go against you.'

'I've not, but Gladys believes that I was the reason for her marriage breakdown, but I wasn't.'

'Yet you, Emily, young and virginal, had all the attributes to turn a rich man's head.'

'I wasn't the second of those, but I suppose it might have looked that way. And I wasn't looking to get married, certainly not to an older man. I was enjoying myself, a good group of friends.'

'Men?' Isaac asked.

'Not only men, although I had a few boyfriends, knew about the birds and the bees, but Joe was special. He knew how to treat a woman.'

'You didn't concern yourself that he could have been married and that there were children?'

'I took his word that he wasn't married, and it was true. I used to get hit on by older men all the time, but I could tell when they were lying, and besides, I never went out with any of them.'

'Why him?'

'There was something about him. I can't say what.'

'Gladys?' Isaac reminded Emily of the reason for their visit.

'I told her that I knew nothing, which was the truth.'

'But you suspected certain things?'

'Not really. I didn't interest myself with Joe's business. The money came into the house, and it provided for myself and the children, ensuring they had a good upbringing, a decent education. Gary's at university, studying law, and Kate wants to be a doctor. Joe was proud of them.'

'His other children?'

'He told me that as he grew older, the need for his children to follow him in the business wasn't that important, and that was probably true, if he hadn't died prematurely, had had a chance to divest himself of what he had, convert it to cash.'

'You said you didn't know what he was up to.'

'I didn't, not really, but sometimes we'd talk. Sure, he was skirting the edge, and I was careful not to mention the massage parlours, nor the strip joints and the gentleman's club, to my friends, although one or two of them had found out.'

'Did they forsake the friendship as a result?'

'My friends are better than that. And besides, everyone's got things they would rather not be known. Mine is that my husband was a gangster.'

'Are you willing to admit that now?' Wendy asked.

'I thought I already had, the day he died. Joe's dead, and Gladys is raking over old coals, accusing me of this and that.'

'Did she threaten you?'

'Not openly, just told me that she intended to wreak her revenge for what I had done to her. For some reason, she had believed that she and Joe would get back together again, but he had no intention. He had bettered himself; she had not. One had risen in class; the other was content to stay where she had come from, although she appreciated the money, but not what it could bring. No designer clothes for her, although she would take off to the Caribbean for six weeks every year, no doubt found a man down there to keep her company.'

'Did she?'

'Ben told me she did, but with him, you can never tell whether he's telling the truth or not.'

'Has he been around?'

'Not yet, but he will soon enough. The man's incorrigible, and there is a certain earthy charm about him. But believe me, he hasn't a chance.'

'That's the second time you've said that,' Wendy reminded Emily.

'It needs repeating. Joe's son, I couldn't. It's almost incestuous. It feels that way to me.'

'Why are we here?'Isaac said.

'Gladys, after her ranting and raving, calmed down, spoke to me as a friend, not as a rival.'

'Do you like her?'

'Not a lot, but she was married to Joe; I have to respect her for that, grant her some indulgence. She told me that Terry's aiming to take over Joe's empire and that he's a vengeful man. Not sure why she warned me, but I got the feeling she didn't have a lot of time for him, although she did for Samantha and Ben.'

'The other two, Tom and Billy?'

'Tom's not amounted to much, and Billy's a rogue and not the lovable variety.'

'We're Homicide. What he gets up to is another department's responsibility.'

'It's Gary and Kate. I'm worried that they'll become pawns in Terry's game. That he'll use them to get to me.'

'Violent?'

'I don't know, and I'm worried. Gladys wanted to tell me more, but she couldn't. After all, Terry's her son, and she wouldn't have been able to act against his interests. If she had to choose between my children and hers, she'd choose hers.'

'Motherly instincts,' Wendy said.

'We can't give you protection,' Isaac said.

'I know, but you need to know. Terry's going to cause trouble, and I worry for my children. They've done nothing, nor have I, but Terry's dangerous and possibly irrational. So much power, it could go to his head.'

'Phone Wendy or me at any time. If Terry comes here, let us know.'

'If he does, I'm not sure I'll be capable of phoning after that.'

The woman was frightened, although why and for what reason, neither of them knew. If, as Emily Foster had said, she was an innocent, then why would Terry Foster frighten her; why had his mother warned her.

Trouble was brewing.

Chapter 5

'Ben, this can't be,' Emily said as she pushed him away, after he had arrived at her house at nine in the evening. 'Joe, your father, not even cold. It's impossible, always will be.'

She was losing her temper as he tried to kiss her, and although she was a lot smaller than her attacker, she was tenacious, and kneed the enamoured man in the groin.

'Why? I wasn't going to do anything against your wishes,' Ben said. 'It's just that I love you, and you need someone on your side to defend you against the family.'

That much was true, Emily knew.

'Ben, if you ever try that again, you'll regret it.'

Ben started to cry. It wasn't the first time he had professed love, but it was the first time he had acted on his impulses, and she hadn't liked it. Before Joe, there had been other men, drunk as she had been, who had forced her into sex. Those had been rape, but the police hadn't been interested, one female officer going so far as to say that she was asking for it with her short skirt and tight top, and drunk.

And whereas alcohol no longer interested her, she still dressed provocatively. On one occasion, tired of the wolf whistles and the eyes of those mentally undressing her, she had gone out with no makeup and wearing a conservative dress and shoes. She hadn't enjoyed the experience, felt naked, more vulnerable than she had before.

It wasn't exhibitionism to her, just the need to look the best she could. As Ben sat on a chair, clutching his groin, Emily had to give a smile, at the thought of what he would think of her if she was naked, as he wanted. The realisation that under the clothing and the makeup was a woman in her forties, the breasts pumped up but starting to sag, the stretch marks, the bulging hips, and what had been firm but tender to the touch was now giving way to age. Another fifteen to twenty years, she would be like Gladys, Ben's mother, a woman who had been attractive once, but wasn't now.

First, the mother, now the son. Who next was going to knock on her door, Emily wondered. She knew of one certainty: she missed her husband. The future, whatever it was to be, was intractably linked to the other Fosters. She needed an ally.

'I'm sorry,' Ben said after Emily had given him a cup of tea.

'Why did you do that?"

'I want you, Emily. I want to take the place of my father in your life.'

'Your family, what now for you?'

The situation was calmer. Emily was confident the man wouldn't repeat his unfortunate behaviour again that day; after all, apart from his fixation, he had always been polite to her.

Emily, even though she had been careful with what she had told the police, knew of her husband's business interests, snippets garnered over the years.

Even he, as much as she loved him, never saw beyond the pretty face, never saw the real person, assumed that intelligence and beauty were mutually incompatible. She knew that she turned a man's head, and when younger, it had served her well, but now it was time for her intelligence to take control.

'Emily, you can't trust any of them, only me,' Ben said.

'I'm not sure I can trust you, and besides, why are they interested in me?'

'You took their father, my mother's husband.'

'Why blame me?'

'The Fosters acquire, never allow anyone or anything to take from them, and you cheated them out of my father.'

'I never did,' Emily said.

'I know that, but they don't. I'm different to them, always wanted to do something better. What's the use of money in a bank account, assets in a safe? You can't eat them or live in them; all you can do it to look at them from time to time. It's the same as a cellar full of expensive wines that you can't drink, frightened that if one bottle is drunk, you've somehow devalued the rest.'

'I've always given you more credit than them,' Emily said, 'but your behaviour here, in my house, is unforgivable.'

'It won't happen again, I promise.'

'Ben, we'll look out for each other, for Gary and Kate. I don't want for much,' Emily said. 'Terry and your mother might not believe that, but Samantha would.'

'I don't want any of it, only you.'

'Ben, stop it. It can't happen, never will.'

Emily Foster was nervous after Ben had left, not only for herself but for her two children. 'Why, oh why, Joe, did you have to go and get yourself shot,' she said out loud.

***

Behind a large monitor and a keyboard, Jacob Morgan, a short, rotund man, his head barely above the level of the tabletop, was slumped in a well-worn brown leather chair when Isaac and Larry entered. If this was the man of importance that Harry Gibson had mentioned, then his initial impression was wrong, Larry thought. To him, the man had a peculiarly Dickensian look about him, a latter-day and overweight Bob Cratchit, Tiny Tim's father, but older and without the humour.

'Mr Morgan,' Larry said. 'Detective Chief Inspector Cook, Detective Inspector Hill, Challis Street Homicide.'

'I thought you'd be here at some time. Who's been talking?'

'You'll not deny your relationship with Joe Foster?'

Morgan continued to type, not looking at either Isaac and Larry, only at the monitor occasionally.

'Relationship? The man came to me for financial advice for which I charged him plenty, invoices if you want to see them,' Morgan said.

'That's not necessary, not now,' Isaac said.

'Good, save me trying to find them. Make this quick and then get out of here.'

'A hostile attitude won't help,' Larry said. He had taken a seat to one side of the stuffy room, a heater on full blast under Morgan's desk, a view out of one window at a brick wall.

'Joe Foster's dead,' Morgan said. 'I didn't kill him, and his death doesn't concern me either way, although the money came in handy.'

'For what?'

'If you're referring to my office, I don't spend money on wasted assets. A fancy office conveys a sense of well-being and expertise to the desperate, but means nothing to the astute.'

If the man was eccentric, with a unique outlook on life, it didn't matter to Isaac and Larry; after all, London was notorious for its colourful characters.

'Joe Foster's murdered, your name's mentioned,' Isaac said. 'Circumstantial, or is there any more to it? After all, we've not heard of you before.'

'No reason to. I mind my own business; advise whoever pays, not partial as to whether they're honest and honourable or not.'

'This advice, was it related to his criminal empire?'

'Hardly. It doesn't pay to become involved, not in my position. Foster, not sure if it's any of your business, was interested in selling up large parts of his assets, setting up trust funds for his children.'

'Which children?'

'Gary and Kate. I assume you've met them.'

'Not yet, although we have the mother.'

'The lovely Emily,' Morgan sarcastically said.

'You don't like her?'

'I can't say I know her, not that well. She was here once a few years back, witnessed some documents, acted as a signatory on a legal document.'

'Surely he would have used a lawyer for that,' Larry said.

'Foster chose his friends carefully. He could trust me, not some money-grabbing lawyer, and besides, I've got a law degree, enough to advise him.'

'Were you a friend?'

'A friend of Joe? Someone you can trust implicitly? If that's your criteria, then yes, I was. Not social, mind you, no time for that. In some ways, Foster

was hard to understand; loyal to his family, even those he
didn't like.'

'Terry?'

'You've heard the adage: talk quietly, carry a big
stick?' Morgan said, more agreeably than when they had
first entered his office.

'Are you saying Joe spoke quietly?' Isaac asked.

'He had a loud voice, but he thought before he
acted; Terry doesn't.'

'He wouldn't appreciate you talking out of turn.'

'He's been here, asked my advice.'

'And what was the advice?'

'Keep his head low; let the police find his father's
murderer.'

'After that?'

'He didn't ask, more interested in what his father
had stashed that he didn't know of.'

'But you do?'

'I've already given an asset register to their
solicitor, although I don't trust the man, any more than he
did me. He can decide on what he tells them; what he
doesn't.'

'That's not his job, is it?'

'I wouldn't know. Or let me rephrase – yes, I
would know, it's not his job, but Joe had assets the family
might not want to know about; assets that might be of
interest to you.'

'And the solicitor is the best man to deal with it?'

'I'm not privy to Foster's will, but I'm damned if
I'm going to sit on secrets, not when others would kill for
them.'

'Literally?'

'It's probable. I told Terry this, even Joe's first
wife. What they do about it is up to them.'

'Why tell us?'

'I told them that if the police came fishing, I'd be open with them, and as you're here now, that's what I'm doing. Joe Foster was not squeaky-clean, but I am.'

'The details?'

'Talk to the solicitor. I'm not involved,' Morgan said as he looked back at his monitor.

Neither Isaac nor Larry left Morgan's office convinced of the man's innocence, although for now it was the solicitor who was of more interest.

Chapter 6

'Asking me questions about Foster is a pointless exercise, DCI Cook,' Gerald Braxton said as he peered over the top of his glasses.

'The man was a client of yours?' Isaac said.

'He was, along with others. Our relationship was strictly legal, conveyancing, the purchase of a property, the sale of another, the reading of his will. Whether he was the devil incarnate or not, is not my concern.'

Braxton, dressed in a pinstripe suit with a white shirt and a dark tie, sat in a room that was insufferably hot, so much so that Larry, overweight and out of condition, was feeling uncomfortable, enough for him to take off his jacket and to place it across his lap. Isaac, fitter than his inspector, kept his on.

'Did you know the man for what he was?'

'If you're implying, did I know that he was a criminal, then the answer, as is the question, is hypothetical and invalid. As I said, our relationship was strictly legal.'

'Were you frightened of him?' Larry asked.

'Why?'

'The man didn't take kindly to those who got in his way.'

'It seems, judging by the freedom he enjoyed, a damning indictment against the police. If he was as bad as you are inferring, and what I suspect may be the truth, then why was he free?'

'And dead,' Isaac said. 'Foster's freedom, his ability to walk the streets or to get driven around in luxury, was dependent on a battery of smart lawyers and his bodyguards.'

'Then it seems as though someone has done you a favour; someone who needs a pat on the back, not incarceration.'

Braxton was right, Isaac agreed. After all, Joe Foster had controlled organised crime in the area, had his grubby hands involved in prostitution, the importation of drugs and standover tactics, all of which were controlled through a network of unseen and mostly unknown men.

'It's what comes after that should concern us all,' Isaac said. 'Joe Foster ruled with a firm and deft hand; his eldest son has neither skill.'

'His son is a fool.'

'He didn't pull the trigger.'

'Maybe he didn't, but you wouldn't be surprised if he had organised it.'

'We're forced to deal with proof, not conjecture. We've nothing on who shot the man, or how they managed to do it on a busy thoroughfare in the middle of the day.'

'That, officer, is your concern, not mine. Explain your reason for being here, what you expect to gain from me.'

'You were the man's legal adviser, someone he trusted. Your insight into him, his family, who may have had a grievance against him would be invaluable.'

'I'm a minor functionary, that's all. I had no interest as to how he had made his wealth; that wasn't my job. I knew what he was; you can't live in this city without learning a thing or two about life, about people. His family, however, present another set of circumstances.'

'Terry?'

'Violent. If he does take control, Joe's legacy, if it is worthy of such a term, will fragment.'

'You have his will?'

'I do.'

'Then you know if he intended Terry to take control.'

'I witnessed the document. Yes, I know its contents, but it is not for me to divulge them. For that, I would suggest you discuss the matter with the beneficiaries.'

'I believe it is,' Isaac said. 'One Foster has died, another might. We need to know if this is a vendetta against the Foster family or only Joe.'

'Joe Foster was aware that his empire would fragment without him, something he had spoken to me about.'

'Why did he trust you? For a man who professes no criminal intent, and a major villain, you two were friendly.'

'He had nothing that I wanted. I wasn't currying favours from him, nor did I want to be involved.'

'Why?' Larry asked. He had adjusted to the climate in the room and put his jacket back on. 'If you're privy to his circumstances, then he must have spoken about where his money had come from.'

'He was not a man to brag. Strictly business, him and me. If you're looking for insight, I can't help.'

'But you know the family.'

'Terry, I do. Gladys, but not recently. The other children, not as much. And, of course, I know Emily and her children.'

'That almost sounds like a recommendation for the last three,' Isaac said.

'It is. Foster mellowed with Emily, and after the coarseness of Gladys, a woman who never came to terms with her affluent lifestyle, the man was better with the second wife.'

'Even though she was a lot younger than him, younger than some of the children from the first marriage?'

'I'm not here to criticise or admire. All I know is that Emily Foster has always been polite, capable and, above all, loving. The attributes that a man looks for in a woman.'

'Samantha?'

'The mother reincarnate – the coarseness of the mother, the smartness of her father. As a person, I can't say I ever warmed to her, but she was nobody's fool, not like the foul-mouthed and violent Terry.'

'Has he been here?'

'Since his father's death?'

'Yes.'

'When the will was read, but not on his own, not yet, thankfully.'

'Worried?'

'I'd prefer not to see him.'

'Joe's other children with Gladys?'

'Tom's a layabout, barely able to tie his shoelaces; Billy's into crime, a few run-ins with the law, but making good money.'

'High-end cars,' Larry said. 'Ships them out of the country, makes plenty on the deals.'

'Proof?'

'Not our department,' Isaac said. 'And besides, Joe wouldn't let any of his children go to jail if he could avoid it.'

'A couple of tame Queen's Counsels from what I've heard. And you're right; Joe would protect them, even Terry.'

'Ben, the youngest?'

'Joe admired him, turning his back on the easy life, putting himself through university. A good job, an attractive girlfriend. Ben's smart enough to take control, but he doesn't want it.'

'He wants Emily.'

'I can't blame him, but she won't besmirch Joe's memory, or upset her children.'

'With someone else?'

'Who knows. She's still young, but she'll wait a long time first. And now, if you don't mind, I'm busy. Talk to Emily; she's the one with the least to hide.'

'We already have. She's the same as you; knows more than she's willing to let on.'

'Smart woman, Joe did well choosing her.'

'You expect trouble?' Isaac asked.

'With Terry, I do,' Braxton said. 'Joe's not the last one to die. I just hope that Emily and her children survive.'

It was Larry who summed up the situation afterwards, in a small café, the chance for the DCI and his DI to talk. 'It's not only Ben who's succumbed to Emily's charms,' he said.

'Who knows,' Isaac's reply. 'Maybe she's not all she seems.'

'Only time will tell,' Larry said as he drank his coffee and looked out of the window at a pretty girl walking by.

***

'That bitch,' Gladys Foster said. 'Taking my Joe from me.'

Samantha Foster looked over at her mother, almost as drunk as she was, not caring whether the second wife was a bitch or not.

It was late at night, the two women in the kitchen of the house, a small dog sniffing around, looking to be given some food off the table. To Samantha, the animal was a damn nuisance, and if she had a chance, she'd get rid of it in an instant, but her mother fawned over the creature.

'Mother, put aside the hatred, focus on the money.'

'Your father said he wasn't going to let any of us get his money when he was dead and buried.'

'He was angry. After all, it was you that kicked him out. And besides, he made sure we all got sufficient, apart from Tom.'

'He was screwing around: that woman in his office, another one who worked in that shop, put her up in a fancy place, went around to see her three times a week, and then he'd be back here looking for seconds.'

Samantha knew one thing for sure: her father hadn't looked for seconds or even firsts with her mother for a long time, years before she had kicked him out.

But then, her mother was a drinker, and telling lies, embellishing the truth and rising to anger were the consequences of alcohol, the reason that her mother often spoke nonsense.

Even though she was drunk as well, Samantha knew she was an agreeable drunk, not belligerent or argumentative.

'Even if he was, and no matter how much you despise Emily, it doesn't alter the fact that he provided for us. Hate Emily, blame her if you want, but don't accuse her or our father of things they haven't done.'

'I still hate her.'

'Mother, now's not the time to talk, but talk we must. It's not only Emily; it's Terry. What's he going to do? Kick us out, have me walking the street looking for someone to lay?'

'You, dear Samantha,' a sneering tone to her mother's voice, 'don't have the bait to dangle.'

'Whereas you, a drunk, fat slob of a woman, smelling of alcohol, do?'

'More than you.'

It was as Braxton had said: coarse women, unable to control themselves when drink took control of their brains, allowing their mouths to talk nonsense.

Gladys picked up another bottle of wine. Tomorrow she would have a savage headache, but tonight she didn't care. She put her arm around Samantha. 'You understand, don't you?' she said.

'I do. Without a man, it's not much fun,' Samantha said.

'You had a man once. What was his name?'

'Six years ago, I did. But they're all the same, always chasing someone fresher and younger. We, who have the experience, an excess of love, something to hold on to, and they want skin and bones with firm breasts, what Emily used to have.'

'She still has, courtesy of Joe's money and a surgeon.'

'You're right, that bitch. Tomorrow, you and I need to talk,' Samantha said as she leant over and took hold of another bottle. No point in sharing, not tonight, she thought.

***

Basing Street was an unusual location for murder, one block from Portobello Road, the heart of Notting Hill, the place to which tourists gravitated. For one thing, Basing Street was a busy thoroughfare, and on the day Joe Foster had been shot, there had been a group of tourists walking around the area, up into St Luke's Mews, the scene of another murder in the past, a couple of women idly chatting on a corner.

While her DCI and DI were following up on people known to Foster, Wendy was out on the street, talking to passers-by, making conversation with those in the shops and restaurants. Someone must have seen something; she knew that. And even if they were reluctant to get involved, not all were locals. Some were from outside the area, others were backpackers earning cash in hand to supplement their travels, and a few had known the man personally.

'You were here. You must have seen something,' Wendy said. She wasn't optimistic. After all, Ted Moulton was known to police; a habitual petty criminal, he lived on the street, under a bridge not far from Paddington Station. He was dressed, as usual, in a gaberdine mac, once beige in colour but now various shades of dirt. With him, an old dog whose party trick was to sit next to him on the pavements in the Notting Hill area and up to Paddington, a pair of large clown glasses on his face, a scarf around his neck.

'I was here,' Moulton said, 'but I didn't see anything, what with my eyesight and an empty belly. My dog may have seen something, but he's not saying much today.'

Wendy looked at the dog, a cross Alsatian and Labrador if she had to hazard a guess. And whereas it wasn't talking that day, or any other, it was a lovable creature that warmed to Wendy when she bent down to stroke it.

'Let's go through what you remember.'

'I could do with a feed, and he's not eaten much for a couple of days.' Moulton said, looking down at the dog.

'McDonald's?'

'Not for me. A good restaurant, decent food, a bottle of wine.'

'Eclectic tastes,' Wendy said. After all, if it weren't for the police paying or a charity handout, Moulton would be rifling in a rubbish bin looking for scraps or picking up cigarette butts off the pavement, and as for the dog, it wasn't any fussier.

'I used to cook myself once. Good, I was, cooked for those with money.'

It was true, as Moulton had been a chef before life intervened, before drugs and drink, a broken marriage, alienation from his children had caused something to snap inside him. It was, Wendy knew, a not uncommon story among the fallen.

Ted ordered filet mignon; Wendy followed suit.

Thankfully it was a pleasant day, warm enough to sit outside as the dog was not allowed inside the restaurant. A plate of raw meat had been ordered for the dog, to be served in a plastic bowl.

'The Savoy,' Moulton said. 'That's where I used to cook.'

'Life's not so good now,' Wendy said.

'I've no complaints. My dog and I, we've got each other.'

'But you were on top of your game.'

'Even so, they still complained.'

A couple at the next table looked over disparagingly at the beggar and the police officer. Wendy thought to flash her warrant card, tell them to mind their own business, but did not.

'You know who was shot?' Wendy asked.

'Joe Foster. Always gave us money. I can't say I knew much about him, but I'm told he was a tough man, not to be crossed.'

'He was a criminal.'

'So what? Half of them in those fancy houses in Holland Park are on the fiddle.'

'Cheating on their tax returns, arguing over the cost of home renovations hardly makes them criminals, not as you'd understand the word.'

'It's the working man who suffers.'

Wendy realised that Moulton was embittered, angry with the world; the only solace was his dog and the street. It wasn't much, Wendy concluded. Although if alcohol had once been a problem, it wasn't now, as Moulton had insisted on smelling the wine bottle's cork, swilling a sample of the wine in his mouth before declaring it fit for consumption.

Disregarding the man's angst against life and certain individuals, Wendy knew that she needed to ease the conversation around to what the man had seen, and why he didn't want to tell her. She had to concede, though, that the food was delicious, and Moulton's choice of wine was superb.

'A man is shot in clear view of a lot of people, you included, and no one's willing to tell us much. Why?' Wendy said.

'A man gets out of a car, shoots another twice, and then drives off. What was there to see? He was gone before anyone registered that something was amiss.'

'A man? A car? That means you saw something, and if you did, why here, why not somewhere less open?'

'I didn't see the man, not from where I was sitting. I saw a car drive off, assumed it must have had something to do with the man's death.'

'You heard the shots?'

'Hard not to. Oh, yes, I heard them, and then there's Foster lying on the street, dead.'

'And people going crazy.'

'A woman screamed, and then there was an ambulance, and then your lot.'

'How do you know this? You weren't interviewed on the day.'

'We left the area. Neither of us wanted to spend time talking to you.'

'You are now.'

'No option, and besides, you're feeding us, and I could do with another bottle of that wine.'

Wendy looked over at the waitress, lifted her hand and pointed to the empty bottle on the table.

'And the dessert menu,' Moulton said. 'The dog's partial to ice cream.'

'If you didn't see the man who fired the shot, what about the car?' Wendy said, attempting to get focus from a man more intent on looking at a menu.

'I'll have the tiramisu, as well as a glass of port to wash it down.'

'I'll have the same,' Wendy said to the waitress.

'Don't forget the ice cream,' Moulton shouted to the woman as she walked away.

'The car? What about the car?'

47

'Mercedes, late model, dark blue.'

'Do you have a registration number?'

'YS18 STV.'

Wendy messaged Bridget; she'd know what to do with it.

Chapter 7

It hadn't taken long for Bridget to find out that the car Ted Moulton had dined out on had been stolen in Kent, and then dumped by the assassin and his accomplice thirty miles north of Basing Street. Forensics would check it out, but Isaac and the team in Homicide did not have high expectations of much resulting from it. After all, a daylight shooting, a highly visible location, showed competency on the part of those involved, not the act of amateurs. They were, the team concluded, men who had killed before.

After she had wined and dined Moulton, Wendy had continued with her enquiries in the street. The only comments she received were 'It was over so quick, never got a chance to see anything', or 'I thought it was a car backfiring', which seemed to be one of the more inept statements. Wendy hadn't heard a car backfiring in years, but for some reason people still thought they did, or maybe it was from television that people got the idea that cars were noisy and unreliable and broke down.

The only piece of information, apart from Moulton's, had been a young lady in a flower shop who remembered a tall black man, something in his hand. Even if he had been the murderer, he would be impossible to identify, and he wasn't Terry Foster.

As Isaac Cook had said about Terry, 'Not the man's style. A cold-blooded killing is not committed in anger, and Foster's only violent when he's had a few. It's more than that: skilfully planned, well-executed.'

Wendy and Isaac met with Samantha Foster, Isaac enjoying the time out of the office. As the senior investigating officer, more time than he preferred was spent in the office, dealing with paperwork, filling out requests for additional staff, writing tedious reports.

Even though only one man had died so far, the nature of the killing was raising media comment that London wasn't the Chicago of the thirties nor was it Somalia. It was a modern cosmopolitan city, where a person should be safe to walk the streets, day or night. Isaac and the team could agree with the sentiment, not the reality.

Isaac cared about such matters. His parents, originally from Kingston, the capital of Jamaica, and now back there in retirement, were always on the alert for roving gangs and criminals. He'd prefer them to be in England, but as his father had said, 'It's our roots; it's where we want to spend our declining years.'

Isaac, who had been born in England, knew where his roots were, in England with Jenny and their child, and even though he wasn't at home with them as much as he should be, he thought about them all the time. He knew that Jenny understood, yet she had shouted at him the previous night, but that was from frustration, the need to get up at three in the morning to feed the baby, an activity that precluded Isaac, even though he had got up. He made her a hot drink, for which he received a weak smile.

Exhaustion, that's what it was, Isaac knew, the same as he felt as he sat down with Wendy and Samantha Foster.

'Miss Foster, we're interested in what you believe,' Isaac said.

'He was a good man, was my father,' Samantha replied.

'Forgive me for saying this, but your father was a man who made enemies.'

'That didn't mean he had to be killed.'

'Live by the sword, die by the sword. Isn't that how the saying goes?'

'Don't quote biblical text at me. My father was an astute businessman, put a few noses out of joint.'

'Literally,' Wendy said.

'If he did, so what? It's a jungle out there.'

'His death would have pleased some, upset others,' Isaac said.

Samantha Foster was a hard woman; both of the police officers knew. If she burst into tears, they would be fabricated. Isaac could not admit to liking her. He didn't have anything criminal against her, other than she was the daughter of a gangster, but Emily had been the man's wife, and he had liked her.

'It's not why you're here, is it? What you want is for me to say something, give you names.'

'It's a line of questioning. We've spoken to Emily, your mother, and now you.'

'It's Terry. You think he did it.'

'He's not a person who thinks strategically, more likely to act and regret it afterwards. Whereas you are more circumspect; you think things through, weigh up the pros and cons.'

'If that's an accusation?'

'It's not. Your father's dead, there's a space that needs filling. Terry's the person to gain the most, or is it you, or another of your siblings?'

'Terry's not up to the task,' Samantha said. 'I'm not saying that for your benefit, but his.'

51

'Would he know this?'

'That's not his style. If he gets control, he'll sell what he can, set himself up in a fancy place, drive around in an expensive car, get himself laid.'

'He's got all three now,' Wendy said.

'Then it'll be more than what he had before.'

'And laid?' Isaac said facetiously.

'Terry is more than capable of satisfying his carnal needs. But with more money, he'll go upmarket.'

'Emily?'

'Not for Terry. He likes them young.'

'We have a car in Basing Street, two men in the car. One of them shoots your father, the other drives the car.'

'Too smart for Terry to organise, and besides, he'd not kill his father,' Samantha said.

'A begrudging admiration for whoever killed your father?'

'Hardly. Although it wasn't the work of an amateur.'

'Your brother? An amateur?'

'If it's enough to believe he's not involved, yes.'

'The problem is,' Isaac said, 'that those who will gain the most from your father's murder are in this family, in particular you and Terry.'

'Then if he didn't organise the shooting, it must be me.'

'Is it?' Wendy said.

'He was my father; I loved him.'

'But Terry didn't, nor did Billy or Tom, and especially Ben,' Isaac said.'

'You're underestimating my family,' Samantha said. 'We may have warred amongst ourselves, seemed dysfunctional to some, but in times of crisis, we were united. If you had met our father, you would have understood.'

'I did,' Isaac said. 'A tough man, loyal to those he cared for, aggressive to those he didn't.'

'The definition of a successful man. Your continuing belief that his kin killed him is abhorrent.'

'If you find out who's responsible?' Wendy asked. She had been a police officer long enough to know when someone was spinning a line, and Samantha Foster wasn't known for restraint in her language. It had been mentioned on several occasions that the daughter, like the mother, had a florid turn of phrase, something that wasn't apparent that day.

'If you do,' Isaac said to Samantha, 'we have a problem, don't we?'

'I don't see how. It's up to you to find whoever committed this act, not us. As for the Fosters, it's up to us to ensure what my father had built up is maintained.'

'And what was that? Is that part of his legacy something you want to maintain, always to be looking over your shoulder for a passing policeman?'

'You, DCI Cook, overrate yourself and your police. Barely able to pull the skin off a rice pudding, most of you.'

'Is that an admission of crime on your part?' Isaac said, not rising to the bait.

'It's an admission of nothing. My father had already started to divest himself of some of the more controversial parts of his businesses.'

'The brothels masquerading as massage parlours?'

'You may well have a middle-class morality, Inspector, but the authorities regularly checked the parlours, and we always ensured that the women were treated well. There was no prostitution at any of them, nor drug dealing at any of the pubs.'

'What about the Vietnamese girl?'

'What about her? She was seventeen, not that we knew, an illegal in the country. And, if your memory serves you right, it was us who reported her to the authorities,' Samantha said.

'She was selling herself in one of your massage parlours.'

'We acted once we found out. After that, who knows what happened to her.'

'I've read the report,' Isaac said. 'According to her, she was trafficked into England, the back of a lorry, set up to do massages, and then forced to give herself to prearranged men. She implicated your father.'

'That's not what I read. It was the manager of the parlour who made her perform those acts. She was prosecuted, six months in prison. It wasn't anything to do with us, and there has been no reoccurrence.'

'Yet they deported the young woman, and eight months later the manager is found floating face down in the river.'

'Guilt by association is hardly sufficient grounds for you to accuse my family of involvement.'

'It isn't,' Isaac said, fully aware that Samantha Foster was not a woman to toy with. She would be a worthy successor to her father.

'The massage parlour?' Wendy asked.

'We sold it off, too much negativity with the place. Besides, they're not good businesses, not anymore.'

'Without the women turning tricks.'

'Another one with a middle-class morality. When was giving massages, or stripping, a crime? It's a liberated world, none of the old-fashioned gentility remains. Even so, strip clubs and massage parlours are passé. It's E-commerce now, that's what I intend to become involved in, assuming Terry's in agreement.'

'Is he to take over? Is he capable?' Isaac asked.

'He's not our father, he knows that, and he's headstrong, impulsive, likely to act without forethought.'

'None of which are ideal traits if you are to be a crime lord.'

Samantha rocked on her seat, a loud laugh. Even Wendy, who did not like the woman, felt the need to smile.

'A crime lord, my father?' Samantha said as the mirth subsided. 'That's the first time I've heard him called that.'

'You've heard worse.'

'I have, but Terry's not my father. He's with me on a strategic realignment of our businesses.'

'Criminal? Isaac continued to bait, realising that the woman was controlling the conversation.

'Even if we had been, not that I'll admit to it, what's the point? Honest and entrepreneurial is the future; the power of the internet, or haven't you heard?'

Isaac had, and Jenny had thought to set herself up online, to do consultancy work from home now that she had a baby. It suited Isaac as he hadn't liked the idea of giving their child over to another person to look after during the day while both parents went out to work to pay the bills. Although for him being at home indefinitely would be frustrating, it would suit his wife's temperament.

'If we concede that your father's death was not a result of family rivalry, a need to retire the old man, not with a gold watch, but a bullet, then who else would have had a motive?' Isaac said.

'My father pushed people, took advantage when they were down, made them ridiculous offers for their business.'

'Which to you is fine?' Wendy said.

'It's called skilful negotiating tactics. It goes on all the time, down at the market on Portobello Road, in the Houses of Parliament, no doubt in the London Metropolitan Police: the powerful taking advantage of those less fortunate.'

'No consideration as to the harm he may have been doing?'

'It's only the scale of it that offends. Do you think of the person you lock up for a crime? Any consideration of his family, what will become of them, whether the children will go hungry, or the mother, the eldest daughter, forced to take in lodgers, to sell themselves to a sleazy pervert?'

'That's not our job,' Isaac said. 'We have people to assist those who are placed in difficult circumstances because of a loved one's actions.'

'It's tokenism, and you know it. You don't care what happens other than the conviction of the individual. Is that so different from my father, that if you go into business, into life, you take the good with the bad, learn from experience, lift yourself up and get on with it? My father wasn't unique, and there was always someone nibbling on the edges, wanting to get an edge on my father, one over on him.'

'Emily, your father's second wife, is concerned over retribution from your side of the family,' Wendy said.

'She doesn't need to be. I might hate her, the same as my mother, but she will be left alone.'

'Terry?'

'Emily might well get a few choice words from him, but nothing more. She's tougher than she looks; she'll know how to handle him.'

'Tom?'

'Useless.'

'Billy?'

'Sharp.'

'Ben?'

'Honest, decent, hardworking.'

'An aberration?' Isaac said.

'Just different, Inspector,' Samantha replied. 'He fancies Emily, not that I can see why, but then, men are unpredictable, seduced by the external packaging, not interested in what is hidden.'

'You, for instance.'

'Not with Ben, but yes. What's Emily got to offer, apart from the obvious?'

Compared to Samantha Foster, a lot, Isaac thought, but then Emily was a more open book. In contrast, the only daughter of Joe and Gladys was intelligent, articulate and, above all, devious in the extreme. She was, to him, capable of anything, even killing her father.

Chapter 8

As the murder investigation progressed, the firmer the team's belief became that Joe Foster's death was caused by someone in his family.

'It's the most logical,' Isaac said. The autopsy had confirmed the pathologist's original statement to Wendy: two gunshots, the first of which would have killed him without prompt medical intervention and the second, to the head, instant death. A professional assassination on a busy thoroughfare, more reminiscent of Chicago and the Mafia of the 1930s, but not in central London. However, Joe Foster's murderer had the courtesy to get out of the vehicle and to shoot the man with a .45 handgun.

'But?' Larry said, confident that his DCI had more to say on the subject.

It was six thirty in the morning, and for the first time in a week, Isaac had managed to get five hours of uninterrupted sleep, although Jenny had been up twice in the night, once to feed the baby, the other just to check.

Homicide, typically abuzz during the daylight hours with people coming in and going out, some filing or collating evidence and others on computers conducting research, was still quiet.

'Too easy, that's why,' Isaac replied to Larry's question.

'I tend to agree,' Larry said. 'After all, what would they have to gain in the short term?'

'That's what I'm saying. We've met with Samantha, talked to Emily, and the first wife, Gladys. Of those three, Samantha would be the only one to gain from it, but she's still got Terry to deal with, and he's no pushover.'

'She's smarter,' Wendy said.

'Brains against brawn?' Isaac said.

'At this time, I'd put my money on the brawn.'

'If Samantha wants to take control, it brings up a couple of points.'

'Which are?'

'How much does she know of Joe's business interests? What has she done to consolidate her position?'

'It's unlikely Terry has done anything, and there would be no point in him killing his father, not without a plan.'

'Not unless the father intended to hand it over to his daughter.'

'What about Ben and Emily?' Wendy said.

'Fancying the woman doesn't seem a motive for killing her husband. If Ben thinks the way to a woman's heart is through arranging the death of her husband, he's mistaken.'

'He wouldn't be the first,' Bridget said.

'He wouldn't,' Isaac agreed.

'Tom?'

'He's a hopeless headcase, addicted to prescription drugs and whatever else he can get hold of,' Larry said. 'If it weren't for his father, he'd be the butt of jokes, someone to push around.'

'His father's dead.'

'Terry's made it known – mess with Tom, and you're answerable to him.'

'He's exerted his influence?'

'Only by acting tough. It's early days, and Joe's violence was covert, skilful manipulation; Terry's is overt. It'll take more than threatening violence; after all, half the villains in the area carry a knife or a gun, and the West Indian gangs, they see the killing of another as a ritual.'

'I grew up with a few of them, including your drinking buddy, Spanish John. What does he reckon?' Isaac asked.

'Apart from not admitting to his criminal activities, not a lot, other than Terry's out of his depth.'

'Any mention of Samantha?'

'Not her, but he said that Billy Foster was a smart operator. I believe that Spanish John and Billy are working together on stealing expensive cars and shipping them off to Africa, no questions asked.'

'Proof?'

'The word on the street.'

'What about Ben? Emily?'

'Ben's not in anyone's radar. He's Mister Clean. Emily's regarded as not involved, although Spanish John reckoned she was a good sort, a classy woman. He said that Jacob Morgan was wily, but we've met him, didn't get much,' Larry said.

'Never forget Emily,' Wendy said. 'There's Ben lusting after her. Who knows what it is between them. Maybe she holds a flame for the younger Foster.'

'Which, if she does, is a motive,' Isaac said. 'Follow through, prove it one way or the other.'

***

Tom Foster, the third eldest of the Foster clan, and someone who came from wealth, was not an impressive sight, the once attractive features having given way to the look of the homeless and the disadvantaged. He neither worked nor had any interest in gainful pursuit.

'The weather's not good,' Larry said, attempting to strike up a conversation with the man. He had found Foster out on the street, close to a pub.

'He was a bastard, my father, always on about this and that.'

'He disapproved of your lifestyle?'

'I can't blame him for that, can I? It's not that I've done much, just loafed around, taking it easy, getting drunk when I can.'

'You could straighten yourself out.'

'Why bother? He was going to die sometime, and I'll get something, enough to get by, even though he cut me out of his will.'

'Your siblings have all got some drive, why not you?'

'Genetics. I got the lazy gene from somewhere.'

Larry recognised the symptoms of a man sinking into an abyss from which there was no return. Years of nothingness, interspersed with drinks and drugs.

'Do you fancy a drink?'

'I don't mind if I do. It's cold today, not the sort of day to be out and about.'

'Not that you intended going back to your mother's house, or did you?'

'Back there, not a chance. What with my mother complaining, my sister running here and there, giving me a lecture, and then Terry acting tough.'

The Duke of Wellington, a pub named after Arthur Wellington who had twice been the prime minister of the United Kingdom and had given his name to Wellington boots, had seen better days. However, it was warm, and it served a good beer, although Larry was conscious of his wife's anger two days previously after another drinking bout, him coming in smelling of stale beer. He didn't want to sleep downstairs again, and after he had got as much from Tom Foster as he could, Larry would leave him to his own devices. If Foster wanted to stay drinking, it would be to his cost.

'Tom, let's get this straight,' Larry said. 'You don't want to be involved; no interest in the family business?'

'None at all.'

'The lazy gene, or do you have an issue with your father's business?'

'You're wasting your time with dumb questions. Look at me, a disreputable character. I had a decent education, plenty of whatever I wanted, but I prefer to do as little as possible, always have, always will. My mother sort of understands, Billy thinks it's a laugh, and as for Samantha, a foul-mouthed and frustrated woman, she barely thinks.'

'Ben?'

'I meet up with him sometimes, have a drink. He's not the preaching type. He's a good person, is Ben; none better, salt of the earth.'

'You've not mentioned Terry.'

'What's to mention? A hard case, thinks he's smarter than he is. I've had a few run-ins with him over the years, and he's not always come out on top.'

'Fights?'

'Serious on more than one occasion. I broke his jaw once, he broke my arm, so that makes us even. Anyway, he leaves me alone. It's Samantha you've got to watch, not that she's the most intelligent.'

'Is that because Ben is?'

'Smart enough to make his mark on his own, to keep clear of our father and Terry.'

'You're not surprised that your father was shot?'

'I'm not upset, if that's what you mean. Another pint?'

Larry didn't ask who was paying, only pushed the two glasses across the bar's counter.

'Our problem is where this is leading to,' Larry said. He was on his second pint, not sure if he could stop. It was alcoholism, he knew that, but he'd not admit it to the team in Homicide and not to his wife. She had dragged him along to Alcoholics Anonymous a couple of times, even had him stand up once and declare 'I'm an alcoholic'. Felt a fool for doing it, and as for the anonymity, of the eleven in the church hall, he knew five of them, drank with three of the five, and only two days later he had shared a couple of beers with their leader.

'If it's going to get serious?' That's what you mean, isn't it?' Tom Foster said.

'Is it?'

'If it wasn't one of us, then yes.'

'If it was your family?'

'I don't see why, but assuming it was, what's the point? Our father, bastard that he could be, wouldn't leave us out to dry. Even me, much as he disliked what I'd become, a disgrace to the good name of Foster – a name to be proud of, to hold up high – he made sure that I had food in my belly, a place to sleep.'

'But you don't eat, not much, and most nights you sleep rough or in a doss house somewhere or on someone's couch.'

'I've got a place, even a woman. Not that either of them is anything special. I'm my own man, making my way in the world, not that I've got very far, although I'm still young.'

Larry didn't see any point in telling the man that he was forty-one years of age, and if he was making his way, as he had said, he had a long journey ahead of him and not much time to complete it. Tom Foster was, as he had heard and could see, not the most intelligent, one of life's drifters, a daydreamer, a drug addict. One day, Larry knew, the journey would be cut short, and the man would be found dead from a drug overdose, or a fight with another degenerate over a place to sleep, or if there was a power play in the Foster family, collateral damage.

'Samantha, what should we make of her? Larry said as he ordered another couple of pints.

'Devious. If Terry intends to take control, he'll need her backing him up, dealing with the flak.'

'And if she doesn't?'

'He'll blow it soon enough. Our father was smart, had a firm hand on the tiller, knew the ins and outs.'

'Streetwise?'

'You knew him. You're a police officer, what do you reckon?'

'He kept us from prying too much.'

'The trouble was you never knew where to look.'

'But you do?'

'You never asked, and I wouldn't have told you anyway. We're only speaking now because you're paying, not that I've given you much.'

'Do you intend to?'

'I don't want my mother hurt.'

'You care for your mother?'

'She deserves better. After all, she raised us, dealt with our father's women.'

'He had others before Emily?'

'Long term, all of them, but yes, a powerful man, good for the image. Not sure if he cared for them, any more than he did our mother, but she knew what was going on, came to accept it.'

'Then why the hatred of Emily? She wasn't one of his fancy women, and she did marry him.'

'That's it. She married him, left our mother on her own. Our mother accepted our father's indiscretions, but with Emily, the man fell for her in a big way, not that I can blame him.'

'You as well?'

'If you're referring to Ben, I'm not. All I'm saying is that she did right by our father. As for fancying her, not me, and besides, I've got myself a woman.'

'Similar to you?'

'Kindred spirits. She's making her way in the world, the same as me. We'll get there together.'

'Does your family know her?'

'Ben's met her, not that he thought much of her, and she's not a beauty, not like Emily or Ben's girlfriend. Rough if I'm honest, but Gwen's had a hard life, a couple of husbands, one who put her in hospital a couple of times.'

'You've admitted to a violent streak. Will you?'

'Not with Gwen; we're compatible, similar interests.'

'Not doing much, screwing when you can, shooting up heroin when you can afford it,' Larry said.

'How did you know?'

Tom Foster was slow on the uptake, Larry realised. The man had just been insulted, a sarcastic comment levelled at him and his girlfriend, and he hadn't reacted or even understood.

'If it's not your family, and it looks likely that it is, then who should we watch out for?'

'You've met the solicitor?'

'Braxton, yes, we've talked to him. Involved?'

'He'd know more about our father than I would, more than Terry, although he would have felt more comfortable with Samantha.'

'But not Ben?'

'Ben wasn't interested. He had his tongue hanging out at the reading of the will, the same as all of us, but he kept away from my father's business ventures, knew them to be dangerous.'

'You're telling me more than you intended to,' Larry said.

'Maybe I am. And besides, our father's dead, and if Terry's up to no good, that's his worry. There's not much you can do with Joe Foster, not now. You weren't too smart when he was alive, and if he's looking down from up above, he'll be having a good laugh.'

'Or below,' Larry quipped.

'Not him. Down below is for losers, people like me, and our father gave to the less fortunate, helped out the local church: a benefactor to some, a tyrant to others.'

'A godfather-like figure?'

'He wasn't Mafia. It was just him, his family and a few trusted advisers.'

'Gerald Braxton and Jacob Morgan?'

'There's one other.'

'Who?'

'Tony Rafter, not that I told you.'

'If Rafter finds out you've been talking, he'll come after you. We need to stay in contact,' Larry said.

'We don't. You've got a name; do what you will with it, but protect my family, my mother,' Tom Foster said. He had had his quota of beers from Larry; he wasn't getting any more.

Chapter 9

There were two Tony Rafters. One of them the general public knew of: a man who by sheer determination and hard work had raised himself from the gutter to pre-eminence as a real estate developer, financier and tireless benefactor of charitable organisations.

The other, carefully concealed and which Isaac had been aware of, but could never prove, was that the man resorted to crime when it suited.

Making an appointment to talk to Rafter about murder could therefore be seen as sheer folly, and potentially a career-impairing move. Isaac was well aware of the situation as he stood in the foyer of the forty-eight-storey skyscraper, the name Rafter emblazoned in twenty-foot letters at the top, brightly illuminated at night.

'Are you sure about this?' Detective Chief Superintendent Goddard, Isaac's senior and mentor, asked.

'We can't run an investigation without breaking a few eggs,' Isaac said.

Given who they were meeting, the chief superintendent had accompanied Isaac – a need for the interview to be conducted correctly, a safety mechanism in case Homicide was forced to explain why they were concerning themselves with Tony Rafter when one murder in Notting Hill was a local matter, not orchestrated from the east of London, and not by Tony Rafter.

A pleasant-looking young woman came out of the lift, approached Isaac and Goddard. 'Mr Rafter will see you now,' she said.

No more was said as the three entered the lift, not until the lift door opened directly into Rafter's office.

'Come in, gentleman,' Rafter said as he got up from behind his antique desk. Isaac had known that the man was short, but hadn't realised how short until he was standing in front of him; he was barely five feet.

'I'm sorry about this,' Goddard said. 'Purely routine.'

Isaac regretted his superintendent's presence, although politically he understood why, and it wasn't as if Rafter was going to fall for any of the usual interview tricks: the rapid-fire questioning, the attempt to confuse, to get the person to talk themselves into a corner, to say something they'd later regret.

'I understand my name has been mentioned concerning the death of Joe Foster,' Rafter said.

The young lady came in and placed a silver tray on the table.

'Tea or coffee?' Rafter said. 'Or would you prefer something stronger?'

The man was smooth, too smooth. Isaac didn't trust him, although there were only rumours that Tony Rafter was behind a lot of the crime in the country, financier to those who'd pay the interest rates he demanded.

The man's story, Rafter not opposed to the truth when it suited, was that at the age of five he'd been fostered out to a family who had nurtured the abandoned child, ensured he went to school every day. And then, at the age of thirteen, thieving from a shop, a packet of cigarettes, and from there, breaking into houses, a prison term at nineteen, until an enlightened prison chaplain had taken the young Rafter under his wing, taught him right from wrong. It was a great story, even on Wikipedia, and parts of it were probably correct, but Isaac, along with Goddard, disputed the official account.

It was true, though, that the chaplain had recognised something in Rafter, and that the man had then gone from success to success, never again coming under official investigation.

'Mr Rafter, did you know Joe Foster?' Isaac asked.

'I did. Not well, I'll admit, but we had the occasional business dealings.'

'His death, did that come as a shock to you?'

'A tragedy, but no.'

'Why's that?'

'He was a tough businessman, a hard man.'

'It's been mentioned that you were involved with him on more than a few deals.'

Isaac was fishing, not sure where the interview was going. After all, it had only been Tom Foster who had mentioned the name of Rafter to Larry.

'We went in together on the building of a block of flats, some trouble with the union later on.'

'The union representative fell off the roof, on a clear sunny day.'

'Accidents happen,' Rafter said. 'Unfortunate, but the man hadn't secured himself, nor was he wearing a safety helmet. Not that it would have done him much good.'

'You're well informed,' Goddard said.

'I had my people prepare a report before you came, on Foster and my involvement with him. No need to burden my mind with the superfluous.'

'Is that how you regard Foster's death?' Isaac said.

'What do you expect me to say? My conscience is clear on this matter. I had dealings with the man, nothing more, and we weren't friends, nor did I know his family. I'm told that he was a good family man, something I can admire, but apart from that, his death doesn't concern me one way or the other.'

'Your honesty is appreciated,' Goddard said. 'However, your name came up, and we felt obliged to follow through. Rumours, you understand.'

Goddard felt that it was up to him to say it before his DCI said it less tactfully.

'The crux of the matter,' Rafter replied. 'I've heard this for forty-five years, ever since I came out of prison. And believe me, I've made enemies along the way, inevitable if you want your name on the building. Those who've failed on account of me, taking a financial hit, are quick to blame my success on an unfair advantage, not on their shortcomings. I can assure you both, Chief Superintendent Goddard and DCI Cook, that I am an honest man, and that I recognise that the two of you are doing your duty. Apart from that, I wish you a good day. This meeting is terminated. My secretary will show you out.'

'What did you reckon?' Goddard asked Isaac out on the street.

'The man didn't appreciate our visit, nor did he accede to it out of a sense of doing the right thing.'

'You'll not get him for a crime, too well connected.'

'If he did arrange for Joe's death, then why bother? What did he have to gain?'

'If Foster had some dirt on him, something that could stick.'

'We're clutching at straws,' Isaac said. 'We've met the man. If we meet with him a second time, we'd better ensure we have some evidence.'

***

Tony Rafter had had to be questioned, a matter of procedure. However, it had proven to be a failure, and feathers had been ruffled. If the man were involved in shady dealings, it would be almost impossible to prove, and if he wasn't, then Rafter was not a man to let it lie. Either way, Isaac knew, as did his chief superintendent, that notice had been served on a powerful man, a man who would resent the inference that he was criminal, involved in a murder, and that such a person, guilty or not, would at some time, when least expected, make sure that pressure was put on officers at Challis Street Police Station.

Richard Goddard, an adroit political animal, retreated to his office on his and Isaac's return to the police station. He had to document the meeting with Rafter, to prepare their justification for putting the man on the spot.

Goddard, frustrated by internal politics, his promotion to commander thwarted every time, considered his possibilities. Yet again his best police officer, a man whose career he had guided on his climb up through the ranks, had landed him in the hot seat. However, as he sat at his desk, typing on his laptop, Goddard couldn't help but smile. If Rafter did cause trouble, it had still been fun watching the calm exterior of the little man with the squeaky voice, wondering about the inner turmoil of a master manipulator and what he would do next.

'Terry Foster met with Emily,' Wendy said. It was the day after the meeting with Rafter, and, as far as Isaac was concerned, the meeting was history. If his chief superintendent wanted to dwell on it, to postulate as to what could have been said differently, that was for him.

As for Isaac, he had never been political, not in the police station, and certainly not at Scotland Yard. To him, there was only one way to show your merit, and that was through hard work and bringing in the results.

'At her home?' Larry, who had not been paying attention, preferring to check messages on his phone, said. It was another early start, and unusually the night before he had not drunk more than two pints, and that was only to be sociable; fishing for information if Isaac asked, a necessary part of policing if his wife did, neither of which was totally truthful.

'Outside of the house, neutral territory. She phoned me last night, calm, no reason to wake any of you up.'

'Emily Foster expected any meeting with him to be acrimonious,' Isaac said. 'What's changed?'

'According to Emily, not that she wanted to go into detail, he wanted to declare a truce, to work together, to preserve his father's and her husband's legacy. As sweet as pie,' she said.

'Did she trust him?'

'She said she did, but I don't believe we can, not totally. After all, she was married to Joe for a long time; some of it must have rubbed off, and she would have had to deal with the first family over the years, maintain the narrow line between civility and rage.'

'Which Gladys has,' Larry said. He was more alert now, listening to what was being said.

'The rage, maybe, but we know she had acted reasonably with the second wife before.'

'Before, it was Joe who was controlling the two families, no doubt reminding Gladys and their children that he was the bank. And that any action against Emily and her children would not be seen favourably, and would result in a reaction not to their liking.'

'But now there's no Joe, only Terry and Gladys, and presumably Samantha. I'm discounting the others,' Isaac said.

'Not yet,' Larry said. 'I've just received a message. We need to investigate.'

'Another murder?'

'Not yet, but Ben's been threatened.'

'Harmed?'

'Not according to him, but he was out with his girlfriend, an early-morning jog. The message is sketchy, but it appears they were running through a park when two men ran by, elbowed him, pushed the girlfriend into a bush.'

'Nothing said?'

'Nothing. No attempt to snatch a phone or grope the girlfriend. It's suspicious; we need to check it out.'

'You and Wendy can meet up with them, give me a report later. What interests me more is Terry and Emily; out of character for Terry to be friendly.'

'It's not as if she's got a hold over him, not now with Joe dead. Terry's got everything to gain, nothing to lose.'

'Is he making a play for her, the same as Ben? Is he carrying a flame for her?' Wendy asked.

'It depends whether he sees her as part of the assets,' Isaac said.

'Which he probably does, and Terry's arrogant enough to think he can charm her,' Larry said.

'I'll talk to Emily; you two, focus on Ben and the girlfriend.'

'Jostling Ben and the girlfriend seems unconnected.'

'We have a violent death, a minor incident and two people unexpectedly being friendly,' Isaac said. 'None of which make any sense, and it worries me. As if something's brewing; something we're not prepared for.'

Thirty-five minutes later, Larry and Wendy sat down in the apartment that Ben Foster shared with his girlfriend. The two of them were sitting close together, holding hands, a picture of loveliness, of love, although Wendy knew that Ben also lusted after Emily. She was sure the girlfriend did not know.

'It might be nothing,' the petite elfin-faced girlfriend said. Compared to Emily's layers of makeup and heaving bosoms, Ben's Swedish girlfriend, Margareta, was waif-like. Why did men want women who advertise the goods, instead of the girlfriend who did not, Wendy thought, aware it was probably primordial.

'We'll be the judge of that,' Larry said. 'You know of Ben's family?'

'Ben's told me everything, or I think he has.'

'She knows,' Ben said. 'No secrets between us.'

Ben was giving an excellent impression of a louse, pretending only to have eyes for Margareta, yet also making up to Emily. Previously, Wendy had liked him; now, she wasn't so sure.

'If that's the case,' Larry said, 'then you can understand our concern that this is more than arrogant and aggressive men in the park. Was anything said?'

'Nothing,' Ben said. 'I might not have told Margareta everything.'

'Okay, a précised version for Margareta. I don't like us talking at cross purposes here.'

Ben removed his hand from Margareta's, positioned himself in front of her, looked her straight in the eyes. 'You remember that I told you my father was a very successful man, a tough negotiator, loving of his family, dismissive of others, and that Terry was a hard case.'

'Yes,' Margareta replied.

'And that Samantha can be a bitch, and that Tom was useless, but I still liked him.'

'I've met Terry and Tom. They were pleasant enough.'

'You've met Samantha as well. Emily, you've not met.'

Wendy was waiting for the revelation that he fancied his father's widow; she was to be disappointed.

'My father wasn't always legitimate.'

'A criminal? But I knew that.'

'How?'

'When we first started going out. It was a hen night, one of my workmates getting married. She was a bit rough, tattoos up each arm, a ring through her nose. It was her that told me; seems that she went out with Terry once and that he had told her things, not that I believed her. No one could be that bad, not if they're related to you.'

'They could, and they are. Terry's violent, and he's taking over our father's empire, and I don't use the word sparingly. Our father, apart from what you and others prefer to see, was an old-fashioned gangster, a man who demanded respect, helped those he liked, ignored those he didn't.

'Disposed of a few,' Larry said.

'As the inspector said. My father looked after his family and his friends, but if you got on the wrong side of him, it was your problem, not his.'

'Is there any more?' Margareta had her hand in his once again, at her insistence. 'It's you I love, not your family.'

'A fair summation,' Larry said. 'The incident in the park could be a warning.'

'My place is with Ben,' Margareta said.

'Six foot under is not where you want to be,' Wendy said, aiming to frighten the young woman who, no doubt, had come from a decent family in Sweden, the worst crime that any in her family would have been guilty of would be a parking violation at most. The young woman didn't understand the reality of the situation, the risk involved.

'It might be best if you go back to your parents,' Ben said. 'For the time being, until this blows over.'

'If you'll come with me.'

'I can't, not now. My mother needs me, and the family has to discuss the situation, what we're going to do with the business, and then there is our father's funeral.'

'Ben's right,' Larry said. 'He can't go now, but you must.'

'I won't.'

Wendy hoped that the young woman, clearly smitten with Ben Foster, wasn't to be an innocent casualty, although with her being pushed over in the park, the scratch marks visible on her arms and face, she wasn't sure.

Chapter 10

Spanish John put it to Larry succinctly. 'It's not if, but when, and everyone's keeping their head down,' he said.

Friday night, the Ladbroke Arms, an excellent place to be and where Larry often went. Outside, youths, some in their late teens, others in their twenties, mingled, forming friendships, lining up partners for the night, but generally oblivious to the area's underbelly.

'Terry Foster causing trouble?' Larry asked. He was determined to keep it to three pints of beer that night, but wasn't sure if he would. After all, the congeniality of the place, the alcohol, the fact that a man sworn to uphold the law and a man determined to break it could meet in a neutral zone. A place to shake hands, slap each other on the back, to skirt around the main issues, until later when the tongues had loosened.

'One of my colleagues is in the hospital,' Spanish John said.

Larry translated colleague for street hustler, pimp or drug dealer.

'Terry Foster?'

'Not directly, but I know it was him.'

'How?'

'The word's out. Anyone interfering with the Fosters is in for big trouble.

'And your *colleague* was?' Larry emphasised 'colleague', half expecting a rebuke, but none was forthcoming.

'A couple of men, white and tough, and my colleague, harmless; they went at him with knuckledusters.

Can you believe it? Here, in this area, such violence. Where's it all heading?'

The pot calling the kettle black, Larry thought. After all, how many people had Spanish John and his cohorts beaten and killed? A man who ruled his part of the city as if it was his fiefdom, and even then, it had been at the discretion of Joe Foster.

Larry knew that Foster had delegated certain areas, expected recompense from others for leaving them alone. Foster was the Mr Big, and Spanish John, a man with aspirations, one of the robber barons paying him compliments, feigning loyalty, scheming how to get rid of the gangster king and to take his place. And now the position was occupied by the former regent, a man yet to prove his worth.

Terry Foster, the heir presumptive, was putting on a display, doing what his father had not, using violence instead of intimidation. It wasn't going to work, not with the West Indians, nor with the East Europeans, and not with the white Anglo-Saxon gangs.

A commotion at the pub entrance; Terry Foster was making his way through.

Spanish John took hold of his glass, grabbed it firmly, ready to smash it down, to break it and use it as a weapon.

Larry, quick to react, took hold of the man's arm. 'Not now, not here,' he said.

Foster sat down at a table, looked around the bar. Outside, the previously jovial and drunk had quietened. The atmosphere in the pub was electric; the uncrowned king was in residence, and he was holding court.

A hand beckoned; Larry complied.

'You look in need of a drink,' Foster said as Larry sat down opposite him.

'Your visit here, purely social?'

'It pays to be seen.'

'Who's next?'

'I've heard that you've seen Ben and his woman.'

'It could have been circumstantial,' Larry said.

'After my father?'

'If you find out who was responsible?'

Larry picked up his glass of beer, took a drink, aware that another awaited him, put there by one of the heavies who had come in with Foster.

'They're answerable to a higher court.'

'It's a police matter.'

'It's not. The Fosters don't shirk their duty, nor do we let others interfere in our business,' Foster said, looking over at Spanish John, raising his hand again and beckoning the man over.

'Terry,' Spanish John said, sitting on a chair at a right angle to both Foster and Larry. It was a neutral corner. The situation was tense.

Outside, the subdued crowd had regained their exuberance and were making a noise as before.

'Spanish John, good to see you,' Foster said.

'And you.'

Two fighters, sparring off, testing each other's mettle, the referee in the corner. Larry felt remarkably calm, but then he often found honesty in criminals. Men who were what they were, not openly admitting to it, not attempting to defend it. But whereas he could admit to liking Spanish John, the same could not be said for Terry Foster. The previous arrogance of the man replaced with a smugness, as if he was turning his nose up at those who would openly challenge him.

Larry was sure that Terry was directing his efforts at Spanish John, the man who was most likely to carve out a large proportion of the Foster empire, given half a chance.

'It wasn't me,' Foster said. 'I didn't put him in hospital.'

'I'll take your word for it.'

If it was intended as a cryptic exchange between the two men, it was wasted. Larry knew exactly what they were talking about.

'Why are you here?' Larry asked Foster.

'A man is entitled to a drink.'

'A drink is when you come through the door, order a pint and sit on your own or make idle conversation at the bar.'

'That's what I'm doing, sitting here with you two.'

'Foster, I don't want any more people getting hurt,' Larry said as he took hold of the full glass placed on the table for him.

'I don't like people killing my family.'

'That's understandable, but taking the law into your own hands won't get any of us anywhere. And if you're involved—'

'Is that a threat?'

'What about my colleague?' Spanish John said.

'I've already told you, I wasn't involved, but someone killed my father, not that I'm blaming you, not your style. But Hill, he's running the investigation, not getting very far, and now Ben's been jostled.'

'If you leave my people alone.'

'A truce? Is that it?' Foster said.

For a man who ruled with his fists, not his brain, Larry thought that Terry Foster was handling the situation well.

A couple in their fifties sat down at the next table. One of the heavies whispered in the man's ear; they got up and moved over to a table on the other side of the bar, the heavy ordering a couple of drinks for them. The man had been polite, but how much that was due to Larry's presence, he wasn't sure.

'For now,' Spanish John said. Even with a police inspector present, the two men felt impunity, the ability to transcend what was right and wrong, legal or illegal. Larry knew that a truce would be transient, soon to be broken by one or the other. He decided that he was neither Foster's nor Spanish John's lackey. He got up, said his goodbyes and left the two antagonists together. Whether their conversation would sour, he didn't know, but that night, his wife would have his company; she would have no reason to complain.

**

Emily Foster, smarter than other people gave her credit for, reflected on her meeting with Terry.

In the twenty-one years since she had married his father, she had spoken to him on no more than a dozen occasions. And each time, it had been cursory and polite. She knew that was on account of his father insisting that his children and the first wife act civilly to the second wife, not allowing any compromise on the subject. And in all those years, Terry, the most aggressive, but not the most intelligent, had adhered to the command more effectively than some of the others.

Gladys had tried, and whereas the two women were natural adversaries, a common ground had been reached. For Tom, there was ambivalence, but then that was the man's outlook on life in general. Billy wasn't worthy of comment, as the man was motivated by money, not by emotion, and of all Joe and Gladys's children, he was the one that Emily understood the least.

Ben was an easy book to read, similar to men she had met when younger. Still did from time to time; the sort of man who would sidle up to you in a shop while browsing, to offer assistance, to give you the benefit of his vast knowledge on any subject, to look down the top of your dress. She liked Ben, similar to his father in many ways. His mannerisms, the way he walked, even the lopsided way he tilted his head when speaking.

Even her mother had said that marrying Joe, an older man, was doomed. Emily made her decisions instinctively, and regardless of the rumours about him, the fact that he came with baggage, as she did, they married. But her baggage had been a succession of bad men, even worse lovers; Joe's had been a family of five children, the youngest fifteen, the oldest twenty-five, and a wife who Joe had still cared for, but not in a loving way.

Samantha was close to her age, and whereas most of the first family had been respectful of the second, she had been the only one who had been begrudging in her respect, with always a snide remark, a disparaging glance.

Two women, one svelte and beautiful, the other heavy-boned but attractive in the right light, as Emily's son would say, frequented the same shops, the same hairdressing salon, even shared some friends. Their paths crossed frequently, and once in the salon, the two sitting next to each other, they had been forced to speak, and Samantha had made it clear that she regarded Emily as no more than the dirt beneath her feet. And Emily, forced to defend herself, had responded in kind, accusing Joe's eldest daughter of being unworthy of the name of a great man.

It had been a tense moment until both women had broken out laughing at the absurdity of the situation. That day, they had left the salon arm in arm, found themselves a good restaurant, eaten a good meal and got drunk. It had been a recreation of Christmas Day in the trenches during the First World War, when the opposing sides had united to play football, drink schnapps and whisky and pat each other on the back, only to kill each other the day after.

Emily knew that family rivalries existed, and to Samantha, her side of the family was all-important. She was the one that worried Emily the most.

Chapter 11

'Sit down,' Gladys Foster said to Terry. 'Learn to be like your father. Weigh up the situation, think it through.'

'It got him killed.'

'Why do you suspect the man? What's he done to you, and why kill your father? Ask yourself, why would he want him dead?'

'Morgan hated my father. You know that.'

'It didn't concern your father, and it shouldn't you. What's he doing now? Nothing, just sitting in his dingy office counting his money.'

'Jacob Morgan, an innocent bystander, advising my father, taking what he could for himself, wanting more.'

'Everybody wants more, your father knew that, and he was willing to spread it around.'

'Not to me,' Terry said.

Gladys looked at her son, knew as his father had that the eldest son wasn't capable of taking on the mantle of leadership. After all, empires created by crime or by honest toil were the same. They both needed a steady hand, someone willing to make the tough decisions when required, to be benevolent when possible. A lot of people, criminal and honest, owed their livelihoods to the Fosters, but with Terry, more than a few would be disenfranchised.

For another twenty minutes, mother and son discussed the situation, as she had with Joe in the early days, and as he had said, she was an excellent sounding board to bounce ideas off. She was also a good wife and mother, cast aside by the man as he rose in stature and influence. An old dishrag left out to hang. She was bitter and not ashamed to show it.

She had tolerated Joe's womanising; after all, her father had been the same, but he had only worked in a factory. As Joe's hold increased in the area, so did the quality of his women, and he even went so far as to put one of them up in a flat in Bayswater, on call when needed, which was most days.

For six years Gladys had waited for him to come home and profess his love for her, to make love, but he never did, and then he was gone, a fleeting peck on the cheek. It wasn't as Samantha had said. She hadn't thrown the man out, only ceased to take any notice of him when he came home.

Gladys sat in the house, realised that Terry was not long for this world, feeling sorry for herself. She moved into another room, opened the drinks cabinet and took out a bottle of red wine. If she didn't have a man, at least she had the solace of alcohol. She was not a happy woman, not that night, not for many years. She thought about Joe and when they had first met, barely more than children, and how he had taken to crime as a duck takes to water, how he planned his forays wisely, two steps forward, one back, never going so far as to aggravate anyone, only to annoy. But then, after so many years at the top, two bullets in Basing Street.

It hadn't made sense at the time; it didn't now. She picked up her coat, put on her shoes and walked out of the house. She needed to see where Joe had died.

***

Gladys walked up Basing Street, past where her husband had died, up St Luke's Mews and along Westbourne Park Road, looking up at the one-bedroom flat Joe and she had rented. Newlyweds, a child on the way, optimistic for the future. They were happy times, even happier when Terry was born and they had moved into a small terrace house in Powis Mews. If Joe had been satisfied with that, she would have been content. A small garden at the rear, a park not far away, and at the weekend, trips to the sea. A chance for the children, three by then, to paddle in the water, to build sandcastles, and then at the end of the day, before the drive back to London, fish and chips wrapped in newspaper.

Joe, she had always known, was driven by a desire to prove to his father, a harsh disciplinarian, that the taunts about his son being the dullard of the family were not true. Sure, his sister was academic and always did her homework, winning the school prize, the head pupil in her last year, but it wasn't intelligence that hampered him. It was frustration at having to learn calculus and French, who was the King of England three hundred years previously. What he wanted was education that taught him about life, how to be successful, how to read a profit and loss statement, to purchase property, to calculate interest rates.

Joe's sister, a schoolteacher in her twenties when Gladys met Joe, a modest life with an unassuming husband and two children, did not contact his family anymore, not after Joe embraced crime. Gladys had met the woman on three occasions and had not seen her for over forty years. She wasn't even sure if she was alive, but if she was, she had no intention of visiting her. Dead or alive, she was gone to her, as she had been to Joe.

Gladys stood outside the house in Powis Mews, absently looking up at the upstairs window. A lady came out of the house, started speaking to her.

'Are you interested? the woman, a similar age to Gladys, a smile on her face, said. 'We're thinking of selling.'

'I used to live here,' Gladys replied. 'Happy memories.'

'You're a Foster?'

'I am. Have you heard of us?'

'Who hasn't. I'm sorry about your husband, not that I knew him.'

'Thank you.'

'You look as though you could do with a cup of tea.'

Inside the house, Gladys imagined herself in the kitchen preparing the evening meal, saw where Tom had said his first word, where Samantha had sat reading a book, and upstairs, where she and Joe had made love. It seemed small in the house, but it had been enough for her; and then Joe walked in the door, telling her he had bought a house in Holland Park.

It was after that, that their life changed. She was busy with decorating the house, he with carving out an empire. Then came the visits by the police, the whispered conversations on the phone, his prolonged absences, and then he was gone, off to another woman, and later divorce and death.

The owner of the house in Powis Mews put her arm around Gladys. 'It'll be alright. Don't you worry,' she said.

Gladys appreciated the kindness. The woman, if she knew of the Fosters, also knew of their reputation, but not once had she mentioned it.

Outside on the street, Gladys took one lingering look at what had been a happy place and walked away.

After aimlessly walking for an hour, she entered a café that seemed warm and inviting, took a seat by the window and ordered a latte. It had started to rain, London rain, a drizzle, enough to chill the bones, not enough to stop people going about their usual activities.

Gladys put down her coffee, not even bothering to finish it, and left the warm café, turning up the collar on her jacket. She needed to talk to someone who, regardless of personal malice, she trusted. She needed to speak to Emily.

***

Jacob Morgan had liked Joe Foster, not that Terry would have believed it, and the two men had forged a working relationship, a grudging acceptance of the other's attributes. And although it was rare for them to socialise, they had often met in Morgan's pokey office or a restaurant of Joe's choosing.

Two men at different ends of the spectrum. Foster, flamboyant, wanting to show his wealth; the other, bank accounts in several countries, an impressive portfolio of stocks and shares. Apart from the office that he had occupied for close to forty years, only once had someone come in and given it a coat of paint, his only other visible asset was a small two-bedroom flat. It was neither pretentious nor decorated with antiques or rare carpets, but had a kitchen with a linoleum floor, a living room with bare walls, and as for the bedrooms, one was for storage, the other contained a bed and a small table to one side. It was the flat of a poor and solitary man, one of which was the reality, the other was the illusion he wished to create.

'My father, he trusted you,' Terry Foster said.

Jacob Morgan neither liked the uninvited intrusion into his office nor the man standing in front of him. Joe Foster would have phoned, arrived at the agreed time, got to the point and left. Terry did none of those, but banged hard on the outer door, wrenched the handle down and pushed the door back until it hit the wall with a thud.

'It's customary to knock,' Morgan had said. He was nervous, but he wasn't going to show it. He understood the psychology. Confronted by a vicious animal, never show fear, only strength; stare them down, don't give an inch.

'I knocked enough,' Terry said. His voice was slurred, the effect of alcohol.

'What do you want?'

With Joe, there would have been an initial conversation about family and friends and the state of the nation, although it wouldn't last long, not for Morgan, as he had no family, and only a handful of acquaintances. As for the state of the nation, what did he care.

Joe had been a gangster but saw himself as an upright citizen, yet he, Jacob Morgan, a man who portrayed respectability, knew more about crime than Joe did, had cheated more out of their money and was richer by a long way. And now in front of him stood Joe's son, a man lacking his father's smartness or his accountant's cunning, hunching his shoulders, attempting to look menacing.

Morgan recognised in the son all the traits of a middle-of-the-road criminal, a man who, had it not been for his father, would have been in and out of jail regularly, and now was trying to run his father's empire with no hope of succeeding.

'I want to know what you're up to.'

'I mind my own business, look after yours if that's what you want.'

'How much money did you steal from my father?'

'I never stole from him. Our business was open and honest. He asked for financial advice; for me to deal with his tax liability.'

'My father never paid tax,' Terry said as he sat down heavily. Just before he collapsed, Morgan thought.

'With judicious planning and my advice, he paid very little, enough to keep prying eyes out of his business.'

Morgan thought to mention the saying that in life there are two certainties, death and taxes, but he knew that Terry, an unread man, would not understand, nor would he have heard of Benjamin Franklin, the man who penned it.

'Someone's trying to get involved in the family's business,' Terry said. 'I reckon it's you, and that's why I'm here. To hammer it out with you, to set the ground rules.'

'To kill me if necessary?'

'It's as good an idea as any.'

'Except that I know more about your father's business than anyone else, including you and your sister. And, with all due respect,' Morgan said, not caring about respect for Terry Foster as the man didn't deserve it, 'your sister is a sharp woman, sharper than you, and she doesn't believe anything is untoward, so why should you?'

'Samantha's trusting, the same as my father. But I'm streetwise. I know a rogue when I see one, and you, Morgan, have been fleecing the family for years.'

'Terry, I suggest you come back with Samantha when you're sober. Then we can open the books, go through your father's finances, the provisions he made, his plans when he died.'

'I don't need any of that. I need the money you've stashed away.'

'A full account has already been given to you: bank accounts, their passwords.'

'I mean the others. The ones that only you know of, and if you're thinking of doing a runner, think again. I'll find you, kill you if I have to.'

'If I planned to do what you're suggesting, and if I had some of your family's money, you wouldn't be able to find me, nor would you ever know the truth of the deception. However, I have no reason to leave or to deceive. London is where I live; where I'll die.'

'You'd better hope that you have a long life, then. Someone killed my father, and you knew about his movements, why he was in Basing Street that day.'

'Did you?'

'Not at the time, but I do now.'

'You've met the woman?'

'He liked it rough,' Terry said. 'Can't blame a man for that.'

After Foster had left, Jacob Morgan sat back on his chair. No longer needing to pretend, he was shaking, his hand barely able to hold the bottle of whisky as he poured himself a drink. He was frightened, aware that Terry Foster was impetuous, capable of acting without provocation, believing what he wanted, not concerned with the facts.

Morgan, calmer after the drink, switched on his laptop, entered a website into the browser and logged in. He was satisfied with the money he had invested, the interest rate that it received, knowing full well that if his recent visitor were aware of what he was doing, he would be dead.

Chapter 12

Emily sat calmly, uncertain why she had let Gladys into the house, although not upset that the woman wanted to talk. After all, both of them were worried about their respective families.

'It was at the old house, sitting with the owner, that it came to me,' Gladys said. 'The knowledge that he is dead, either at the hand of one of my family or an outsider. I'm not sure which of those options I prefer.'

'Neither,' Emily replied, feeling fuzzy-headed, the result of worry and a bottle of wine. Never a big drinker apart from in her teens, when drinking and raving were the accepted norms.

Joe's death had signalled a change in her life. Even though Joe had left Gladys years before, he had still retained a soft spot for her, keeping a photo of them as teenagers, arm in arm. It had not concerned Emily previously, but now as the woman spoke, helping herself to a glass of wine, she was jealous, even though it made no sense. After all, she had had the man for twenty-one years, good for most of them, although they had separated six years back for a couple of months, not that she could remember why.

'It could only be Terry,' Emily said, not sure if it would offend his mother or not, beyond considering if she even cared.

'Terry, compared to his father, is just a boy,' Gladys replied.

A boy who, if given half a chance, would seduce his stepmother, Emily thought, but did not say.

'Do you suspect him?'

'I don't want to, no mother does, but Terry's wild, likely to do something stupid.'

'He didn't shoot Joe; the police know that.'

'Terry wouldn't be the first to consider his family expendable,' Gladys said.

'Not even my two children, who want nothing to do with the business.'

Gladys took hold of another bottle of wine, removed the screw top and poured Emily and herself a full glass each.

'Did you understand the extent of Joe's business?' Gladys asked.

'We never talked about it, but I knew enough. A lot of it was legal; some of it wasn't.'

'You weren't concerned?'

'Not when I was younger, and then the children started to grow up, at school, doing well. If what he did gave them a good upbringing, I'm afraid I ceased to care, decided that it wasn't important.'

'Apart from the clubs and the massage parlours, he distributed illegal drugs. Did you know that?'

'What's that got to do with your being here?'

'Everything. Joe had a partner, a man in the shadows.'

'Not Terry or Jacob Morgan?'

'Joe didn't think much of Terry, and as for Morgan, he's a man to be careful with. I wouldn't trust him an inch.'

'They were friendly,' Emily said.

'In business, but no more. He never came to our house, nor yours, I assume.'

'Never, but Joe, if he mentioned him, told me that the man was antisocial, adept at his job, but neither interested in luxury nor overt displays of wealth. Joe reckoned the man was loaded.'

'If Joe made more as a result of using Morgan, and as long as the man was upfront with him, Joe would have looked the other way. Rub him up the wrong way, and Joe was ruthless, but if you were of benefit to him, then he was your friend.'

Emily filled Gladys's glass; the two women inebriated.

'Did Joe ever kill anyone?' Emily asked.

'What do you reckon?'

It wasn't the reply that Emily wanted, but she knew that honesty was important.

'I believe he has.'

'Joe dealt with dangerous individuals at times.'

'Proof?'

'Joe wouldn't have done it himself, too smart for that.'

'Would Terry have killed Joe, honestly?' Emily asked, drunk, her mouth moving too freely, saying things it shouldn't.

'He would know people who would for a price.'

'And why was Joe on his own in Basing Street?'

Gladys, more practised with alcohol, although drunk as well, but still retaining some control, stood up and hugged Emily.

'You'll find out soon enough,' she said as she closed the front door of the house behind her.

Emily, unsure of what had just transpired, finished her drink and settled herself down in a comfy chair in the living room. She knew that what Gladys had said was important; she just wasn't sure how to respond.

***

The revelation that Joe Foster had been meeting with another woman who lived on Basing Street came as a surprise. To the team in Homicide, a new avenue of enquiry after stagnating for a week.

The room where Isaac and Wendy sat with Samantha Foster was warm, the woman wrapped in a blanket, continually wiping her nose with a handkerchief.

Isaac, fearful of taking the flu to Jenny and their child, sat at a distance from her, straining to hear her voice. Wendy had no such issue and sat alongside the woman.

'Our father knew I could run the business, but I needed help. Ben's never been interested…'

'He's an honest man,' Isaac said.

'He's got other interests.'

Isaac knew that to many Joe Foster was the palatable side of crime. A man who used his illicit gains wisely, for the betterment of those down on their luck; for the church where he prayed every week, and put more in the collection plate than anyone else.

Samantha was rambling, not addressing the issue, skirting around what Isaac and Wendy had come for.

'Basing Street?' Wendy said for the second time.

'What do you know?' Samantha said.

'Your father and Emily; not all there is to it, is it?'

Neither Isaac nor Wendy wanted to say what they had found out from Jacob Morgan: an early-morning phone call, telling them to talk to Samantha, she knew the truth about Joe's mistress.

'Our father had a roving eye, even when he was with my mother. Is that what you're referring to?'

'How long have you known?'

'About Basing Street, four months. Terry knows.'

'It explains why your father was in the street, not who he was meeting. Any ideas?'

'There's only one, Eileen Cavendish.'

'Emily always believed that her husband was faithful.'

'If it's Eileen, then he was. No emotions wasted on her; she's not worth it.'

'Sex, nothing more?' Wendy said. 'And according to you, that's not being unfaithful.'

'Powerful men have egos that need stroking. That's the way it's always been. If he was spending time with Eileen, it was all about proving that he was young, full of zest. Emily's in her forties, not the fresh-faced peach anymore, and she knows it.'

'So did your father, is that what you're saying?'

'He did love Emily and her children, even us most of the time. A credit to the woman, but our father needed the occasional outlet, the need to let down his guard, to walk the street on his own, nobody watching his back.'

'He could have done that somewhere else,' Isaac said. 'On holiday, another country where he wouldn't be recognised.'

'He could have, but our father was a local lad made good. He didn't want to travel far; this was his place, and he was perfectly content to stay.'

'If Terry knew, that meant others. Was it such a big secret?

'Our father wouldn't have wanted it bandied about. As for Emily, she must have known.'

'She didn't seem to believe it was possible, the times we've spoken to her,' Wendy said.

'Emily was married to the man; knew what he was before she married him, or maybe she believed she had changed him. After all, she was one of his playthings before he married her. There were others.'

'Eileen Cavendish?'

'She's younger than Emily, and back when our father married Emily, she was just a child. Not sure where she came from, but she's attractive, made a name for herself when she first arrived in the area.'

'As a prostitute?' Isaac asked.

'Prim and proper little miss, a goody-two-shoes, a prick teaser Terry used to call her, and he tried it on more than once.'

'Succeeded?'

'Not Terry. Eileen knew what she had, played it well; not giving her favours to any drunk, but waiting for a sugar daddy, someone to set her up, give her the good things in life.'

'Your father?' Wendy said.

'How is it that I've never heard of her?' Isaac asked. Morgan had been open when it had suited him; he wondered if Samantha was doing the same.

'Why should you? She never did anything wrong, was perfectly polite to everyone she met, did her job and went home.'

'To Basing Street?'

'She worked for my father. She managed the accounts, strictly above board.'

'Morgan dealt with the other side?'

Samantha didn't respond, only stared back. To her, she was helping the police to find a murderer; to Isaac, the woman was playing a strategic game. Either way, Eileen Cavendish was of great interest.

***

'Good on the man,' Spanish John said after Larry had quizzed him about Joe Foster and a probable woman. It was late afternoon, Larry conscious that meeting in a pub at such an early hour was dangerous. The West Indian gang leader was a heavy drinker, seemingly with bottomless legs, as Larry had been in his youth, eight pints of beer and still walk a straight line. But with age comes the inability to drink as before, and after five pints, Larry would be feeling lightheaded; at eight, he would be slurring his words, straining to focus.

It was then that he was at his most defenceless, the probability of arrest if he attempted to drive, another caution from his DCI. Larry knew the risk, but the information from Isaac and Wendy was red hot, and he had been charged with finding out who else knew about the Cavendish woman.

Wendy had instantly regretted phoning Emily, as a visit would have been better, but her DCI had wanted to know if she firmly believed in her husband's fidelity.

After the brief chat with Emily, Wendy wasn't so sure of her innocence. It wasn't as if Emily was naïve, but Wendy remembered the night her husband had come home late from work, a supposed farewell for a work colleague. She had known that it was a female, and as for the few drinks and nothing else, she had never been sure; not that she had ever pursued the matter or questioned her husband about it or waylaid the woman to put her on the spot, to get to the truth.

As far as Wendy had been concerned, it was best to let sleeping dogs lie, and the truth would only bring further complications. Although, after that night, whenever her husband had mentioned an after-work get-together, she had accompanied him.

Emily, she knew, would have been able to tell if her husband had been unfaithful; the sheepish look, the wanting to turn over in bed and to go to sleep, and Joe Foster had not been young. He wouldn't have been capable of inexhaustible stamina, of satisfying two women of a night, especially if Eileen Cavendish was as delectable as Samantha Foster had said.

'Do you know her?' Larry asked. It was his first pint; he was taking it easy, determined not to falter. The investigation was at a crucial point, and if he weren't there to do his duty, then someone else would be.

'I've seen her around. She kept to herself, polite to those that said hello, but classy, not from around here.'

'Why do you say that?'

'I would have known her. As well as Foster did apparently, from what you're saying.'

'I'm not saying anything. So far, it's only been mentioned, not confirmed.'

'It will be.'

'Why?'

'If she worked for him, was willing to put out for him, financial sweetener or not, what man's going to resist?'

'I would,' Larry said.

'That's because you're a boring flat-foot, an upholder of law and order, although Isaac Cook, he wasn't a slouch when he was young.'

'Nor when he got older, but now he's married, a young child.'

'It wouldn't have stopped him in his youth. He wasn't Mr Squeaky-Clean.'

'Crime?'

'Not Isaac. But he'd come out with the boys, get drunk, even if we were underage, and if there were any willing females, he'd be into them.'

Anecdotes about his DCI were entertaining, but Larry hadn't met Spanish John to discuss the past, only the present.

'If Joe Foster was involved with Eileen Cavendish, how come you didn't know about it?' Larry asked.

'Who said I didn't?' Spanish John's reply.

'Is that a yes or a no?'

'It's maybe. I knew she worked with the man, not that they were involved. Although you can't blame him, can you?'

Larry could. He had his faults, he knew that, but cheating on his wife wasn't one of them.

Larry always found Spanish John good company. The man had a charm about him that attracted people, but he was still a vicious man, capable of extreme violence at times, yet sympathetic and kindly at others. As with others in the area, he saw crime as a vocation, no different to a police officer or a nurse. If asked, and Larry had posed the question before to others, he knew the man would respond that it was a harsh world, a rough part of London, and either you were part of the culture or you weren't.

It was, however, no longer a valid view. In the late fifties and sixties, Notting Hill and its surrounds were slums owned by malevolent racketeers, and violence and crime were rife. But that was over fifty years ago, and Notting Hill and the area around it were, on the whole, affluent and expensive, no longer the haunt of the disadvantaged and oppressed, but of an educated middle and upper class. Spanish John was a criminal because he enjoyed it.

'What else do you know about the woman?' Larry asked. He had drunk two pints, but although Spanish John was downing the pints rapidly, so far he hadn't revealed any previously hidden facts. The pub and the beer were Larry's best chance of a revelation.

'She's not the only attractive female around here, and more than a few of them are available. I focus on them; no time to chase the others, and besides, her working for Joe Foster wasn't a recommendation for folly.'

'You feared the man?'

'Not me, but there was no point in riling the beast.'

'Was he?'

'Not personally, ruin his manicured nails and his expensive suits.'

'But others would do it for him.'

'We've spoken about this before, but yes,' Spanish John said as he thrust his empty glass forward.

Larry knew that keeping to two pints to ensure a welcome at home that night, and no chastisement from his DCI, was in vain. His drinking pal had information, and he wanted it. Larry took the phone out of his jacket pocket, messaged Isaac to let him know the situation, and then phoned his wife, receiving, as expected, an ear-bashing.

'Collar and chain, got you under control, has she?' Spanish John laughed.

Larry, in return, laughed, but it wasn't with humour. He knew that his attempts to kerb his drinking and smoking had done him good and neither the smell of tobacco nor the taste of beer had the same allure as before: he felt guilty.

Three more pints followed in quick succession; the initial reluctance overcome by the drunkenness that was fast approaching. Larry placed his hand on the gang leader's forearm. 'What's the truth?' he said.

In all the time that the men had been in the pub, no one had approached them. It was ominous, Larry had thought earlier, but now he gave it no thought.

'Foster wasn't the only player around here.'

'You included,' Larry said.

'Crime exists, not only here in our neck of the world, but in politics, in business, in the police.'

Larry knew the man was correct, but it didn't alter the fact that Spanish John's activities could send him to prison if there were proof. Not that Larry had dug too deeply for it, knowing that the man was smart; according to Isaac, who had sat alongside him in the classroom, he was gifted even, the possibility of a scholarship to a better school.

'We're not talking about what you get up to, not now,' Larry said. 'It's Joe Foster's death that I'm interested in.'

'His family?'

'They're suspects, especially Terry. It seems too obvious.'

'Is it? Terry's not that bright; subtlety's not his strong point. He beat up one of my people once, a couple of years back, an argument over something or other; I can't remember what.'

'A drug deal gone wrong, one of Foster's women in one of the massage parlours?' Larry said in an attempt to stimulate the man's memory.

'That's it, the massage parlour. He'd paid his money, didn't even get a happy ending.'

'Are you saying it was a front for prostitution?'

'My man thought it was, but then, he was always too stupid for his own good. Anyway, after the woman had given him his money's worth, without what he thought he was entitled to, he's out in the street hurling abuse.'

'Terry Foster?'

'He hears about it, arrives within ten minutes with a couple of heavies. Anyway, to cut a long story short, Foster's in a mood, and he's been drinking. He lays into my man, and then when he's on the ground, the three of them are kicking and stamping on him.'

'His condition afterwards?'

'Unconscious, a broken leg, internal bleeding. Foster had least had the decency to phone for an ambulance before leaving.'

'Courteous of him.'

'Not at all. He knew that my man wouldn't talk, and at the hospital, there for five days, he continued to claim it was a mugging, nothing to worry about, happens all the time.'

'The police?'

'A couple of uniforms questioned him, but they weren't much interested. After all, a barely-literate black man of no fixed abode didn't interest them.'

'Prejudice?' Larry said.

'It exists.'

'You've not explained about Terry after the savage beating.'

'I met him the next night. He gave me the details. I couldn't disagree with him. He then gave me a thousand pounds, told me to make sure my man got the best medical treatment, another couple of hundred pounds to go and get himself laid at his expense with a whore he knew.'

'Did he?'

'Once the pain had gone away, my man was there with the woman; reckoned the beating was worth it if he got to screw such a woman.'

'Terry's got a streak of decency, but it still doesn't explain why he would want to kill his father, assuming he did, and why when the man was on his way to meet Eileen Cavendish,' Larry said.

'The two heavies that night. Check them out. They'd be capable of murder, not that I'm saying they shot the father, but who knows.'

'You do.'

'Maybe I do; maybe I don't.'

It wasn't an answer, and Larry wasn't sure if he had been fed a tale or whether Spanish John had given him a lead without being too direct. Was the man playing his cards close to his chest, or was he involved?

Larry downed his pint, shook the gang leader's hand, although the man's eyes were closing as he sat down on a chair in the corner of the pub.

At another table, three of Spanish John's men. Larry was inclined to ask which of the three men had been beaten by Terry Foster, got laid at his expense, although, as he studied them through beer-glazed eyes, he knew it was the one in the middle, shorter than the other two, and with a vacant look. He was, as Spanish John had said, not too bright.

Outside the pub, as Larry fumbled for his car keys, not that he intended to drive, only to sleep off the effects of the beer, a voice came from the other side of the road.

'Who is it?' Larry said.

'We're here to make sure you don't get into trouble,' Isaac said. Alongside him stood Wendy.

'I'll be alright. Just getting information, that was all.'

'Leave the car; Wendy will look after it. As for you, a good feed and black coffee. A couple of hours and we'll drop you off at home.'

'Let's hope he found out something worthwhile,' Isaac said to Wendy. 'It's not always easy defending him to the chief superintendent.'

Wendy said nothing; only knew that DCI Isaac Cook would support and defend his team whatever the cost. That was the measure of the man, the reason that Homicide worked so well: a loyal team, a caring boss.

Chapter 13

Eileen Cavendish sat calmly. She was, as had been described, an attractive woman in her mid-twenties, neither blowsy in appearance nor cheap in her dress.

She was not, to Wendy, who had accompanied Isaac to the third floor flat, typical of either a wanton woman or someone's bit of fluff. Although, according to Jacob Morgan and then Samantha Foster, she had been Joe Foster's mistress.

'Miss Cavendish, we have a few questions,' Isaac said as he pulled up a chair alongside her in the flat. If it was the woman's prize for sexual favours, it was below par. It was a two-bedroom flat, with a kitchen-diner, a flat-screen television on one wall, a flower in a vase, and cream-coloured walls. It was neat and tidy, no better than the place Isaac had sold in Willesden.

'I imagine you do,' the woman responded in a gentle voice.

'Your relationship with Joe Foster?'

'I'm so sorry that he died.'

'Since his death, what have you done?'

'I have stayed here most of the time, other than to go to the supermarket.'

'Not to the office?' Wendy asked, surprised by the woman and her surroundings.

'I went once, only to deal with some outstanding paperwork, but it wasn't necessary.'

'Why?'

'I can continue my work from home, which I have been doing.'

'Why hasn't the Foster family mentioned you before?' Isaac asked.

'I worked for Joe, nothing more. Why would they mention me?'

'Do you know Jacob Morgan?'

'Yes, I've met him on a few occasions, purely professional.'

If it weren't for Eileen Cavendish, Wendy would have been concerned about what 'professional' meant. She couldn't believe that this conservative young woman had been the mistress of a notorious gangster. It just didn't make sense.

'Joe Foster was coming to visit you the day he died, wasn't he?'

'He was. I suppose I'm a suspect, the scarlet woman.'

'Were you Joe Foster's mistress?' Wendy asked the question that she and her DCI had been skirting around.

'Is that what people think?'

'Only two people, maybe a third.'

'They couldn't be further from the truth.'

'Your story?' Isaac said. Eileen Cavendish, to him, didn't fit the archetypal look of a gangster's moll. He was intrigued.

Eileen moved to another chair, more comfortable than the wooden chair she had been sitting on, and took a deep breath. 'Joe Foster was not what you think,' she said.

'What does that mean?' Wendy asked.

'Of course, I knew what he was, and what others thought of him, but believe me, behind that harsh exterior was a compassionate man, a man that people could love.'

Wendy thought the woman was heading to a confession: that she had been the man's lover, even though she had just denied it.

'He was a gangster, dealt in drugs, had people killed,' Isaac said, tired of yet another person justifying their association with a criminal. It was facts that Homicide needed, not a reason why and how and when, and Eileen Cavendish was wasting time.

'I can't believe that. He was a tough man, played by a different set of rules to most people, but that doesn't mean he was a criminal, only that others are jealous.'

Either the woman was delusional, Isaac thought, although he couldn't believe it, or else she somehow perceived the man's better points as being more important than how his charitable acts and benevolence were funded.

''Miss Cavendish,' Isaac tried again. 'We know that Joe Foster was a major crime figure, and that he visited you regularly. Either you were sleeping with him, or you weren't, but this pretence that the man was something he wasn't, does you no credit. You're intelligent, and you don't look or act like the man's former lover, but then you seem unable to grasp the seriousness of the situation, the probable danger this places you in.'

'He has known of me since I was four years old,' Eileen said. 'And regardless of what others might say, our relationship was platonic; it couldn't be any other.'

'Are you saying you're his daughter?' Wendy asked.

'I'm not. Before he married Emily, and after leaving Gladys, my mother and Joe had been lovers.'

'So why did he employ you?'

'Joe had loved my mother, the same as she had him, but life got in the way. My grandparents were both very ill, and my mother went north to look after them, not realising that she would be gone for a long time. In that time, my mother married another man, a good man, my father.'

'It still doesn't explain why you are here in Basing Street, visits from Joe Foster.'

'It does. After six years, my father died in a car accident. In desperation and sadness, and after a suitable period, my mother contacted her first true love only to find that he had married another. Whereas he had loved my mother, he now loved another, and he wouldn't cheat on Emily, that was how much he cared for her.'

'He supported your mother?'

'He helped us both, not that I ever saw him, not until I had become an adult.'

'You contacted him?'

'I did. We met, realised that we liked each other, and he offered me a job.'

'Who else knows about this?'

'About my mother and me? Nobody. It was our secret; I hope that it can remain so.'

'It's murder. The truth can't be hidden. And besides, if people believe you are the man's mistress, that places you in danger.'

'I will stay here for another week, and then I will go somewhere else.'

'A job?'

'I'm not sure, maybe move in with my girlfriend. As you can see, neither Joe nor any other man interests me, and if those with minds in the gutter want to believe the worst of me, there's not much I can do.'

'Not a lot, but why did he come here regularly?'

'He liked to talk, nothing more. With me, he could be open, talk about nonsense or politics, even music, but never his business. If he was as bad as others believe him to be, then I never knew, nor would I have thought worse of him. To my mother and me, he was a good man, someone we could rely on.'

'Did he meet your mother after she had contacted him?'

'Never. They only spoke on the phone. Does his wife believe that he was unfaithful?'

'We're not certain, not yet,' Isaac said.

'Terry knows his father was involved with you, and Samantha wasn't surprised, not that she seemed to like you,' Wendy said.

'Terry's a rough man. And as for Samantha, what more could you expect?'

'I'm not sure what you mean about Samantha.'

'Isn't it obvious? Samantha is more capable than Terry, but she's got a bad attitude.'

'Joe told you this?'

'He planned to put Samantha in charge at the right time, but he wanted me to deal with the day-to-day paperwork. He didn't trust Samantha, not while he was alive. He always suspected that she was fiddling the books, not that he blamed her, but he would have preferred it if she hadn't.'

'He intended to give her control of the business?'

'Who else? He understood human nature. Once she was in charge, she wouldn't let anyone cheat her, but while he was alive, a little bit extra to her didn't matter. And besides, she pulled her weight, more than could be said for Terry.'

'You don't like him?' Wendy said.

'Never, and he was always trying to rub against me in the office, if he got half a chance.'

'He'd not be the first,' Isaac said.

'No, but his leering made me feel unclean.'

'Could he have been capable of killing his father?'

'Terry would be capable of anything.'

'Joe was unprotected on Basing Street, any idea why?'

'I told you. Sometimes he wanted to relax, to be a regular person.'

'What about the other family members?' Wendy said. 'A brief summation.'

'Gladys, rough around the edges, good mother.'

'What about Tom and the other children?'

'Tom, a great disappointment to his father; Billy, smart, dishonest, but not a leader.'

'Ben?'

'His father admired him, even if the son didn't want to be involved. You'll want to know about Emily?'

'We do. What do you reckon?'

'A good mother, devoted to her children, to Joe. Easy when she was younger, Joe knew that, but she never let him down, nor him her.'

'Your feelings for the man?'

'I admired him for what he had achieved.'

'Even if it was criminal?'

'Subjective. He hadn't been charged for any crimes, and who knows where the fine line between sharp and astute and criminal is. Joe played the game, was successful. Made some nervous, others jealous.'

'What you've told us about your mother and Joe Foster. Can it be proved?'

'If you have to, yes. He was a friend, nothing more, not that anyone will believe you or me,' Eileen said.

Isaac nodded his head, agreed with Eileen Cavendish, not sure if he had been spun a tale or whether it was the truth. For now, he would give the woman the benefit of the doubt.

***

Emily Foster had been quick to jump to conclusions. Wendy had checked after the visit with Eileen Cavendish, found out that the mother had lived in Notting Hill before the birth of her only child. And that she had left to look after her parents, staying for longer than expected, marrying a local man, before he died tragically late at night after a drunk driver had slammed into the side of the vehicle he had been driving.

For the time being, Eileen Cavendish was off the hook, a minor character in the saga. However, Emily's outburst of expletives aimed firstly at her dead husband and then Eileen was disconcerting, so much so that Wendy was forced to reconsider whether her favourable preliminary judgement of the woman had been wrong.

'We have no reason to believe that your husband had been unfaithful,' Wendy said. 'On the contrary, it appears that he had been honourable, although his time away from home must have concerned you.'

'Not really,' Emily said, a mug of coffee in her hand.

It was mid-morning, and outside the window it was raining. A miserable day made worse by the doubts forming in Wendy's mind about Emily.

It was Larry's conversation with Spanish John and Isaac's and Wendy's meeting with Eileen that had caused concern.

After all, Terry Foster had been in the area throwing his weight around, beating up a man outside one of the pubs, getting into a car soon after.

It had been Isaac, at an early-afternoon meeting instead of the usual 6 a.m., who summed up the situation.

'We've got a young woman who professes that Joe Foster visited her just for a chat, yet nobody seems to believe it, and you can't blame them.'

'You don't think it's possible?' Wendy asked.

'It's illogical. If Joe Foster was a committed family man, in love with Emily, why was he visiting Eileen Cavendish and not telling her.'

'I'm not sure if Emily knew, not at first,' Wendy said. But now, Wendy could see that Emily had possibly been jealous and believing the worst of her husband; after all, she had been one of his fancy women back in the day, and she would have known the tell-tale signs.

The protestations of love that Emily insisted on, were they entirely accurate, Wendy thought. Even though it was unusual to leave an office meeting before her DCI had brought it to a conclusion, Wendy stood up, took hold of her handbag, checked her car keys and phone and left the office, a garbled response when Isaac asked the reason for her actions.

Isaac and Larry sat for a minute, puzzled, trying to make sense of what had just happened.

'Not like her,' Larry said.

'Wendy's thought of something. She'll phone us soon enough,' Isaac said.

At the door to Isaac's office stood Bridget, so far underutilised in the current homicide. In her hand, a folder. 'You'd better read this, look at the photo,' she said.

Isaac opened the papers he'd been handed: Larry read through his copy.

Neither man spoke after reading their two sheets, only Larry letting out a deep breath.

'It's damning,' Bridget said.

Isaac picked up his phone and called Wendy, told her to get back to the station immediately.

'How did you get this?' Larry asked.

'It was what Wendy told me about Eileen Cavendish, too good to be true. An attractive woman, a gangster, supposedly platonic, chatting about the weather. It made no sense, not to Wendy, although she had liked the woman, but then Wendy's a soft touch.'

'I'd agree with Wendy on that score,' Isaac said, waving his two sheets of paper. 'But this changes the situation.'

'I did some checks on the woman, ran her photo through the database, found out that she had a past.'

'And what a past,' Larry said. 'It just goes to show what you see is not necessarily what you get.'

'And with Eileen Cavendish, it's more than we would have thought.'

Wendy came back into the office. Isaac pointed to a spare seat, handing over his two sheets as she sat down. 'Read this,' he said. 'And where were you off to?'

Wendy didn't reply to her DCI, only looked at the photo in the centre of the first page, the name below it. 'I needed to talk to Emily,' she said after she looked up from the paper.

***

'What else does it say?' Eileen Cavendish said in the interview room at the police station.

The room was cold and the woman was wearing only a summer dress with a light-blue cardigan.

'It's correct on every count,' Isaac said. 'You did go to university, a degree in accountancy, and your mother checks out; how she married your father, your birth two years later. However –'

'It doesn't state that at university I had a stress-related illness, and that I had taken ecstasy, even tried heroin, though never addicted to the latter.'

'It doesn't mention that,' Wendy said. 'But why?'

'Economics, not what I was studying, but life in general. My mother was poor, especially after the last man in her life had cleaned out her bank accounts, and she couldn't afford to finance me through university.'

'There are government loans to help.'

'Not enough to survive, but yes, there are, and I did take advantage of them. Either I could work in a shop part-time to feed myself, keep a roof over my head, or I could do something else.'

'You chose the else,' Isaac said.

'It wasn't such a big deal. I told you before I wasn't into men, but if they wanted to pay for my time, that was up to them.'

'How did you get into escorting?'

'I wasn't the only one. Some enjoyed it, others didn't, but it was better than working the midnight shift at a fast-food joint or stacking supermarket shelves. I was studying accountancy; I knew that two and two equal four, and that a mundane job at seven pounds fifty pence an hour while also studying three to four hours a night, five days a week, wasn't going to work.'

'Your decision was purely financial?' Wendy asked.

'What else? My girlfriend at the time was doing it, and I had no moral issues with it. Why work thirty hours in a dead-end job just to get by when I could tart myself up, get two hundred pounds for a couple of hours; an occasional six hundred for an overnight?'

'You were attractive in the photo,' Isaac said.

'I still am, although I prefer to downplay it. I did what was necessary, no shame about it, but it's not

116

something I want to talk about. And besides, my mother, even though she's had her fair share of men, is conservative by nature. It would have upset her if she had known at the time.'

'Does she know now?'

'I told her. I don't like to keep secrets from my mother. After all, she brought me up on her own, apart from my father when he was alive. She wasn't happy about it, that's why she contacted Joe, asked him to help out.'

'How can we trust you after this?' Isaac asked.

'Because it's the truth. I'm a lesbian, not interested in men, not for sex or romance. I got my degree, and I did have a good job with Joe until he died. Life's choices: some are good, some are bad.'

'Working for Joe Foster? Good or bad?'

'He knew the truth.'

'If he had tried it on with you?'

'I owed the man a lot, but he never did.'

Apart from the woman concealing her past as an escort, she hadn't lied. However, she had worked for Joe Foster; she must know more, but for now, there was no more to be gained. Eileen Cavendish, a one-time prostitute, left Challis Street by a side door and walked off down the street.

Isaac looked at her as she left, certain they had not seen the last of her. Somehow, she was integral to the investigation, and her arrangement with Joe Foster was still bizarre.

Chapter 14

Terry Foster reacted angrily when Larry met up with him.

'We've spoken to Eileen Cavendish,' Larry said. 'She worked for your father.'

'And screwed for him. Did she tell you that?'

'She denied it. Why should we believe you over her?'

'Pretty and sweet, is that it? Bamboozled the police into thinking that she was a vestal virgin,' Foster said, affecting a mincing, mocking tone.

'Not at all, but she was open and honest. We've no reason to doubt her and her story checks out.'

'The mother, university, a degree in accountancy? What about the rest?'

'You seem to know a lot about her. What else do you have?'

'My father had her checked out before employing her; needed to know she could be trusted.'

'And?'

'She was a whore, or didn't you know that?'

'What we know isn't important. It's what you do that interests us.'

'She sits up there in that flat, prim and proper, but she's still on the game, I know that.'

'How?'

'I just do.'

'Are you inferring that you've paid her for her time?'

'I'm not.'

Foster wanted to throw stones at the woman, Larry realised, but when pressured for evidence, he didn't have any. Larry remembered the father: decisive, not prone to violent outbursts, not promising on something he couldn't deliver, not brokering dissent. The son was not the natural inheritor of the father.

'Terry, you're wasting my time,' Larry said. 'Eileen Cavendish, even if she sold herself in the past, hasn't done anything wrong around here, and you trying to accuse her does you no credit. Not unless these aspersions serve you some purpose, although I can't see what. And if she was still on the game, so what? She wouldn't have committed a crime, not unless she's sticking flyers in telephone boxes.'

'You're out of touch with reality, Inspector. They don't do that anymore; it's all done online.'

'Do you fancy Eileen?'

'Who wouldn't, but she gave me short shrift, but back then I was a nobody.'

'Some would say you still are,' Larry said. He was baiting the man, hopeful that his reaction would not be violent; not concerned overly if it was. There were still the two heavies who had gunned down the father, although the two who lounged against Terry Foster's Mercedes weren't them. One of the two was a squat body-builder who went by the name of Mad Angus; the other, well over six feet tall, was an ex-wrestler who had spent six years in Maidstone Prison for grievous bodily harm.

Another significant difference between the father and son – that Joe Foster, careful to maintain his honest businessman status, ensured that those close to him had no criminal record. Of the two who had protected him, one had been a hard-as-nails ex-policeman and the other a Nigerian from Lagos, the largest city in the country, a polite and attractive man who always dressed in a suit and didn't drink.

'Maybe they would, but they might regret it,' Foster said.

'You knew about your father walking up Basing Street the same time once a week?'

'I did, even told Morgan, which I assume is where you found out about my father and Eileen.'

Larry did not reply. The information had been given in confidence, and he didn't want Morgan dead, not yet at least.

'It doesn't matter,' Foster said. 'Morgan's been fleecing the family for years, and we don't need him.'

'He also knows your secrets, possibly who would have killed your father, who the two men were. Do you?'

'I've got my suspicions.'

'Then it's for you to tell the police,' Larry said.

'Am I? What if I'm right? What then? You arrest them, charge them with murder, and then an expensive lawyer in a suit and they're out within ten years, maybe less.'

Larry could see the conversation was going nowhere, and sitting in a café drinking coffee with a man he didn't like wasn't his idea of a good time.

'Level with me,' Larry said. 'Eileen Cavendish. Your father's lover or wishful thinking on your part; an attempt to discredit her, to put the blame elsewhere?'

'I've got nothing against the woman, not even that she doesn't fancy me, but then, there's no accounting for taste.'

'None at all. Besides, her sexual orientation wouldn't favour you.'

120

'So what if she fancies women. Give her a real man, and she would have changed her mind.'

A crudity about the woman that Terry thought appropriate, but which Larry did not like. If she was a lesbian, if she had sold herself to survive during her university years, what did it matter? The woman, according to Isaac and Wendy, was pleasant and intelligent, charming even, not like Joe Foster's son. For a moment, Larry hoped that the man was guilty of his father's murder, but Terry Foster was at least smart enough to make sure that his alibi was secure and that anyone paid to kill on Basing Street wouldn't be local, and would no longer be in the area.

***

The first night of uninterrupted sleep in two weeks, and Isaac was feeling fresher than he had since Jenny and child had come back from the hospital. However, Jenny reminded him as she prepared his breakfast that she had been up three times during the night.

He hugged her as he left, kissed her and promised to be home early; neither of them believed that to be likely.

In the office, at five thirty in the morning, Isaac switched on his laptop, scanned through the emails, answered some, deleted others, and read the news: a war in the middle east, a tornado in America, a tsunami in Japan, rioting somewhere else.

Even though murder was depressing, the world wasn't much better, he concluded as he closed the laptop and made his way over to the small kitchen area. The biscuit tin was empty – remiss of Bridget who usually made sure it was full – and even though he had eaten breakfast at home, an early-morning coffee and a biscuit would have set the tone for the day.

It was a day when he felt something was going to happen, good or bad. For too long, the team had interviewed and theorised, and now the leading players were known, apart from the two that had shot Joe Foster.

Larry came into Homicide at ten minutes to six looking the worse for wear, although he was earlier than Wendy who came in nursing a sore leg. Bridget had told Isaac that her housemate had had a rough night with arthritis, and no more was said on Wendy's arrival.

Isaac knew that if he made an official report on his sergeant's condition, she would be subjected to a medical, an examination she might not pass. And the one thing he cherished above all else was the cohesive team he had moulded, even Larry, who had got drunk the previous night.

'Now we're all assembled,' Isaac said. He wasn't in the mood to chastise, only to encourage. The pieces were falling into place. The evidence, not complete but sufficient to postulate possibilities, the time for the team to put forward theories, no matter how ridiculous, to separate the wheat from the chaff, to see what falls out.

'Larry, rough night?' Isaac said, remembering he was not going to complain, but when his DI was on a drinking binge, it invariably meant he had been chasing information.

'I met with Terry Foster, not that I got far. Only found out that the man's got a foul mouth, and that he sees himself as God's gift to women; reckons he could turn Eileen Cavendish given half a chance.'

'He's not likely to get a fraction of that,' Wendy said.

'Does anyone believe her story? That Joe Foster used to go up there once a week for a chat, especially given that she saw him every day in the office,' Isaac said.

'Nobody with half a brain would,' Larry said as he held his head.

'Larry, do us a favour. Go out and splash cold water over your face.'

'I paid a visit to Jacob Morgan after I left Terry Foster. He's a strange character.'

'You got drunk with him?' Wendy asked.

'Our wedding anniversary last night. Just the two of us, the children with my wife's sister. I'm afraid we both got a little drunk.'

'More than a little,' Isaac said. 'Clean yourself up before the chief superintendent pays us a visit.'

'Is he coming down?'

'Who knows, but it's been more than a week since we gave him something worthwhile.'

'Then you'd better phone him up, tell him he'll have a report on his desk this morning, something to pass on to his superiors,' Larry said as he got up and walked out of Isaac's office.

There was a cockiness about Larry that Isaac liked. The man was proud of himself; he had uncovered evidence.

Wendy took the opportunity to go and make coffees for everyone. She returned within ten minutes, a selection of biscuits on a plate as well.

Larry, looking refreshed, his tie straight, his hair patted down with water, took hold of a mug of coffee in one hand, a biscuit in the other. 'Terry reckoned his father and Eileen weren't playing monopoly, although he had no proof. He also knew about her selling herself,' he said.

'It wasn't for long,' Bridget said, 'and if she dresses conservatively, minimal makeup, then most men wouldn't have made the connection between the escort and Foster's accountant.'

'But you did,' Isaac said.

'Facial recognition technology helped, but a woman looks deeper than the superficial.'

'Great detective work, finding her.'

'Not really. I knew when she had been at university, and that she didn't have a lot of money. It was a four in a hundred chance that I'd find her.'

'Four in a hundred?' Larry said.

'Statistics show that close to four per cent of female university students are using sex to pay their way through university, either by art modelling or stripping, or in Eileen Cavendish's case, prostitution. Higher than most people would think, more than I would, but then, they don't go telling their parents or friends.'

'Eileen Cavendish did.'

'She used a different name, a city thirty minutes away by train. If it hadn't been for me, no one else would have found her. She had been picked up by the police once, her photo on record.'

'You mentioned Jacob Morgan,' Isaac reminded Larry.

'I know you've spoken to him, but Morgan's not normal. I'd heard of him once in the past, not about his association with the Fosters.'

'Then what?'

'Rumours mainly, but Rasta Joe, when he was alive, mentioned him, reckoned Morgan was a smart man.'

'More so than Rasta Joe,' Isaac said.

'Not something to be proud of, a former classmate of yours,' Larry said.

'So was Spanish John. Not everyone turned out bad. Some even made chief inspector.'

Larry didn't take his senior's remark as anything other than office repartee. He hadn't intended malice, and he knew his DCI would not take offence.

'Spanish John's not someone I'd take home to meet my wife, but we have the occasional drink,' Larry said. 'He's worried as to what's going down. After all, an assassination always raises the spectre of more deaths, of open gang warfare.'

'Not this time, we hope,' Isaac said.

Larry did not respond. Jacob Morgan was of more interest.

'Morgan wasn't pleased to see me, but he let me into his pokey office, offered me a whisky.'

'Which you accepted,' Wendy said.

'Rude not to, and besides, the tongue loosens when liquored. Not that he was giving much away, but I got the impression he was glad of the company. Good timing on my part.'

'What do you mean?' Isaac asked.

'Morgan's frightened. He told me that Joe Foster had his finger in many pies, none illegal, he emphasised, but then we'd expect him to say that.'

'Did he admit to being afraid?'

'He did, not sure why he told me, other than he thought we could protect him.'

'Not without a good reason.'

'I told him that, although he said it was important. How Terry Foster was threatening him, even sent one of his heavies around earlier in the day to intimidate. Morgan's a private man, no wife. Celibate, I'd say,

125

although why I wouldn't know, but no one's ever seen him with a woman or a rent boy in the area.'

'Is it only Terry?' Isaac asked.

'Joe Foster's business empire is being carved up piece by piece, not that Terry Foster wants that, but some of the women in one of his massage parlours have left, gone to another place run by another gangster.'

'Who?'

'Spanish John, not that I've asked him yet. We don't talk about what he gets up to, only others.'

'Is that it?'

'Morgan's been visited by others, not that he'd say who they were. I got the feeling he wasn't sure who they were or he was too frightened to open up to me, knowing full well that he'd be snitching.'

'Any details as to these other people?'

'He said it was just the one man: white, English accent, strong voice. He said he wouldn't know him again.'

'He's lying.'

'Morgan said he had his suspicions as to who had sent the man.'

'He may as well have given you a name.'

'He did, not in as many words. Told me the man had an office in Canary Wharf, his name on the building.'

'Tony Rafter?'

'That's who I'd reckon, although it doesn't make sense. Tom Foster mentioned the name, and now Morgan. Why would Rafter break cover? Foster's empire would only be petty cash to him.'

'Unless there's something else,' Isaac said. 'What if Morgan has dirt on Rafter? After all, the man knew what his primary client, Foster, got up to. Knew where the illicit gains were stashed, the crimes committed, the hidden faces.'

'If he knew what Rafter was up to, and with us sticking our noses in, digging in the dirt, unveiling hitherto hidden secrets, the man might be considering his options.'

'Will Morgan open up, give up facts?'

'I doubt it. He thinks we can protect him without him doing anything.'

'He's not that naïve. Morgan's too devious to open up to a police officer without due consideration as to the consequences.'

Isaac remembered his encounter with Tony Rafter; a man with political influence, a person who would stop at nothing to cover his tracks.

It had to be done, although another interview with the friend of politicians, a man who mingled with royalty, would not be easy. It was proof that Homicide needed, and it was only Jacob Morgan who could provide it.

Whatever the day would bring was subject to intense scrutiny and a degree of trepidation. Upset an important person, and the powers on high would be down on Challis Street like a ton of bricks, Isaac knew only too well as did his chief superintendent. They had been there before, but Isaac was determined, and if it was his job on the line, then so be it.

Some in Challis Street would have weighed up the pros and cons, decided on the least difficult road, but that wasn't Isaac's style.

'Bring Morgan into the station,' Isaac said. 'Read him his rights, make sure he's safe and secure. The man's going to talk.'

Larry nodded his head, but he wasn't so sure. And he was equally certain that his DCI wasn't either.

Chapter 15

Jacob Morgan sat in the interview room at Challis Street.

Isaac went through the formalities, told Morgan his rights – the man had declined legal representation.

'You gave us a tip-off about Eileen Cavendish,' Isaac said.

'Terry Foster's throwing his weight around. He's going to do something stupid, and I don't want to be accused by you or him of being involved, hiding facts. There's a war coming, but you must know that already. Terry's not too subtle, more bash and burn, guaranteed to lose out in the end.'

'If Joe Foster's empire is legitimate, something you've insisted on, why war?'

'He asked me for financial advice. As to his empire, I don't know either way, only that trouble's brewing.'

Isaac thought back to his schooldays, the English teacher attempting to hammer into delinquent teens and diligent students alike the beauty of the English language, the quote from Shakespeare's *Hamlet*: 'the lady doth protest too much, methinks'. It seemed to sum up Morgan, a man quick to defend his innocence, only too ready to accuse others.

'This war, between who?'

'Many a person disappeared due to Joe Foster,' Larry said, sitting alongside his DCI, knowing full well that the man was winding up the accountant.

'If they did or they didn't, it wasn't any of my business,' Morgan replied, a little surer of himself in the interview room.

'Larry's talking about murder,' Isaac said. 'Something you must have known about.'

'Joe Foster was the subject of a lot of innuendoes. Rumours on the street are hardly proof.'

'You admitted to Larry to being frightened.'

'Not frightened, concerned. Terry is wild, likely to rile the wrong person, inflict pain where it's not warranted or wanted.'

'Rile who? The West Indians, someone we don't know?'

'The empire is disintegrating from within; the barbarians are at the gate,' Morgan said.

'A student of history, the fall of the Roman Empire, Machiavelli, or something more?'

'Joe Foster's business empire was an autocracy with no clear successor.'

'He told you this?'

'I've mentioned this to the police before. Joe couldn't trust Terry, not totally, and of the others, Samantha was the only one savvy enough, but she was female.'

'The age of equality. Are you saying her sex was against her?' Isaac said.

'I'm saying nothing, only that Terry wouldn't have been able to accept it, not his sister, not someone younger than him.'

'And that, family aside, someone would be hurt, possibly killed, the same way as Joe was?'

'I'm not sure what I'm saying. My involvement with the father was not criminal, but Terry might see the situation differently.'

'Are you saying that you knew Joe was a criminal? And what about Eileen Cavendish? You told us about her, and from what we can tell, her relationship with Joe Foster was not sexual.'

'Which one do you want me to answer?'

'Both.'

'Yes, Joe was involved in crime,' Morgan admitted for the first time.

'Proof?'

'No proof, but I'm well aware of the money he was moving out of the country; more money than the books he gave to me to audit showed.'

'You're aware of Tony Rafter? You hinted the man's name to Inspector Hill.'

'Did I? I can't remember that I did. I know him by reputation, nothing more.'

'This money that Joe Foster sent out of the country? Drug money? Extortion? What sort of money? What do you reckon?'

'It was more than I advised him on.'

'How do you know this?'

'Joe trusted me, a trust I would never violate. He knew that.'

'You're aware of this money, but you don't question him. Unusual, I'd say.'

'To an officer of the law, it might be. As long as my clients sign a declaration that the information they're supplying is correct, then my conscience is clear.'

'Even if it's drug money, garnered from a heinous activity?' Larry said.

'You're friendly with Spanish John, share a few drinks with him from time to time,' Morgan said.

'In the course of my duty, I do.'

'Yet the man peddles drugs. How do you square it with your conscience?'

'I don't need to. I need to get the feel of the area, know who's up to what.'

'You know about his activity, direct knowledge. Maybe not enough to put the man in jail, but from what I hear, you and he are friendly. It could be that your lifestyle benefits from the acquaintance.'

'It does not,' Larry rebuked Morgan, angry at the aspersion.

Morgan looked away from Larry and directly at Isaac. 'Are you aware that your detective inspector is believed by more than a few to be on the take?'

Larry sat stunned, not sure what he had just heard. Isaac felt a pang of disbelief; a realisation that there might be an element of truth in what Morgan had said.

Isaac sat back on his seat, looked over at Morgan, not willing to glance at Larry, not able to give him a reassuring pat on the back.

Did that explain how Larry had afforded the deposit on another house, a property beyond an inspector's pay scale, Isaac thought. The social-climbing aspirations of Larry's wife were known in the department, and even though she was an attractive woman, a good wife and mother, she continued to give Larry anguish.

Isaac knew he needed to conduct an internal investigation; he would need the advice of Detective Chief Superintendent Goddard.

'That's a serious accusation,' Isaac said.

'It's a rumour, not proof; no more than my criminal involvement with Joe Foster. It's easy to throw verbal bricks, another to back them up with something solid. For all I know, your inspector is as honest as the day's long.'

Isaac wasn't sure what to make of Morgan's flippant reference to the inspector's honesty. Was it just that, a passing remark, or was it intended to reveal a previously unknown truth? Whatever it was, it was serious.

Regardless, Jacob Morgan was sitting across from him. With no charges against the man, he could get up at any time and walk out. Mentally compartmentalising the man's previous remarks, Isaac focussed on the matter in hand.

''I repudiate what Mr Morgan just said,' Larry interjected as Isaac prepared to continue his questioning.

Isaac did not respond. He looked back at Morgan, concerned that the man was trying to lead the police down a false trail, to deflect from his wrongdoings.

'Before we were distracted,' Isaac said,' you were referring to war in the area.'

'Foster is consolidating his power. Some of the gangs are up in arms, not taking kindly to Terry and his tactics. And then there's Samantha, nobody's fool. She could be behind the scenes plotting against her brother, stirring the gangs, feeding them information.'

'Loyalty to the father implies loyalty to the family. Joe Foster wouldn't have had you denigrating one of his children.'

'Joe's dead, his children aren't.'

'Can you prove that any of Foster's offspring are guilty of a crime?' Isaac asked.

'That's for you, not me.'

'What about Ben?'

'The youngest child of Joe and Gladys. He could control the gangs, but he's always preferred not to be involved in crime.'

'He could run the legitimate side of the business, leave the other to Terry.'

'Terry would soon stick his nose in on what Ben was doing. No wonder Joe hated Terry, thought he was deficient in the brain, cast doubts on his parentage.'

'Is there any way that he's not Joe's? After all, the other four children of him and Gladys are not known for violence.'

'He was Joe's; he admitted that much. The man's a throwback to Gladys's father, an Irishman with a foul temper and not much between his ears.

'This war? The family or someone else? Specifics, what do you have?'

'Ask your inspector,' Morgan said.

'We're asking you,' Isaac said. 'If this gets nasty, you could get caught in the crossfire, collateral damage, assuming you're friendly to one side or the other.'

'I'm friendly to no one, only self. I'll admit to liking Joe, but as for the others, apart from Emily, I wouldn't give you tuppence for the lot of them.'

'That's not the tone of an innocent man, wishing ill on people,' Isaac said.

'What you sow, you reap. Joe made his way in life, the same as I did. He preferred sociability and family; I didn't, but we understood each other.'

'Why Emily?'

'An innocent, that's all. If she gets caught up in it, don't expect me to shed a tear.'

'Why?'

'I live on my own in a little flat, work in a pokey office, store my money where it's to my advantage. I don't care for people, not as you would understand.'

'There's a term for that,' Isaac said.

'Don't bother with a psychological evaluation, not with me. I'm antisocial, nothing more. I bother no one; no one bothers me.'

'Yet you were friendly with Joe Foster. Does that mean you didn't care what he did?'

'To you, I'm a horrible little weasel of a man, not worthy of pity or admiration. Correct?' Morgan said.

'It still doesn't explain what you know and how we should proceed.'

'Talk to your inspector's friend, have a few pints with him, ask him about Terry, the threats he's making. And as for that cock and bull story from Joe's fancy woman, he was screwing her; I know that.'

'How?'

'He told me. Not that he didn't love Emily, but he was ageing, as was she. He needed fresh meat, good for the libido, the self-esteem.'

'Not for you?'

'No interest in physical contact, male or female.'

'Tony Rafter?'

'You'll not prove anything,' Morgan said.

'That wasn't the question.'

'That's the only answer you're getting. Cross Rafter and woe betide you. As for me, I'll wish you both a good night.'

Jacob Morgan got up from his seat, shook hands with Isaac and Larry and left.

'You could have held him,' Larry said.

'He told us as much as he intended,' Isaac said. 'Too much, in fact.'

Both of them knew what Isaac was referring to: Larry's possible criminal activity. The next few days in the office were going to be difficult, both of them knew.

Chapter 16

A shadow had descended over Homicide. Although Jacob Morgan's aspersion had been just that, a disparaging attempt to distract attention away from him and his relationship with Joe Foster, it had resonated with Isaac. Not that he was comfortable with the situation, but his DI's easy rapport and friendliness with the villainy in the area had drawn comments before. And once Morgan had raised the possibility, Isaac could not ignore it.

It was not the first time that a police officer had been accused of taking bribes, but now it was personal, it was Detective Inspector Larry Hill, a man that both Isaac and Chief Superintendent Goddard respected. Isaac had brought him into Homicide, and whereas there had been concerns over his inspector before, it had been his drinking, nothing more.

Morgan had mentioned it in passing, and only two days previously Larry had been in the office showing photos of the house he and his wife were purchasing. Proud as punch he had been, saying how happy his wife was, not once mentioning the strain to pay the mortgage, an almost weekly gripe before. Isaac, not wanting to, but unable not to, smelled a rat, and not just a small scurrying animal, but something large and menacing; a creature that could tear the good reputation asunder that Challis Street Homicide had built for itself. Undermined from within, brought down by a corrupt police officer, the most despicable of all men.

Chief Superintendent Goddard sat in his office on the top floor of Challis Street. Behind him the panorama of rooftops, and in the distance, the London Eye. The weather was menacing, dark clouds, the threat of rain.

The mood in the office was equally gloomy.

Goddard, a man Isaac regarded as a friend, even if he was his superior, spoke. 'We can't hush this up. Too many questions asked if we do.'

'It's a distraction,' Isaac said. 'We've got a turf war in the making, and Larry, apart from this, is vital to the team.'

'Suspension, subject to an internal investigation. I can't see how you can avoid it, and if we're remiss, it's our heads on the chopping block. You know that as well as I do.'

'Larry deserves the right to defend himself, and besides, Morgan's not a man to trust. He was cornered, said something to throw us off the scent.'

'It worked.'

'We're all tarred to some extent by association, and Larry's been mixing with the wrong crowd,' Isaac said, more as a means of justifying to himself his inspector's innocence than anything else. 'It could be nothing.'

'And it could be. Many a person condemned at the altar of indecision; the rumours allowed to flourish. We've got to nip this in the bud now. Where's DI Hill?' Goddard said.

'Downstairs, making out he's busy.'

'If we don't act soon, we leave ourselves open. Have you spoken to him about this?'

'We've spoken, not that he took it well. Accused me of believing the word of a rogue over that of a police inspector of nearly twenty years standing; a man whose record is unblemished.'

'You can't blame him. Others have besmirched both of us before.'

Isaac knew what his chief superintendent was referring to. On two occasions, Isaac had been sidelined, and the superintendent sideways promoted to remove his influence in the police force, to isolate him from his mentor in the House of Lords, a former commissioner of the London Metropolitan Police. And now it was two men who had felt the rough end of incorrect justice who were about to act on a villain's assertion, and no one was in any doubt that Morgan qualified for the epithet, and to risk destroying the career and reputation of one of their own.

Two hours later, the three men gathered in one of the station's meeting rooms. Isaac sat at the head of the table, Richard Goddard to his right, and at the far end, directly facing Isaac, Detective Inspector Larry Hill. None of the three showed any friendliness, none of the light-hearted banter that usually preceded a formal discussion.

To those assembled, it was a sad state of affairs, something that none of them wanted to deal with, conscious that inaction after Morgan's visit to the station would leave them open to the charge of dereliction of duty.

'I'm innocent of any crime,' Larry said. His voice was tremulous, an indication of the strain he found himself under.

'A man is innocent until found guilty,' Goddard said, not showing emotion, knowing that if one of his team was guilty of a crime, then he, as the senior officer, was by default guilty, the sword readied by others for him to fall on. A political animal, the superintendent knew that others would be baying at the door, pressuring him to act or to be acted on, not caring that outside a war was in the making, the troops lining up on each side. It was an impossible situation, only to become further confused as the first skirmishes commenced.

Whatever the outcome for the inspector, Goddard knew that his own future in the police force would either rise meritoriously or sink into oblivion. He would have preferred to have ignored his inspector's possible crimes until the war abated, but that wasn't possible, not now.

Isaac read out the areas of concern, Bridget having typed up the necessary paperwork, after having taken her laptop to a secure room away from prying eyes.

'Your friendship with the gang leader known as Spanish John,' Isaac said first.

'It's hardly a friendship,' Larry replied.

Isaac had no issue with meeting a criminal if it served the investigation, but it was a friendship. Whether it was criminal was another issue, but it was still unwise.

'High levels of alcohol consumption,' Isaac continued. Not a crime in itself, but a possible disciplinary matter, and if Larry was subjected to an investigation, then it was better to be thorough. The man was a good police officer, and he didn't want to lose him, but now was not the time to be shilly-shallying. It was the time to be decisive, so much so that if questions were asked now or in the future, he, as a chief inspector, had acted with due diligence and care.

Larry said nothing, only looked down.

'Financial improprieties, the third issue.'

'What does that mean?' Larry said.

'Your purchase of a house that appears to be outside of your ability to pay.'

'Shrewd money management is hardly a crime.'

It wasn't, Isaac knew, but his inspector wasn't a man who had shown financial acumen before.

'Due to the seriousness of the matter, hopeful that all issues raised will be resolved, I suggest that you continue in Homicide,' Goddard said. He knew that the inspector should be on suspension, but Larry Hill had his ear closer to the ground than anyone else in Homicide.

'Thanks,' Isaac said, turning to Larry. 'I hope this can be resolved.'

'It will be. Of course, I'm friendly with criminals, but it's a two-way street. They scratch my back; I scratch theirs. It's how policing is done out on the street.'

'Inspector, I suggest you take advice from your DCI,' Goddard said. 'The realities may be that, but in this politically correct and increasingly sanctimonious world, mentioning it's a two-way street, scratch my back, scratch theirs, is tantamount to a confession.'

'That's not what I meant,' Larry said.

'Maybe, but the interpretation, especially if the matter goes further than us three, would be distorted. I wouldn't want opinion of you prejudiced by what you say.'

'Then am I innocent in your mind?'

'Every police officer, every criminal, is innocent to me. It's up to the courts, or in this case, the Department of Professional Standards, to decide otherwise.'

'That's not an answer,' Larry said, a little more impertinent than he should have been with the chief superintendent, Isaac thought.

'It's the only one I can give. As a police officer, you are exemplary in your duties in bringing in criminals, solving homicides, but…'

It was the only answer that Larry was to get; to him, it wasn't satisfactory, and he was worried. He knew how the system worked: a scapegoat found if needed, and he was it. And out on the street, the villains would take advantage, become more reluctant to open up with a police inspector if the man was under suspicion, not that they cared either way. Still, they knew that a police officer under investigation was liable to act for his survival, not theirs.

It was a complication that Homicide didn't need, not at this time.

***

It was, Jacob Morgan realised as he sat on a chair in his small flat, a mistake to make a comment about a police inspector, knowing that, guilty or not, the organisation behind him would rally to protect the man, and if not him, the reputation of the police force.

He was a marked man; it was for him to make plans. It was ten in the evening, too late to leave his flat, but it couldn't be delayed. Even so, Morgan showered and shaved, combed his hair and put on a suit, a freshly-pressed shirt and tie completing the ensemble. To him, a tidy man led to an orderly brain, a discipline instilled in him by his strict Methodist father. It was a discipline that had served him well.

Outside on the street, the late-night traffic was starting to reduce, and there was an aura of tranquillity. In the office, a five-minute walk, it was as quiet as a grave, almost as cold. Morgan turned up the collar of his jacket and moved over to the other side of the room, stooping down to switch on a small bar heater. As he stood up, a twinge in his back, a reminder that age was catching up with him. He knew he should have left five years before when he had been still young enough to enjoy the benefits, cognisant that choosing frugality over imprudence might well prove to have been wrong. He thought of Joe Foster, possibly the only person he could have called a friend.

Sure, he knew what the man had been, the crimes he had committed, the bodies he had buried, but even so, the man had lived well; two wives, both enjoyed while they were young and supple, and then, unbeknown to either of his two families, Eileen Cavendish. Morgan wished he had been more like Foster, and he hoped that once free of England and his office and austere flat, he would be able to embrace a more befitting lifestyle. After all, money wasn't the issue, although a lack of energy may prove to be an encumbrance.

Seated at his desk, he switched on his laptop, entered the codes, appreciated the technology. Even so, at his side, a pen and paper, as he checked bank account after bank account, writing the amounts and the countries where they were. Once completed, he totalled up the amount before finally leaning back into the comfort of his chair. He then closed his eyes, let his imagination have free rein, saw himself surrounded by women, by Eileen Cavendish if she was willing. They had met and had been comfortable in each other's company, and money could be a motivator, but he wasn't so sure.

For some unfathomable reason, the woman, even though she was Joe's mistress, appeared to cling to him, and he to her for another reason. In all the years, when his belief in the security of unfettered money had been important, Jacob Morgan had rarely sought the solace of a woman, but now he could feel the need for Eileen.

Morgan smiled and thought that maybe he wasn't that old at all. It wasn't the police that worried him, not much, as he regarded them as staid and laborious, following procedures, obtaining warrants, looking for indisputable proof, but others: others not concerned with right or wrong. To such people, suspicion was proof enough, and as he went back to the computer, he knew that he was about to do something that wouldn't be open to dispute. He was about to cheat the Fosters. None of them was as smart as Joe, but concealment would not be so easy, not if one of the more capable siblings decided to check.

Morgan once again looked at what he had: fifteen bank accounts, a portfolio of shares in the name of a company he had set up, and the deeds to a mansion in Portugal, an office block in Malta, and a block of apartments in the South of France.

Morgan knew that if Joe had been alive, he wouldn't have considered what he was about to do. It was all so simple; an easy exercise to travel around the world, selling stocks, buying others, disposing of the properties, buying others with cash in another name.

Jacob Morgan, a man who had skirted crime, was about to make his mark, but it would be secretive. If only he could entice Eileen to come with him. She was the only thing he would miss of London. He decided to visit her; he was confident of success.

Chapter 17

Larry's wife took the news badly when he told her that night. He had thought to keep it from her, hope that the investigation would be handled discreetly and that his record of service would work in his favour. But as Isaac had explained after the chief superintendent had left, it wasn't that easy. Due diligence was essential, and one bad seed could upturn the apple cart, and Challis Street was under close inspection by others.

Isaac knew the reason, assumed that Larry had some idea, that Detective Chief Superintendent Richard Goddard, desperate for promotion to commander, was using all in his arsenal to secure the rank. He was even willing to go so far as to circumvent senior management at Scotland Yard and to encourage Lord Shaw, his mentor, a former commissioner of the London Metropolitan Police, to put in a word here and there, to smooth the promotion.

Others wanted the upcoming commander's position. Some of them competent; others devious and not afraid to get in the dirt, knowing that mud sticks and a corrupt police officer at Challis Street was very sticky and would reflect on the chief superintendent.

Goddard had left the two in the room, shaking his head in despair as he climbed the stairs to his office, preferring it to the lift, a failing attempt at staying fit.

In Homicide, even though nothing had been said officially, not by Isaac or Larry, certainly not Bridget, it seemed that everyone knew. Isaac, once he had taken stock of the situation, called Wendy into the office, as she was the one who was most likely to engage with Larry, and told her that he'd been accused of corruption, of taking bribes.

'Not to me, he isn't,' Wendy said. 'I've met a few in my time who were on the take, but Inspector Hill, his own worst enemy sometimes, isn't one of them.'

She told Isaac about her early days as a constable in Sheffield, the blame passing when a truant girl that Wendy had found had been returned to her parents on the advice of an inexperienced social worker, only to die at the hand of the father. And how some of those in authority, one of them an inspector known to take bribes, had tried to blame the constable, even attempting to pervert the course of justice.

'Not so easy these days,' Isaac said. 'More accountability, more processes in place.'

'Bridget would disagree. Give her a computer, and she could do it, for or against. Back then, we didn't, unless you regard a machine the size of a car with reels of tape that used to churn away as a computer.'

Isaac had to agree. Bridget would have made a first-class fraudster if that had been her bent; thankfully, it wasn't, and also privy to Larry's dilemma, she rallied to his side. The next morning, a freshly-baked cake for him in the small alcove that served as a kitchen.

With Larry in limbo, his mood changed. No longer the cheerful demeanour, more of a sullen manner, not communicative as he had been, terse with those he met.

Spanish John was the first to comment as the two of them met for lunch at one of the pubs in Notting Hill. 'What's up?' the gang leader said.

Larry didn't feel as though he wanted to respond and would have preferred to be back home with his wife, the one person who after her initial alarm had affirmed her confidence in him. He appreciated that when the cards were laid out on the table, she cared more for him and the children than her upwardly mobile friends. To him, they were shallow, always bragging about how well they were doing, the places they were going to on holiday, the Porsche in the garage next year. Larry was sure that most of them were up to the hilt in debt.

The husband of one of them had a lifestyle, flush with money one month, struggling the next, which did not indicate a business plan, but probably crime. Larry had checked him out, found out that he had done time for embezzlement, nine months in jail before early release. And then, his wife's closest friend, a woman that Larry liked, had committed adultery, only to confide it to Larry's wife and to have the wrath of God visited on her, a lecture on Sodom and Gomorrah.

His wife, Larry knew, had a narrow view of the world, detached from the grimness of it; the reason he did not come home and talk about his work, not about the bodies he had seen, the people he had arrested. And if her close friend's husband was involved in illegal activity, he'd find himself in handcuffs soon enough. It wasn't for Homicide to deal with it, but even though he shouldn't have, he had told the drug squad to be on the lookout for the man. And now, Larry thought, they are willing to condemn me without a trial.

It wasn't often that he felt sorry for himself, and whereas Bridget's cake had cheered him, he knew that as he looked at the others, the peripheral staff in Homicide, he could sense that behind the bonhomie their faith in the inspector had been shaken.

'Morgan has inferred that I'm on the take,' Larry said. In his hand, a pint of beer, although he didn't want to drink, not that day, not ever again.

'You'd not be the first.'

'I know of others, but the proof is not so easy. You're not about to tell me who you're bribing, are you? I need a win,' Larry said. 'You're holding out on me. I need something solid, to prove that you're not paying me.'

If Isaac had been there, he would have said that Larry's approach was foolish, open to misinterpretation. But Larry saw a possibility to reach into the soul of Spanish John, still a man with a soft side, even paying for the heart surgery of a child of poor parents, not even West Indians, but Asian and Muslim. It wasn't something that the man wanted to be known generally, as acts of generosity did not necessarily work in a gang leader's favour.

However, it didn't stop him from inflicting wretched violence on those who crossed him. Julius Rios was one such person, not that it had ever been proven.

Larry had never warmed to Rios, who was from Barbados, an island in the Caribbean. Taller than most of his compatriots, with a slim build and a penchant for sharp suits, gold jewellery and a Panama hat that he wore at a slant, the man had been born and had grown up in the Caribbean, and London was not to his liking. He was vocal on the subject if he had more than a few drinks in him, only ever drinking rum.

Rios had appeared in London four years previously, cutting a swathe through the area, and money never seemed to be an issue with him. He had a cultured accent, not the dialect of the islands, and with his soothing tones, he had soon found a job as a disc jockey in a local club. After nine months and a succession of girlfriends, he was spinning the turntables at raves around the country, making a lot of money, getting laid most nights.

And that was the problem; Rios, who didn't like England, but enjoyed the lifestyle it afforded him, had a problem with women. The more, the merrier for him: groupies if they were available, not that he checked their age, only their willingness, or the girlfriends of other men if he could, the wives, the more the better.

Julius Rios was a man who had it made, but a man who didn't know when to stop, which line not to cross.

And then, three Christmases before last, the man had disappeared, no forwarding address, his belongings intact in an apartment he rented in Bayswater.

Over that Christmas, the talk in the pubs and out on the street was about what had happened to Rios. Some speculated that he had gone back to the Caribbean, but that was soon discounted; others thought that maybe he had tired of the life, and had hung up his sharp suit, thrown his hat in the river, and just gone back to being an average Joe. The wildest of the speculations was that he was dead, the victim of a jealous lover, a disgruntled boyfriend, a violent father whose daughter had lost her innocence to him.

Larry had known the truth four weeks after the last time Rios had been seen in the area. The man was unique in dress and character and in bearing; he could not be mistaken for anyone else.

It had been a Thursday night, after the murder of a local hooligan, his mother the only person sad about his demise. She was pleading with Larry and Wendy to find the killers of her son. 'Mickey was a good boy, always kind to me,' she had said.

149

'When was the last time you saw him?' Wendy had asked. She could sympathise with the mother, although the woman was known to the police: a prostitute who had been in trouble with the law on several occasions, a dead child whose father could have been one of a dozen men. The deceased had been doomed from the start; statistically, the odds had always been against him, only it wasn't a rival group that had killed him.

'I could see him from my bedroom window, out on the street, talking to Julius Rios,' the mother said.

Two weeks later, with no more seen of Rios, and enquiries conducted in Barbados, the man's background became known. A cosseted childhood, the best of educations, and Julius, the favoured son of a senior Barbadian politician, had been destined for business and politics, a possible prime minister of the small country. However, the young Rios, apart from his obvious advantages, also had a frivolous nature, preferring from the age of sixteen to drink and dance and socialise and to get any willing female into his bed; the last one, the daughter of a political rival of his father. With the shame of it to the Rios family, let alone the blow to the father's political aspirations, Julius Rios found himself on a plane to England with enough money to survive.

Back home in Barbados was a young child, Rios's child, who would never know his father. And then the indisputable proof that Rios had murdered Mickey, his body found in a shallow grave just outside Woking in Surrey, Rios's fingerprints on the knife in the young man's chest.

On reflection, Larry realised he hadn't been as diligent as he should have been. After all, it had been Spanish John's girlfriend who had been in bed with Rios on a Saturday morning when the gang leader had walked in on them. Rios had had the good sense to jump out of a window and to make a naked dash through the streets until he made it home.

And now it made sense. Rios was encumbered to Spanish John, a man who would use it to his advantage, and he had got Rios to kill the hapless Mickey. Once that was done, someone else killed Rios, thus killing two birds with one stone.

The only thing that didn't make sense was why Mickey had been killed. Rios, Larry could understand. The man, like the French philosopher Jean-Paul Sartre, much to the consternation of the women he seduced, would give a detailed account of his amorous undertakings to all and sundry.

Larry felt a chill run through his body as if someone had run over his grave. He was sitting down sharing a drink with a man who had been responsible for a murder. In the past, it hadn't weighed too heavily on his conscience, but now, it did. He wasn't sure how to proceed, but one thing was for certain: his friendship with the gang leader was at an end. He picked up his beer, downed it in one go and waved over to the barman for two more drinks. He knew that the police investigation was the least of his problems.

Now he had to deal with Spanish John, to arrest him for crimes committed. It would create an unbreachable wall between the police inspector and the villains in the area.

Whatever the future, Larry decided, it would be of his making. He'd show those who doubted him that he was an excellent and incorruptible police officer.

***

Eileen Cavendish's reputation, tarnished as it was, took a turn for the worse after Jacob Morgan had visited her. She felt the need to contact Homicide.

Unnerved as she was, she managed to sit still on one of the chairs in her flat. On the other side of the room, Wendy sat upright, conscious of the other woman's trauma. Isaac, not so easily taken in, looked hard and long at the woman, either Joe Foster's lover or friend. He still wasn't sure which.

'Why call us?' Wendy asked. 'After all, he didn't touch you, or did he?'

'I had no one else to turn to. That's why I phoned you.'

'No one in the area; not the Fosters?'

'Maybe Ben, but mentally he used to undress me every time he saw me.'

'He fancied you as well?'

'He's a young man. They're all the same.'

'You don't mind people looking, assuming that you and Joe were involved?'

'Of course I mind, but I needed to talk to someone about Jacob Morgan's visit, what he said.'

'Not the police necessarily?'

'No. And besides, it might be nothing, but Morgan left me unnerved, not sure what to do. He wanted to buy me.'

'In as many words?' Isaac said.

'That was my past when I was desperate for money, but not now. And no, he didn't want a quick fumble, a leg over; he wanted me to go with him, to be there on call.'

'A concubine?'

'I've been to university. You can say it. He wanted a whore to have sex with him when he wanted.'

'We've checked out Jacob Morgan. What makes you so certain that you understood him correctly.'

'If a man stands close to where you're sitting and says he's going away and he wants you to join him, then it's not conversation that he wants.'

'You told us that was what Joe wanted, not that we've ever believed it.'

'I may have screwed for money once, but I never did with Joe, not with anyone for a long time.'

'If Morgan hadn't wanted you for sex, would you have gone?' Wendy asked.

'There's not much for me to do here, and the lease runs out on this place in a couple of weeks. I can't see any of the Fosters paying for it.'

'Terry?'

'He wouldn't want to talk, not with him. He's just a lout.'

'Financially, you're in a dilemma, the same as in university. Easy to return to the tried and trusted once you've done it. No issues with morality for you; you've said that before.'

'I've got money. I can always find another place, another job, but never another Joe.' Eileen Cavendish raised a handkerchief to her eyes.

'He was a friend, yet you still cry for him,' Isaac said. 'A woman of your age, you should have a boyfriend, a husband even, yet you pine for a man old enough to be your father.'

'He was,' Eileen said. 'Now you finally understand why he and I could be nothing more than platonic.'

Wendy could see the truth in it, although Isaac remained mystified.

'That's not what you told us before,' Isaac said.

'I told you what I knew as the truth. I hadn't lied.'

'The man you thought was your father wasn't. Is that what you're saying?'

'I have no memory of the man who was married to my mother. He died when I was four, as you well know. My mother always told me that he was a good man, and every birthday and at Christmas, his name would be alongside my mother's on the card.'

'Why did she tell you the truth?'

'I suppose I always suspected it from the first day I came to work for Joe. He was a hard man with everyone apart from his family. Not disrespectful of the other women he employed, not a chauvinist or a bully, not like Terry. But with me, he always had a tenderness about him.'

'And you hadn't met him before?'

'Never.'

'You prostituted yourself, something Jacob Morgan wanted from you.'

'He's an evil little man. Joe, or maybe I should call him father now, told me about Morgan, as to how he used to cheat him.'

'I thought nobody cheated Joe Foster and lived to tell the tale,' Isaac said. 'You're aware of how violent he could be?'

'Not with me, not with his family, not even with Jacob Morgan.'

It wasn't an answer, but Wendy could see that the woman was struggling with the dilemma of Joe being her father.

'Why are we here?' Wendy asked. Apart from the woman's revelation and Jacob Morgan's proposition, nothing more had occurred. It hardly seemed a police matter.

'Joe knew that Jacob was cheating him, but he used to say, "he makes more for me than he takes", which was how Joe's mind worked. If one of his men was taking a little extra on the side, Joe was willing to turn a blind eye. To him, loyalty and competence were all-important. But anyone who cheated him and then came up with lame excuses, he'd be down on them like a ton of bricks.'

'Joe had men killed,' Isaac said. 'Others might want to avenge their deaths.'

'Joe never sullied himself with doing it personally.'

'But you knew about it. And why are you telling us this now? Before you were reticent, feeding us a lame story about you and gangster Joe. What's changed now?'

'Nothing's changed, but Morgan, he told me how much money he had.'

'How much?'

'Over thirty million pounds and Joe was no fool with money, nor was I. I believed that he had taken only just over four from him, both honestly and cheated. Which means that Jacob Morgan has stolen a lot more, something I can't believe, and the man wasn't stupid, or else he was involved in something else.'

'It still doesn't explain why we're here,' Wendy said.

'It does. If Terry finds out, he'll suspect me of involvement with Morgan, assume that the two of us were scheming against his father. If that happens, I'll be forced to reveal that I'm his half-sister, something I don't want to do.'

'Why? You could have a claim to some of the money.'

'I don't want it, none of it. Besides, Morgan never touched me, but he was menacing. He repeated that the truth about the money he'd taken would come out

155

eventually. He didn't mention blackmail, but that's what it was.'

'To coerce you into agreeing to his demands?'

'If Terry found out about me, and he will, then what will happen? Ben might come to my defence, but it's unlikely. Not because he doesn't fancy me, but he wouldn't want to be involved.'

'He has a girlfriend,' Isaac said.

'Ben has a wandering eye. He was after Emily, and Joe knew that, not that he would have acted out of order, not with his father's wife, but now, who knows. And Terry's after her.'

'If Ben made a play for you?'

'If he did, I'd have to tell him the truth. Regardless of the hate within the family, they remain close. Look at how they treat Emily and her two children; pariahs, they are to them, and none of them have acted against the first family's interests. On the contrary, Emily was always on to Joe to spend more time with Gladys and their children, but he never wanted to, apart from Ben, who he admired, Samantha, he respected, and Tom, who he pitied.

'You've met Billy. Hardly a charming man, not even a lovable rogue. The man's made a career for himself, but more than ten minutes in his company, you're rushing for the door. Bore the hind legs off a donkey with his monotone voice, his endless babble about profit and loss, how much it costs to organise a shipping container, the people he has to pay.'

'He speaks openly about his crimes?' Isaac said.

'To Joe, he did. I used to see Billy from time to time; the most I got from him was a leering look and "is the old man around?".'

'His leering? Worry you?' Wendy asked.

'Not much.'

Isaac had it figured. All this beating around the bush was leading up to the truth.

'Eileen, why didn't your mother tell you about your father before, before you became his lover?' Isaac said.

'She said it was because of the memory of the man who I had thought was my father.'

'Did Joe know the truth?'

'As far as he was concerned, I was the child of a lost love. He respected me for that.'

'Your mother has done you an injustice, hasn't she?'

'An injustice that can never be righted.'

Wendy looked over at her DCI and then back at Eileen Cavendish. 'You're pregnant,' she said.

Isaac sat back on his seat, stumped as to what to say. Opposite him, a young woman, the mistress of an older man, carrying her father's child, oblivious of the truth until she had confronted her mother.

'I phoned my mother for advice as to whether I should keep the child or not. Believe me; I didn't know. To me, Joe was a friend of my mother's, a former lover.'

'Did you love him?'

'Yes, I did, but now we know, it was not the love of a woman for a man, but the love of a child for a parent.'

Wendy, unable to remain seated for any longer, went over and sat beside Eileen, put her arm around her. 'It'll be alright,' she said.

Isaac knew it never would be.

Chapter 18

Larry knew that if he continued to associate with criminals, he was stoking the fire of damnation; and if he didn't, he would not be able to prove to his accusers, and to those that had placed faith in him, that he wasn't the most heinous of all, a bent copper.

There had been one at his previous station, an overweight sergeant who'd take his favours, either in money or sex, to overlook the girls out on the street selling their wares.

The sergeant, Tony Molloy, had grown up in Manchester, and when questioned by his colleagues, had replied that where he came from, there was more give and take. And if the route to solving a crime was through the auspices of a woman down on her luck, then why not enjoy it while you could.

Larry had never taken favours in London, although there were plenty of opportunities, and Molloy had been the only one in the station, but to snitch on a colleague was a two-edged sword, in that the snitcher would be ostracised in the police station, his position untenable.

Larry had spent just over two hours with Spanish John in the pub. It was one o'clock in the morning, and he was back at Challis Street, after spending an hour with his wife and children. Sleep eluded him; worry had taken its place. In front of him, his laptop; to his side, a cup of coffee and a slice of the cake that Bridget had made for him. Not an emotional man, he felt a lump in his throat, a tear in his eye; he was, he knew, at the lowest point in his life.

For ten minutes, he surfed the net, found nothing that interested him. Eventually, entering a password, he found Julius Rios on the police database, including a picture of the body after it was exhumed from the shallow grave where it had been buried. He had seen death before; he was unmoved by the sight.

Larry scanned through the documentation, unsure why Spanish John's girlfriend had given a statement, but there it was, a photo of the woman attached to the right-hand corner of the first page. Even though no proof had ever been found of Spanish John's involvement in the man's death, he had been the prime suspect until his alibi, a mixed-race woman of Jamaican and English blood, had come forward and made a statement. He had been with her for the previous two days and nights. If it wasn't cast iron, then it was as close to it as it could be. The woman wasn't a whore or a floozy or someone who chose gangsters for lovers, but a solicitor with a good reputation and a soft and melodious voice. Spanish John was off the hook.

Julius Rios, a man that interested people when he was alive, had become in a matter of months a cold case, filed as unsolved, forgotten by everyone but the doting parents back in Barbados.

Larry knew that his survival depended on solving murders, and whereas Joe Foster was of prime importance, Julius Rios was also.

Larry was about to embark along a road from which there was no return; he was to sever the cosy relationship that he had with the criminals in the area. He hoped he was up to the task.

With resolve in his heart and fire in his belly, he printed out the last known address of Julius Rios's girlfriend, switched off his laptop and went home. Even though it was close to three in the morning, he felt sure he would sleep well for the next few hours.

***

Terry Foster walked the length of the garden at the rear of his house, a phone in one hand. He was a worried man, unable to fathom what was wrong, why the Fosters' hold on crime was weakening.

'Are you saying we've lost our stranglehold in Hammersmith?' he said quietly, attempting to emulate his father's style: talk softly, carry a big stick, Joe Foster's adage. Terry had tried the reverse. For all his efforts, including tough arm tactics, frightening a few, one man in the hospital, it hadn't worked. He had racked his brains trying to understand, but maybe it was right what his father had said, he wasn't bright enough.

Terry wondered if it was true. School had bored him, and at sixteen he had walked out of the school gates for the last time, never once picking up a book since, other than a comic or two. Adept at video games, handy with a billiard cue, whether it was to pot the black or to smash it over someone's head, an accomplished street fighter and drunkard, but that was it.

His sister always had her head in a book, always studying, and once he had tried to read one that she had said was exceptional, but after five pages he had thrown it to one side.

'What use is Charles Dickens? *A Tale of Two Cities*?' he asked Samantha, only to be told that it was a classic of English Literature, the selfless sacrifice of

160

Sydney Carton, guillotined in place of Charles Darnay out of his love for Lucie Manette, but he had not heard what she said. He had already switched on the television, another sword and sandals epic to watch.

He remembered the look on her face even to this day: stupid she had thought him. And then there was the youngest, Ben, studious, a credit to his parents his father had said, but when was his father ever there, always spending time with one woman or another, and then, as an old man, with Emily. It was wrong, Terry had thought at the time, and now Emily, still as beautiful as ever, was on her own.

What would his father have done, he thought, regretting he had not listened to the teacher, to his father, to Samantha. Downing his whisky, he hung up on his man in Hammersmith. A temporary downturn in business, Terry consoled himself with that thought. He'd deal with it tomorrow. He did not consider that his father would not have waited; he would have dealt with the issue immediately, but the son had more important things on his mind.

Emily Foster attempted to hold back the door, but the man on the other side was too strong. Once inside, Terry, who had downed another couple of whiskies on his way over to her house, pushed her against a wall in the hallway.

'Stop, please stop,' Emily screamed.

Unable to control himself, and well beyond the point of no return, not that he had a lot of control even when sober, he continued with his unwanted amorous and drunken advances.

From another room, a commotion. The door at the end of the hallway opened. In the light emanating from the kitchen, Terry could see a silhouette, but just as with a shark, that once it has locked onto its victim it can't be stopped, neither could he. A shark attacked out of hunger; not lust or hatred, but a primaeval need for sustenance.

Terry Foster's need wasn't food; it was sexual, but also primaeval, instinctive. Unable to stop, unable to rationalise, he continued to focus on Emily, pinning her harder against the wall.

He hardly noticed the pain in his side, but within a matter of seconds, he relaxed his grip on the object of his lust, staggering back and then collapsing.

'Gary, what have you done?' Emily said, attempting to catch her breath, to pull her dress down.

'He wouldn't stop,' Gary, Emily's eldest child, said.

Emily looked at her son. 'Phone for an ambulance, contact the police,' she said.

Gary took his mother into the kitchen. He sat her on a chair and then dialled 999, the number for emergency services. A woman answered; Gary gave the address and the reason for the call.

'Five minutes,' she said. 'I've got your number. I'll inform the police as well.'

'We already have the number,' Gary said as he looked over at his mother. With trembling hands, she scanned through the saved numbers on her phone.

'It's Terry,' she said. 'My son has killed him.'

Isaac phoned Larry and then Wendy.

In the hallway, before the ambulance had arrived, a groaning.

'He's still alive,' Gary said. 'I only stuck a knife into him to stop him.'

Emily breathed a sigh of relief, hoped that Terry, regardless of his previous actions, was not dead. She didn't care for the man but she did care for her son, and now he had stabbed a man in her defence.

Regardless of anything else, whether Terry lived or died, and notwithstanding the reason for knifing the man, it was a crime. Joe's son's future jeopardised through no fault of his own, only because his mother had loved a gangster.

Emily fetched a pillow, put it under Terry's head and held a towel to the wound in his lower torso. There was blood on him and the floor, although not as much as she would have expected.

'I've phoned for an ambulance,' she said.

'Thanks,' Terry mumbled. 'Gary?'

'I don't want him involved.'

'I'll not hold it against him. I would have done the same for my mother.'

Emily didn't expect any compassion or remorse for his actions, and she knew it was the closest that Terry would ever get to an apology.

A knock at the door, two paramedics stood there, a man and a woman. There was no need for them to ask where the victim was; he was in front of them. Apart from saying a couple of words, they went straight to where Terry was lying.

Out on the pavement, a couple of uniforms were establishing the crime scene; the tape strung around two poles, one for lighting, the other for the telephone, the ends secured to the fence.

'He's stable,' one of the medics said. 'We'll take him to the hospital.'

'He'll live?' Gary asked.

'It's not for us to say, but it doesn't look too serious. It'll hurt like hell, but then, judging by your mother, he probably deserved it.'

'He did, even so…'

'We only deal with the people, not the motive.'

The medics placed the injured man on a stretcher, passing Wendy on the way out. A crowd was starting to form on the street.

'You look as though you could do with a sedative,' Wendy said as she arrived.

'I'm fine,' Emily said. 'It's Gary that I'm worried about.'

'DCI Cook and DI Hill are on their way. We could wait for them if you prefer.'

'It was Terry. He was drunk, determined to take me at any cost.'

'Not the sort of thing for a son to hear of, let alone witness.'

'It's fine, mother,' Gary said. 'Don't worry about me.'

Both women did. It was an attack with a deadly weapon, premeditated or not, justifiable or otherwise. Wendy thought it would not result in a custodial sentence, not even a fine or a police record, but it wasn't for her to say; that was for others to decide.

'He was intent on rape,' Emily said.

'Your son stabbed him?' Isaac said as he walked into the house.

'Gary wasn't meant to be here. If he hadn't been—'

'If he hadn't,' Isaac said, 'Terry Foster would have committed a crime, and your son wouldn't be answerable for what he's done.'

'Protecting my mother,' Gary said. 'What else could I do?'

'DCI Cook is the devil's advocate, stating the situation from our point of view,' Wendy said. She thought that Isaac was harsh, although she knew that was not his nature. However, he was correct. A crime had been committed; a caution would have to be given.

'If Mrs Foster is up to questioning,' Isaac asked, looking over at Wendy.

'I believe so,' Wendy replied.

'I am,' Emily said.

'You're more than likely to experience delayed shock. We don't want your testimony prejudiced by your ability to think clearly, to remember the details.'

'I can corroborate what my mother says,' Gary, a fine-looking man of twenty years of age, said. Dressed in jeans and a white shirt, with shoulder-length hair, he looked to be a credit to his mother. However, in his blood flowed the DNA from his gangster father. If that had, in part, been responsible for an overly violent reaction to his mother's attacker, then it would go against him.

Larry stayed outside, the crowd forming, lemmings to a cliff, most of them interested in the ghoulish, a death. However, none admitted to it, only expressing out loud that they hoped everyone was safe inside.

'You knew the people?' he asked a middle-aged man dressed in a heavy jacket, a flat cap on his head.

'In passing. She was a beauty, and I don't mind saying so, although my wife didn't like her.'

Larry took the man off to one side. Usually, it would have been Wendy out on the street, conducting a door-to-door, asking people passing by what they knew and what they had seen. But this time, Wendy's place was in the house, the compassionate shoulder, and if it was indeed an attempted rape, she would know what to do more than him.

'What didn't your wife like?' Larry asked.

'My wife's no oil painting, not that she's vain about such things.'

'That's not an answer.'

'I was coming to it. I'm no oil painting, either, but you don't like to be reminded of it. And there's her in there, all hair and breasts, and my wife, greying and putting on weight.'

'If you keep reminding her, no wonder she's not pleased.'

'Not me. I'm no better, but her inside, Emily, she's always friendly, a smile on her face, or at least, she used to be. Her husband died; did you know?'

'We knew. What about him?'

'There was a rumour that he was a bad man, but you've seen his wife, the children, not that they're young anymore.'

'This rumour?'

'He rarely left the house without a couple of men with him.'

'That doesn't make him bad.'

'They were protection, not that I've got anything to say against him or his family. Perfectly fine neighbours, minded their own business, we minded ours.'

'And you lived next door, never went in theirs?'

'Never. My wife's not a socialiser, mild agoraphobia, and as for me, a good book, a movie on the television at the end of the day, and I'm fine.'

'Joe Foster has been on the television occasionally,' Larry said.

'If what they said about him was right, what was it to me? At least we didn't have barking dogs or hooligans in the street.'

'You think he dealt with them?'

'Rape? Is that it?' the neighbour no longer interested in himself and his wife, more interested in what was going on at the Fosters' house.

'Attempted. How do you know?'

'We could hear her through the walls.'

'Yet you didn't do anything about it?'

'It wasn't for long, not long enough for me to knock on their door. I did phone the local police station, told them what was going on, but then I heard the son's voice, and then it went quiet. Anyone I should know?'

'The son or the wife?'

'The rapist, who did you think I was referring to?'

'Her husband's eldest son,' Larry said.

'He's been around a couple of times since the father died. No doubt felt he should take over his father's duties.'

'The father, what else do you know about him?'

'Apart from the rumours and the television, not a lot. As I said, a chat over the fence. He came home once with lipstick on his collar. I pointed it out to him, and he cleaned it off, smelt like a French boudoir though. She must have known.'

'Emily?'

'Mind you, she lays the makeup on thick, but hers is a different smell. He was putting it about, but then, that's what men do.'

'Even you?'

'Why not? No harm if the wife doesn't find out, and a man's got to have a hobby.'

'I thought yours was reading and watching the television.'

'One's cerebral, the other's inane. Short rations at home, has been for years, no conscience to worry me.'

167

'You're very open, unusual for a member of the public.'

'Unique, I'd say, but in my younger days, before I set up my own business, did well with it, I was in the army, military police. I got to learn a thing or two, realised that those that hold back often do it for a reason. Ask me what you want. I'll give you the truth.'

'Emily Foster? Faithful to her husband?'

'One of the other sons used to come around every few weeks. No screaming when he was there.'

'Which one?'

'The youngest, Ben.'

'You believe that they were having an affair?'

'I don't believe anything. If they were, that was up to them; if they weren't, bad luck to him, but the father would have been upset, and I never liked the look of his two men.'

Chapter 19

As for Terry Foster, it was clear that even though it had been an attempted rape, neither Emily nor Gary would corroborate that with the police. When asked to put it in writing, they stated that it had been a misunderstanding: a drunken man falling over Emily in the hallway, Gary misinterpreting his mother's screams, rushing out from the kitchen, imagining the worst, acting in her defence.

As Emily sat down and wrote her statement, Wendy looked at her, saw the woman raise her head. Their eyes met: both women knew the truth. But for the sake of peace and harmony in the extended Foster family, Emily had chosen to lie.

Isaac, with no other option left to him, although he could have pursued the matter, tried to get Emily to alter her testimony, cautioned Gary, but decided not to take him to Challis Street Police Station. After all, the facts were clear, even if the young man's mother had compromised his defence. And the advice from the hospital was that the would-be rapist was sitting up in bed, heavily bandaged and sedated.

Gary Foster's lunge at his half-brother had been in defence of his mother, using a knife from the kitchen. It could have resulted in death, and if it had, then Gary would be in a prison cell.

At the hospital, Isaac stood at the bottom of Terry Foster's bed. The man opened his eyes, rubbed them to focus. 'Just exercising my rights,' Foster said.

'Raping your father's widow, hardly the act of a gentleman, more that of a master and a slave,' Isaac said.

'Did she say it was?'

'On the contrary, she said you had slipped, drunk as you were, and that she was screaming for help. It doesn't explain why her dress was torn, though.'

'Gary?'

'He'll say what his mother wants. If it was me…'

'But it isn't. What with you and that inspector of yours, a fine pair of chumps. Why you bother for the pittance they pay you, I don't know.'

'Sleeping easy at night comes into it.'

'I sleep well enough,' Foster said. 'Why are you here? You've got nothing against me, and I'll be out of the hospital tomorrow.'

'Gary stabbed you, doesn't that count for something?'

'It's not the first time I've been stabbed, not the last. Gary over-reacted, that's how it is, isn't it?'

Isaac knew it was. As long as the three kept to their stories, there wasn't a lot more that he could do.

Wendy had remained at Emily's house, ensured that she and her son were fine, curious as to why they had lied.

'We're fine; honestly we are,' Emily said. 'We just want to forget about tonight.'

'It's not the first time that Terry's been here,' Wendy said.

'No, but he's not been as drunk as he was tonight. He likes me no more than I like him.'

'He likes you enough to rape you. Doesn't that count for something? Doesn't his behaviour appal you?'

Gary Foster looked away. It wasn't something he wanted to think about, not with his mother. Emily put her arm around him, pulled him in close. 'Maybe it's best if you go in the other room,' she said.

'If you're sure?'

'I am. Women sometimes need to talk without a man present.'

'Emily,' Wendy said after Gary had left, 'the truth about you and Terry.'

'Tonight? I've told you that already.'

'If you continue with this charade, there's not much more I can say. But Terry's a dangerous man, capable of more violence. I wouldn't want you and your children placed in danger out of your fear to tell us the truth, not only about tonight but of what you know about Joe and his other family.'

'I want us to be left alone. I've spoken to Gary and Kate about it, a family discussion, the three of us.'

'And what was decided?'

'Kate would like to stay in London. I'm planning to sell this house, not that I want to, but I must, can't you see that?'

'As long as you stay around here, you're inextricably linked to the Foster dynasty.'

'We'll always be marked out as repugnant. We weren't with Joe, but with Terry, he'll drag the good name of Foster down into the gutter. I don't want to be around when that happens.'

'The Fosters' crimes will be revealed in time, even Joe's,' Wendy said. 'However, we're Homicide, and Joe was murdered. Your defence of your dead husband is admirable, but it doesn't help you or your children. Think about them for once, not the memory of a man that doesn't deserve it.'

'He does to me.'

Wendy had to admire Emily, although her loyalty was ill-founded, given to a man who had killed or had given the orders to kill, a man who had prospered through crime, a man who had cheated on his wife. Wendy realised that shock tactics were required.

'Eileen Cavendish?' Wendy said. She needed the woman to open up. A murderer or murderers were still on the loose, and behind Emily's attractive façade there was a wealth of knowledge, some suppressed, not believing ill of her husband.

'She worked for Joe, a plainly-dressed woman, although she could have been attractive.'

'Anything else?'

'Joe told me that she was the daughter of an old friend. He employed her as a favour, found her trustworthy and eventually indispensable.'

'He used to meet with her at her flat.'

'Wendy, I might appear silly and frivolous, but I'm not that naïve. If you're asking me, did I suspect my husband of having other women, then come out with it.'

'Then, yes. Was your husband ever unfaithful?'

'It's not something a woman wants to think about, but yes, he was. Not often, you must believe, and I never confronted him about it.'

'Why?'

'For the sake of the children when they were younger; for myself when they were old enough to deal with the truth. Whatever he may have been, whatever he had done, I loved him. I wasn't willing to break up the family over my husband's occasional indiscretions.'

'But Eileen, she was something else, wasn't she?'

'I thought he would get over it, but there was a connection between the two that I don't think he even understood.'

'We know what the connection was. Her mother told her recently, too late as it turns out.'

'I'm not sure I want to hear,' Emily said.

172

'I don't want to tell you, but I must. Joe died for a reason, and up until now, we've thought it was to do with crime. We've long suspected Terry, or if not him, possibly Tony Rafter, although that's stretching the possibility. And now we have Jacob Morgan, a man with more strings to his bow than previously thought.'

'Jacob?'

'On first name terms?'

'Joe liked the man, trusted him as much as he could trust anyone.'

'Morgan stole from your husband.'

'Joe knew that.'

'He didn't know that it was more money than any of you suspected. The man's got the key to the treasure chest. If he wanted to, he could deplete the Foster fortune with ease.'

'Tell me,' Emily said.

'You said you didn't want to know,' Wendy reminded her.

'I didn't, but I must know the truth. He was having an affair with her, am I right?'

'He was, but he still loved you. The connection between the two was misguided, a love that can't be spoken, to be melodramatic.'

'Are you saying?'

'Joe was her father, not that he or she ever knew, and now she's pregnant.'

'Joe's?'

'According to Eileen.'

'How tragic. What's she going to do?'

'We never got that far. I assume she'll not continue with the pregnancy, but that's for her to decide, not us. It does, however, bring another dimension into the equation, the possibility of a religious zealot, aware of the truth, determined to slay the sinner.'

'Both are guilty of the crime,' Emily said, her face pale and drawn, not sure how to react. Compassion, on the one hand; disgust on the other.

'Jacob Morgan knew about the affair,' Wendy said.

'Then he's the murderer. Don't you see it? So easy for him to kill Joe, take the money.'

'He wanted Eileen as well. Has he ever approached you?'

'Not with Joe alive, and besides, I wouldn't be interested.'

'Neither was Eileen, but her circumstances are changed.'

'The woman's mother is to blame, not telling her daughter about Joe.'

'Even if she is, the unborn child complicates the situation. How would any of us deal with such a situation?'

'Badly,' Emily said. 'I need to see Eileen.'

'Your husband's mistress, his daughter?'

'She's still a woman. I cannot hate her. She needs a friend.'

Wendy knew she was in the presence of a truly good person. She hoped that Emily was innocent, apart from falling in love with a gangster. However, reality suggested that behind the façade was a vengeful woman, a woman who regarded Joe's indiscretions with disgust. If that was the case, then the loyal wife had missed her vocation; she should have been on the stage.

***

The suspicion remained that behind the scenes Tony Rafter lurked. But without further proof or a line of enquiry, neither Isaac nor Chief Superintendent Goddard was willing to take the battle to a man whose defences were unassailable. A man who would have a battery of lawyers to issue defamation writs, to complain of police intimidation and of besmirching the name of a prominent citizen.

It was one law for the rich and powerful, another for the rest. And in the middle, not influential, but rich and astute, was the figure of Jacob Morgan – or it should have been.

On a Thursday, three days after Eileen had revealed the unthinkable, two days after Gary Foster had thrust a knife into his half-brother and one day after Terry Foster had checked himself out of the hospital, Jacob Morgan received another visit.

With so much to digest, the intervening days had been spent in Homicide, the team brainstorming what they had, the progress of the investigations – perilously little as it turned out – and the way forward. It wasn't the first time that a murder investigation had ground to a shuddering halt. Isaac knew it wouldn't be the last, even though Chief Superintendent Goddard was on his back again, but that was the man's style.

Larry, accompanied by two uniforms, had knocked on Morgan's office door at nine-fifteen in the morning. The man was known for his punctuality, never arriving later than eight forty-five, rain or shine. It was unusual that he wasn't there, but there was still his flat, or maybe he was ill, or elsewhere.

'You'll not find him at home,' a woman hollered up the stairwell as Larry stood outside Morgan's flat.

'Where is he?' Larry asked.

'We don't see him much, keeps to himself most of the time. He packed a case and left, no idea where.'

'We're the police, Homicide.'

'I figured you were that, what with the police car outside. Has he done anything wrong?'

'A few questions, nothing more. What can you tell us about him?'

'Not a lot. He causes no trouble, no more than a mouse, but then we've got one or two of them. No idea why he stays here, but then, he is miserly.'

'How? What do you mean?'

'Have you seen inside his place?'

'Only his office, nothing special.'

'Once a week, I clean for him. It's tidy in there, but the furniture's seen better times, and the place could do with decorating. I open the windows when I'm up there, but he doesn't.'

'And he's left? Coming back?'

'Not soon. The suitcase was big enough. I'd say he might return, but then you're here. He must have done something.'

'It's important,' Larry said.

'I can't help you,' the woman downstairs said as she closed her door.

'Leave her,' Larry said to the uniform. 'Inside is where we need to be.'

'We'll need a warrant,' the uniform, fresh out of training, eager to follow the rules, said.

'We're Homicide. The man could be dead inside.'

Larry leant up against the flat's door, felt movement. He pushed a little harder, the door springing open.

'You forced it,' the uniform reacted with alarm. 'We can't go in.'

'Welcome to the real world,' Larry said. 'He's either incapacitated or dead, or else he's done a runner. Exceptional circumstances require a degree of latitude on how the rules are applied, don't you agree?'

The uniform nodded his head weakly. He disagreed, but then Larry recognised himself at that age, full of innocence, a belief in the police as the purveyors of truth and justice, not intrigue. The man had a lot to learn, but learn he would; Larry knew that.

'I'll go in on my own,' Larry said. 'In case there's evidence in here.' He took out a pair of gloves from his pocket, put them on and entered the flat. It was as the woman downstairs had said, clean and tidy, but unloved and unwelcoming. It also had the smell of a bachelor, musty on account of the windows not being open, the lingering odour of tobacco smoke.

In the main rooms, nothing seemed out of order. In one of the two bedrooms, a computer and printer on an old wooden desk, bookcases to either side, a view out to a small untended and unloved garden. In the larger of the two bedrooms, a double bed, its top sheet pulled back, signs of the bed having been slept in.

Larry carefully opened a wardrobe, only to find himself staring at a row of coat hangers, and apart from an old and heavy coat, the sort ideal for a British winter, there was nothing else. Searching further around the room, and behind an oil painting, definitely not one of the old masters, not that he was an expert, Larry found a safe. It was closed.

Larry phoned Isaac first. 'He's taken off,' he said. And secondly, he called Gordon Windsor to prime a couple of his best people to get down to the address, to check the flat for evidence of Morgan and anyone else who might have been in the place.

Two miles away, two women sat down to talk. One apprehensive that her lover's wife was sitting opposite her; the other feeling sadness for the woman who had been a confidante of her husband, then a mistress, and finally a daughter. It was a room of heightened emotions, each woman anxious to apologise and to show remorse, not sure how to say what needed to be said.

'Tradition dictates that I should scratch your eyes out,' Emily Foster said.

'And that I should, if I have a modicum of decency, beg for your forgiveness, but as much as I want to, I can't. Joe was unique, a man larger than life. Such people do not behave like others, a different set of rules apply,' Eileen Cavendish said.

'But for you, they don't.'

'I can't express what I feel. You are aware of my condition?'

'I've been told. It's a dilemma. The child, the result of a forbidden relationship, regardless of the ignorance of both parties, will be the recipient of condemnation.'

'My mother is a religious person, campaigned for the rights of the unborn child, and now I'm contemplating going against her wishes.'

'You don't share her views?'

'I do, and if it weren't for the obvious, I would feel no compunction about letting nature take its course.'

'Then I will side with your mother. But you cannot be on your own, not when it begins to show. You must come and live with me. Whatever you decide, I will respect your views.'

'Joe said you were a good person.'

'Not always. I have a past, the same as most people, but it's where it belongs, the same as yours, and no one need ever know the parentage of the child.'

'It's a murder. It's bound to come out, the same as my past at university when I was short of money.'

'You sold yourself?'

'I did.'

'Well, Eileen Cavendish, seducer of husbands, a fallen woman, and now friend, you and I will have a lot to talk about over the next few months,' Emily laughed.

Eileen laughed in return, a feeling of relief, a concern that the friendship of someone who should be an enemy did not feel right. Regardless, she would not ruin the evening; she went to the kitchen, brought back a bottle of red wine, some biscuits and a slab of cheese.

'Tonight, we will get drunk,' she said.

Emily nodded in agreement, kicked off her shoes. From a bird's eye view, it would have all seemed perfectly harmless and harmonious. Emily hoped it was.

Chapter 20

Nothing prejudices a murder investigation more than the disappearance of a key person. However, the team still believed that Jacob Morgan, missing for three days now, was the least likely candidate of those who could have arranged Joe Foster's murder.

He was, however, apparently a wizard at embezzling money, and Samantha Foster confirmed that Morgan had emptied two overseas bank accounts already and changed the password on three others, although, to the police, she only acknowledged that the family had taken a substantial financial hit.

Ben understood how, but then he had had the benefit of university education. Samantha, equally adroit, could also see how easy it would have been for Morgan. Terry, barely able to read a bank statement, impatient with social media passwords, and hopeless at the video games he enjoyed, rarely getting past the second level, could not.

Terry shifted in his chair. The wound from Gary was still sore, but true to his word he had not contacted either Emily or Gary. He continued to tell Gladys, his mother, that it had not been rape, only a misunderstanding.

Billy, another visitor that night at the house, reluctantly took his place next to Samantha at the long table.

'Time's money,' Billy said impatiently.

Tom said nothing, not concerned either way. Samantha could see he was high on drugs.

Samantha stood up, exerting the power of her expertise over Terry. 'Jacob Morgan has cheated us,' she said.

'How much?' Terry's response.

'Somewhere in the order of fifteen to eighteen million pounds.'

'Can you be more precise?' Ben asked. Crime might not have interested him, but money did.

'I can only go with the bank statements I have. Who knows if they are truly accurate? It might be even more.'

'The police are looking for Jacob,' Gladys said. Money wasn't her strong point, having only limited education and a lack of interest in the subject. Even when the family had been flush, able to buy the best, she had still shopped at high street discount shops, always looked for a bargain in the New Year sales.

'If the police find Morgan before us, he could reveal all he knows,' Ben said.

'Our father trusted him,' Samantha said. 'What makes you think Morgan would act against our interests?'

'Self-preservation.'

'What do you mean?' Terry asked. To him, it was clear cut. Jacob Morgan had stolen from the Fosters, answerable not only to the family, but to him, and he had a solution if the man was found.

Samantha glanced over at Terry, a look of condescension for someone of low intellect. She then directed her eyes over to Ben. 'You can explain it better than me,' she said.

'In simple terms,' Ben said, 'has Jacob Morgan committed a crime?'

'Okay, you two think you're so smart,' Terry said. He felt anger rising in him, a need to lash out.

'Sit still,' Gladys said.

Terry sat back in his chair, still respectful of his mother.

'If Jacob Morgan has falsified the bank accounts,' Ben continued, 'there is the question of whether our father was party to it. I believe that's the first matter.'

'Why would our father do that?' Terry asked.

'It depends if he had been sharing any of the accounts with a third party, or if it was important not to show the true worth for logistical reasons.'

'So?' Terry still didn't understand.

'Has Morgan committed a crime? Helping himself to overseas funds is not a concern of the police, not necessarily.'

'Are you saying that even if the police found him, he might get off?'

'Of cheating us, it's probable. The police won't have a lot of sympathy for us, not if the money's offshore, and if it can't be linked to a crime in England.'

'But is it?'

'No doubt, but the proof is what the police need. And besides, the police are looking for a murderer, not who stole what from whom, not unless it's relevant, and Morgan taking the money seems a smart move to me.'

'If I get my hands on him,' Terry said.

'And what will you do?' Billy's input to the discussion. 'String him up by his balls, make him talk, or would you kill him, not considering that the man has our money.'

'Billy's right,' Samantha said. 'Your bull in the china shop approach isn't going to work, not with Morgan, and if you find him, which seems improbable, he might decide to take his own life before you can question him.'

'Listen to your sister, to the others,' Gladys said to Terry.

Terry seethed. He was the senior male member in the family, and two women and his younger brothers were telling him what to do.

'Very well,' he finally said, reluctantly.

'Find Morgan before the police, ensure he's somewhere very secure and comfortable. No rough stuff, not until we've had a chance to discuss matters, not until Samantha's put together a more accurate report of what we know, what we believe and a strategy to get the man to hand over the money,' Ben said. It was not what he wanted. After all, he had just proposed to his long-time girlfriend, and she had made him swear that he would not become involved in the family business, but now he was, and it was impossible to stop. A lot of money was at stake, and he could lay claim to some, hopefully to that which had been gained legally, but even he knew that was unlikely.

'Even if I go along with this,' Terry said, 'it doesn't alter the fact that Morgan could have been involved in our father's death.'

'The money first,' Gladys said. 'After that, do what you want with the man, get the truth out of him, whatever way you reckon.'

'I might have to string him up, not that Billy would like it, to find out about the money.'

'Think like your father, reason this through. If Morgan is going to suffer, and believe me, if he killed Joe or arranged for him to be killed, then he will, we don't want the police to know where he is. Afterwards, the man has to disappear.'

'We kill him,' Terry said.

'We keep him on ice till we've got the money; until we're sure he is of no further value,' Ben said. It was clear to him that what the family needed was him at the helm. He had so far steered clear of crime, but at the back of his mind, the possibility of legitimising the family business, pushing Terry to one side, his sister as his loyal second. But until then, he would keep to the agreement he had given to his fiancée. It would be for others to find Morgan, not him.

With the meeting adjourned for the present, Billy left, in a hurry as usual. Samantha returned to her laptop; there was an asset register to compile, a profit and loss analysis to conduct, and a more accurate account to prepare of monies received, monies owing, monies invested, and most importantly, money that Morgan had absconded with.

***

To Homicide, Jacob Morgan's disappearance was of grave concern. If Morgan was to be found, and at present that seemed unlikely, even though there was an All Ports Warning out for him, he had a lot of questions to answer.

'No one's talking on the street,' Larry said. Isaac knew that meant no one in the pub. The possible further action on Larry and his easy association with criminals was in abeyance; after all, his accuser was now on the run, the accusation defused by his actions.

'Not unexpected,' Isaac said.

'He had been in Basing Street.'

'Only your friend would have known him.'

Larry did not respond.

The lady living downstairs from Morgan's flat had reiterated that the man never brought anyone home, and as far as she was concerned, the man was chaste. She admitted to Wendy, when Larry had excused himself for ten minutes, that she had tried it on with Morgan, only to have the man close the door in her face.

'Meat on a plate,' the woman said. 'Twelve years back. My husband had just left, took off with his fancy woman, and I had my needs. He wouldn't be much of a catch, not Jacob, no oil painting, a bit on the weedy side, but smart, knew his way in the world, plenty of money, mark my words.'

And even though the woman would have been no Eileen Cavendish twelve years ago, she wasn't unattractive, but Jacob Morgan had rejected her, never brought another woman back to the flat. Then, a few days ago, he had been at Eileen's, offering to take her with him.

It was hard to believe that a disciplined man could abstain from the pleasures of the flesh until he had reached an age where the libido would be waning, and then decide that he wanted Eileen. It was like those people who say they will travel when they retire, but never do.

Bridget spoke. 'I've put together a report on the man; you all have a copy.'

'Give us the précised version,' Larry said.

'Jacob Morgan, no middle name, sixty-seven years of age, a sister in Suffolk, although she's not seen him for over twenty years. Their childhood wasn't idyllic, a philandering father, a stern mother. An accountant since his mid-twenties, he had worked for a firm in Mayfair until branching out on his own once he reached thirty.'

'Any irregularities?' Isaac asked.

'The firm he worked for is still there, although most of the people from thirty years ago have retired.'

'Any names that should interest us?'

185

'Only one, Tony Rafter.'

'The connection?'

'They both worked at the same firm, similar ages, similar backgrounds. According to one person at the firm, the only one that I could find from back then, Morgan and Rafter were friends, spent time in each other's company. One went on to fame and fortune; the other buried himself in financial ledgers.'

'Different personalities yet friendly. It doesn't make sense,' Wendy said.

'It gives us a reason to meet Rafter again,' Isaac said. 'Could it be that Morgan was the conduit between Rafter and Joe Foster, the power behind the throne, the master manipulator pulling Foster's strings, directing his actions?'

Isaac called the meeting to a close. Bridget was to continue with her research into Jacob Morgan; Wendy was off to meet with Emily Foster, and Larry was at a loose end. He wanted to meet with his contacts, but he had decided to not only prove his innocence but to ram it down the throats of his doubters. Even though he did not like being in the office, that was where he'd stay for the day, researching, compiling a dossier on Spanish John's crimes. He was fearful of what he was about to do, rousing sleeping dogs from their slumber, placing himself in danger, but there was no option.

Meanwhile, Isaac climbed the stairs to Chief Superintendent Goddard's office. Tony Rafter needed to be questioned about a one-time colleague of his; the man wasn't going to be happy, and Isaac did not want to take the inevitable flak on his own when Rafter made a formal complaint.

Chapter 21

Richard Goddard's response was as Isaac had expected. After all, it wasn't the first time the two men had come up against people of influence and importance, even going so far as to want to question the prime minister of the United Kingdom on one occasion.

It had been early in Isaac's time in Homicide, the deaths of a man and a woman, a clear case they had been silenced to protect a senior member of the government. At first, it was believed to be the prime minister, but it wasn't. However, the senior government minister was close enough to the prime minister to have caused severe embarrassment, an almost certain electoral defeat. The case had left a sour taste in Isaac's mouth after he realised that he had slept with one of the government-sanctioned assassins.

In the end, Goddard, a man who had guided Isaac's career, reminded him that an imperfect system, weighted in favour of certain individuals and institutions, wasn't unique to London or the country. It was universal, since time immemorial, the strong riding roughshod over the weak, imposing rules and restrictions over the masses while they acted with impunity.

Jacob Morgan was missing. He had been an adviser to Joe Foster, a former colleague of Tony Rafter. To Isaac, it was more than circumstantial. And Rafter had had business dealings with Foster, legal on the surface, but down low, in the underbelly, scratching around in the dirt, there would be the three men. But where was the proof? No one knew, and of the three, only one was available.

Rafter was visible most nights on the television, at one charity event or another, announcing another business success, drawing ever closer to being anointed by the Queen, a tap on the shoulders with a sword. And now Isaac wanted to take the man on with flimsy evidence, attempt to pin him down with adroit questioning, knowing full well what had happened the last time he and his chief superintendent had met him.

'He's our best chance of finding Jacob Morgan,' Isaac said.

The chief superintendent sat back on his chair, looking across his desk at Isaac, turning around to check the weather outside. 'Even if I agree with you, we'd never get a straight answer from the man,' he said.

'We need Morgan, and now.'

'Even if you do, what do you expect from Rafter? He's hardly likely to give you the man's address, even if he had it. And besides, why this fascination with Rafter? No one's ever been able to pin anything on him, though others have tried.'

'Then how do we go about finding out what we need to know from him?'

'He won't consent to an interview, and without something substantial, we'll not get a court order to make the man comply.'

'And if we did, his people would go through it with a fine toothcomb, is that what you're saying?'

'You know it is. Men such as Rafter are protected. Sure, he let us in the once, a pretence that he is just a humble law-abiding citizen, but he'll react quick enough if he's pushed too hard.'

'He's criticised on social media.'

'They can't be sued, not easily, and Rafter knows that. After all, the extreme left is always lambasting those they disagree with. Even you've come in for invective after you arrested a person they approved of.'

'Who turned out not to be a murderer.'

'Did they retract their comments?'

'Never. The law is not only there for the powerful, and nowadays, an internet-savvy person of no great intelligence can be influential, money or no money,' Isaac said.

'And Rafter will be surrounded by his people, willing to sue the London Metropolitan Police, you and me. How do you think Jenny will feel if you're sued? After all, a new baby, a new house, your career dashed by Rafter, damned by social media. It's hardly a good reason to take the man on.'

'We can't let a murder go unpunished because it might cause us trouble.'

Goddard called in a legal adviser from Scotland Yard, a smartly-dressed woman in her forties, who drafted a list of questions for Rafter on his relationship with Jacob Morgan, the nature of his financial dealings with Joe Foster. It was, Isaac concluded, a waste of time, in that the document from Challis Street would go to Rafter's legal team, more experienced than the person who had drafted the document for the police.

Isaac had seen the document before it was sent, initialled it to confirm his agreement, stating on the record that this wasn't the way to conduct policing, not when people had died, aware that the police had no option.

It had taken two days for the final document to be prepared, two days lost, but in Homicide the sun never sets, and the team were working longer hours than usual, and most days were twelve to thirteen on average.

Larry continued to work his contacts, drinking less than usual, much to the consternation of the locals in the pubs he visited. After all, a police inspector who downed his beer with gusto couldn't be all bad.

***

Charmaine Bradley, Julius Rios's girlfriend, had not fared well over the years. The last time Larry had seen her was at the inquest into her lover's death. Back then, she had been dark, with a wig of blonde hair that hung down over her shoulders. Rios had been a player, definitely not faithful to Charmaine, but as was known, neither was she to him. A stripper in one of Joe Foster's clubs, she serviced those who paid well, even offering a free sample to Larry as he conducted a search for drugs at the rear of the premises late one night.

Money had been spread around, Larry knew, as no drugs had been found.

'On the house,' Charmaine had said. He remembered it well, and now, as he stood on the doorstep of the woman's house, depressingly downmarket, he reflected on the difference between the woman then and now.

Charmaine stood before Larry as the door opened. In the background, two children: one still crawling, the other older by one or two years. Both were neatly turned out, but time and heroin addiction had wrought its worst on their mother – the blonde hair, incongruous on a woman from the Caribbean, no longer there, only a mop of black curly hair.

The body that had been firm and succulent, the lecherous men reaching out to touch, the money thrust into her bra and panties while she was wearing them, thrown on the dance floor if she wasn't, now gone to fat and sag.

If she hadn't answered to her name when Larry had shown his warrant card, he would not have recognised her.

'I'm clean,' Charmaine said as Larry sat down in the kitchen.

Larry knew what she was referring to.

'No drugs,' Larry said.

'Not with the children. I was a tart back then, but now, a husband, two children, and I'm fine.'

The woman's voice said one thing; her expression said another. Back then, when Rios had been around, it had been exciting, and being his woman came with a great deal of pride, even if Rios was an unscrupulous individual and Charmaine's naked body had been seen by most of the men in the area, used by more than a few.

In her day, and she had been discretionary as to the men, she had charged plenty for an hour or a night, not that Rios had ever cared. If asked where she was, he would only say 'busy'.

No one, not in the crowd that the two of them hung around with, criticised her. Most of them had done whatever had been necessary to survive, and to them, criminality was a necessity, as were prostitution and theft and dealing in drugs.

'I want to reopen the inquiry into Julius Rios's death,' Larry said.

'You've come to the wrong person. I'm not the same that I was back then. Julius died, that's all that I know. As to who is responsible, I couldn't care less, and even if it sounds callous, he did me a favour.'

'Murder, a favour?'

'I was heading downhill fast, caught in a whirlwind, no way out. Regardless of how much any of us pretended to be enjoying the experience, few of us were.'

'Julius was,' Larry said.

'Julius was unique. He hadn't come from a broken home, hadn't been abused as a child, passed around. There weren't many like him.'

'Spanish John?'

'Is he still around?' Charmaine said as she wiped the nose of the younger child.

'You don't keep in touch?'

'With two children, a husband who works nights, what do you reckon?'

'If he works nights, what are you doing here on your own with the children?'

'He has a day job, two or three hours, helping out with a fruit and vegetable wholesaler. He doesn't like me talking about my past.'

'Does he know?'

'I met him soon after the inquest. It was around the time that I decided to sort myself out.'

'A good man?'

'He's not been in trouble with the law, if that's what you mean. He's as white as you, treats us well, even though he's not much with making money, nights manning a helpline for those struggling with life.'

'You used to live well.'

'I did, but it was an illusion. Drugs to stay happy, spending money when I wasn't, stripping most nights.'

'And prostituting on the side.'

192

'Look at me now, fat and not so desirable, is that what you mean?'

'Charmaine, credit to you if you've found a good man, and if you're satisfied with your life. However, I've got a problem, and I need your help.'

'Not if it means revisiting the past. I keep busy, don't dwell on what was or what could have been. If it weren't for the children, I'd be out working.'

'Stripping?'

'Not anymore. Money is not the great motivator. We've got enough, and in a couple of years, I'll find a job in a shop if I can.'

'I've been accused of taking bribes,' Larry said. It was clear that the woman wasn't going to help the police, but she might help him, personally.

'I offered you a bribe once.'

'I didn't accept, tempted though.'

'Not many would have refused. I was easy on the eye back then; men would fantasise over me when I was on that dance floor.'

'You're still an attractive woman,' Larry said. 'More homely. It lends allure to you.'

'They'd not be stuffing money in my underwear now, more likely to boo me off the stage.'

'Don't go back. Stay with your husband. It's better than what you used to do.'

'I've no shame about it, still got some photos. Mind you, it's not something I talk about at the church on a Sunday. Not sure they would understand, probably give a few of them apoplexy.'

Larry had to laugh. The woman was charming, with a wicked sense of humour. He had to admit to liking her, and yes, not telling the church was a good idea. His wife took him to the local church occasionally. Once, he had mentioned that he was in Homicide, then came the inevitable questions as to murders he had seen, people he had met and was it true that most murders were committed by relatives, which he had said was often the case – even citing one murder where the murderer, a fifty-two-year-old man, had sliced up a fellow workmate over the affair the man had been having with his wife, only to find out that the jezebel was one of the churchgoers.

After that, with the woman breaking down in tears of sorrow and shame, he rarely spoke about Homicide, and never to anyone outside of his family and fellow police officers.

'Charmaine, even with your new-found morality and you, an upstanding citizen, I'm asking your help. Consider your duty.' Larry knew it was a corny line to use, but he could tell that pleading to her good nature would not go amiss.

'You think it's Spanish John, don't you?' Charmaine replied.

'I like the man, but he's dealing drugs, and I'm certain he's behind Julius's death, not that I've got any evidence.'

'Nor have I. Julius never trusted him, but then Julius didn't have a lot of confidence in many people, the reason we got on well.'

'Both honest with each other.'

'He knew what I was doing on the side; but Julius, he was ambitious, a cut above the rest, and the flamboyant clothes, the charisma, were his disguise. Behind them, a smart man, smart enough to have taken control in the area. People gravitated to him; instinctive, it was.'

'A threat to Spanish John?'

'A threat to others. Don't labour too much on him, look to others.'

'Who? Rasta Joe was alive then, so was Joe Foster.'

'One black, one white, both vicious.'

'I was good friends with Rasta Joe, more so than with Spanish John,' Larry said. 'Rasta Joe was a killer, although I preferred to see another side to him, Spanish John is worse.'

'You need proof, not that I can give you any. If I could, I would, but Julius was the smart one, not me. I wasn't dumb, but Julius could make calculations in his head, sum up whether it was a good deal or not; I'd have needed a calculator.'

'If he hadn't died?'

'I wouldn't have met my husband.'

'Is that it? Did you love Julius?'

'In between drugs and stripping and screwing, I suppose I did. But how can anyone know when they're confused. I love my husband; I know that. Not that he's a Julius or a Spanish John or a Joe Foster, but he's dependable, and the children love him.'

'Joe Foster, what can you tell me about him?'

'He used to frighten Julius. It was what he used to say to me: "watch that man, he's dangerous, and if you find me dead one day, don't look past him".'

'Are you suggesting that Joe Foster was involved?'

'I don't know, and that's the truth. And how did you find me? I don't use Charmaine anymore. A different surname as well.'

'Bridget in Homicide. She can find anyone.'

'I'd prefer it if you don't come here. If you want to talk, make a time and a location, nowhere near where I'm remembered, and I'll come. Apart from that, the past is the past. It's the present that interests me now, and my husband will be home soon, and the youngest is way past nappy changing, and the other needs a feed.'

Larry left Charmaine and her children, walking past a tall, skinny white man at the gate to the front garden of the house, a brief nod from one to the other.

Charmaine would have a few questions to answer to her husband. Larry hoped the man was as good as she believed him to be.

Chapter 22

With Jacob Morgan conspicuous by his absence and Tony Rafter protected by an invisible wall in Canary Wharf, the routine in Homicide settled into a disturbingly familiar pattern. The early-morning meetings, Larry out on the road meeting with his contacts, Wendy using her people-tracing skills, Bridget making sure the paperwork was up to date, and Isaac ensuring that the department was left alone to do what it did best – solving murders.

Isaac was aware that the efficient running of a police force needed bureaucracy and accountability, meticulous reporting and indisputable evidence before a trial, although he wished there was less of the back-stabbing politics. Within Challis Street Police Station, the critics were waiting for their chance to make their mark, to unseat him, to take control of Homicide, the prestige department at Challis Street.

Out on the street Larry's behaviour was starting to become a subject for concern. Previously magnanimous and friendly to rogue and honest citizen alike, he had taken on an air of indifference, his manner to some haughty, to others downright bizarre.

Spanish John, increasingly isolated from his previously tame police inspector, was worried. Before, at least once or twice a week, the two men would meet, if not for a drink in one of the local pubs then at least for a coffee, but now there were reports that Larry Hill was asking questions where he shouldn't.

First, the once lovely and promiscuously easy Charmaine, and then a friend of Julius Rios's, and thirdly, a phone call back to the man's home country, a chat with the brother of the deceased.

'A drink?' Spanish John said on the phone to Larry, a chance to clear the air, to give him some information, to test the police officer's mettle. Spanish John believed himself to be a good judge of character, the reason he had been more open with Larry, the reason he had come to like the man, although like and respect and fear were not usually mutually compatible characteristics. And even if he was a police officer, Spanish John had ways of dealing with him.

'Sure, six in the evening, the usual?' Larry's reply, not that he wanted to go. On his laptop, on paperwork locked in his drawer at Challis Street, disturbing new evidence. The case was firming, and it filled Larry with trepidation.

Larry was in Isaac's office, a run-through on the murder of Joe Foster, aware that a meeting with Spanish John would get him out of the meeting soon enough.

It should have been Wendy as well in the office, and Bridget if she had any input, but it was just the two men, the smartly-dressed Isaac and his less than sartorially elegant inspector.

'Hunch or proven?' Isaac said.

'With what?' Larry's reply.

'Your visit to Rios's former girlfriend.'

'If I raise the tempo, prove that Rios died on instructions from Spanish John.'

'Is Rios's death relevant to the current investigations?'

'It could be.'

There was a vagueness about his inspector that Isaac didn't like. A previously good policeman, his behaviour had changed, now more a vigilante than an officer of the law. Vendettas and throwing caution to the wind weren't how Homicide worked, not as long as he was in charge. Isaac knew that he needed his inspector focussed on the current investigation, not one that had been filed as unsolved.

'Even if you can prove that Spanish John was involved in the death of Julius Rios, it doesn't do this department any good, nor you.'

'It could be construed that I'm solving a murder to prove that I'm innocent of other charges. It's easy to preach from a pulpit in Challis Street, listening to a man who's no longer around, not so easy out in the real world, and that's where I know. Internal machinations bore me, results don't, and I've got Spanish John on the run.'

'Have you?'

'I found a witness, willing to testify that he was there when Rios was marked for elimination.'

'We know that Rios was messing around with Spanish John's girlfriend, a good enough reason to get himself killed, but it's old news. Unless you can tie his death into Joe Foster's, then forget it. And that's an order.'

Isaac didn't like to rule his team by command, preferring to ensure they operated together by consensus, each playing off the others' strengths, but now his inspector was cracking up.

Even though less alcohol and cigarettes had improved Larry's appearance, it was clear that withdrawal from one or the other had also affected his temperament, misaligned his mental sharpness. Some people, Isaac knew, were destined for self-destruction, the inability to make the decisions vital for long life. If Larry was one of those people, and it was a choice between beer-swilling, cigarette-smoking and competent or teetotal, nicotine-free, irrational and vacillating, Isaac knew he would choose the former.

'Very well, meet with the man, do what you can to get him to open up, or else drop it.'

'Even if it impacts on the other investigations?'

'Does it? Spanish John has kept us informed on what happens in Basing Street. Maybe he knows more than we think. Open up to the man, not that he'll give up crime, but murderers loose on the street do him no favours.'

***

Eileen Cavendish had not wanted anyone else to know the truth about her unborn child, but Wendy had told Emily Foster, and after that Gladys had been told by Emily.

The three women of Joe Foster; there were known to be more, but to the trio, they weren't important. Previously ostracised by the Fosters, Eileen was now integral to the family, in part because she was carrying another child of Joe's, but also because Joe's empire was more complicated than had been previously thought. Jacob Morgan had stolen from them, and Eileen knew more about the finances than anyone else did, barring the vanished man.

Terry had been less than subtle in saying that if he got his hands on Morgan, he would be dead. Gladys, as much as she loved her children, knew that there were defective characteristics in all of them, especially Terry, the most criminal of the four that had resulted from her marriage to Joe. He was the least astute, the man most likely to cause the empire to collapse. Already he was into the funds, a Mercedes no longer suitable, a green

Lamborghini in the driveway, and he had more speeding tickets than most; one more and he would lose his driving licence. His bodyguards, not in the car with him, but driving behind him as he cruised around his domain, often had palpitations.

Eileen would admit to liking Emily, but not Gladys. With Emily, there was a warmth, and although Gladys was sympathetic to her plight, the conversation soon returned to the missing money.

As to how much the Fosters would welcome her back, Eileen knew it came with conditions, and once she had given them what they wanted, she'd be out on her ear.

When it had just been the two of them, Eileen had been willing to drink a couple of glasses of wine with Emily, but with Gladys present, she felt she could not.

'Joe's left us all in the lurch,' Gladys said. 'And you in a delicate state. Are you sure about this?' she asked.

'That I'm his daughter, conceived in a hotel room in Windsor, not far from the castle, yes, I am.'

'Are you laying claim to any of his money?'

'Enough to survive, and I'll be content.'

'Not happy?' Emily said. A stupid remark, she realised, after saying it.

'My mother has never been interested in money, unable to see the worth of fighting to succeed. I follow after her in that respect, not my father. One day, when this is all over' – looking down at her, as yet, flat belly – 'I will take stock. Until then, I will survive.

'If you want me to check your finances, attempt to circumvent the damage caused by Jacob Morgan, I am willing to do so, subject to satisfactory compensation and a guarantee that Terry will not come near me. If he does, I will delete all that I find out.'

'I'll give that promise,' Gladys said.

'And keep him away from me,' Emily added.

Even though there was cordiality, it was evident to Eileen that all of them, including her, had ulterior motives. She would work with the Fosters, but with conditions. One of those was the child she carried was not to be speculated over by anyone. But then, she knew that Gladys knew, as did Emily, and the police at Challis Street. She put on her coat and left the flat five minutes after the other two women. Although not a regular churchgoer, barring Christmas and Easter, she had a lot of praying to do, hopeful of guidance, not sure that she would receive it.

***

As one woman walked to the church, a man in another country strolled from his hotel to the beach, to a bar that had been his home from home for five days now. Jacob Morgan wanted to say he was pleased with his decision, but he wasn't so sure.

The hotel had five stars, the suite he occupied twice the size of his flat in London, and the weather was warm and balmy, a gentle breeze blowing from the sea. It was a holidaymaker's idyll, but as a man who had lived a modest life, occupied a mediocre flat and had spent his days in a darkened office surrounded by ledgers and books on finance, he was finding it difficult to adjust.

He reflected on that last time with Eileen, her rejection of him; it angered him, the life he could have given her, whereas now there was a surfeit of women looking for an ageing lothario who was flush with money, even if not so with libido. He qualified on all counts, and although he had dreamed of shaking off the singular dreariness of his previous life, he couldn't.

'Buy me a drink?' the woman who had taken the chair next to him said.

She was attractive and scantily dressed. It wasn't friendship she wanted, but he bought her a drink anyway. Loneliness had never concerned him before, too many distractions to bother, but he had felt it the first day he exited the plane, when he was hit in the face by a furnace, and still wearing a suit.

'Where are you from?' the woman asked as she came closer.

He wanted to respond, to enjoy the lifestyle that he had thought about for so long. Money wasn't an issue; he had plenty for three lifetimes, although this one would be shortened if he continued to drink at the same rate. Previously, a whisky of an evening, the occasional pint of beer in the pub, and now he was on his third rum and coke, and the woman next to him was downing them at a rate of two to his one.

Even so, she was company, even if she came at a cost, the cost of his dignity. A man of modesty before, increasingly lured by the promise of exotic delights and weakened by the alcohol, he saw himself as the young Adonis.

'Are you hungry?' he said.

'I know a good place, not far from here.'

He knew that he had to make an effort, to shake off the staid and modest mentality that had shaped his life: a life of hard work, never leaving the office of a night until his desk was cleared of all papers, and then home and soon to bed. The woman, younger than him by about forty years, became more desirable, the age difference losing its significance as the alcohol dulled his senses.

He relaxed for the first time since he had passed through security at Heathrow, a false passport in another name, his hair black where it had been grey, the moustache that he had had since twenty-five shaved off.

The officer at immigration had stamped his passport, wished him well, made a comment about how lucky he was. And that he was; a beautiful young woman on his arm, a bulging bank account, and no one in England knew where he was.

'Wait for us,' the woman said to the taxi driver after they had arrived at the restaurant.

'Better to pay him,' Morgan said. 'No point in running up the bill.'

'Here an Englishman is king. No need to worry. He won't charge us much.'

The meal was superb, the company divine. All the negatives that he had felt were gone. It was the first time he had smiled in a long time, not thinking about England, other than how he had cheated the Fosters; how the police had eaten out of his hand, believing every word that he uttered.

He went to sleep that night with the woman at his side. It hadn't been a total disaster, not a success, either. The last thing he remembered was the door to his room opening, another person coming in. Too tired to respond, he imagined it a dream.

It wasn't.

Chapter 23

Larry, conscious of the conversation with his DCI, pressured Spanish John about Joe Foster's murder; attempted to persuade the man that it would be better for all concerned if the murderers were apprehended. The gangster's reaction had not been favourable, and after two pints, Larry had left the pub, unable to feign the friendship he had once felt for the man. Larry knew he was in trouble when he rounded the corner to where his car was parked, two minutes after leaving the pub.

'You've been asking questions,' the man said.

'Not me, and besides, who are you?' Larry had replied. It wasn't the first time that people in the area had taken a distinct dislike to him; after all, it was a rough area in places, and street muggings weren't unheard of, although a lone police officer wasn't the usual target.

'It depends on who you are, not me,' the man said as he grabbed Larry and shoved him into a narrow alley around the back of the pub.

Larry's instinctive reaction was to push back, that was until he was hit in the stomach by a fist, and then his head was united with a wall as another man thrust him into it.

Bleeding, confused, out of breath and hurt, unable to fight back, Larry collapsed to the ground. He was prepared for a kicking, but it didn't happen. Instead, two of the three men grabbed him by the shoulder and propped him up against the wall.

'You're making enemies around here,' one of the men said.

Larry took a handkerchief from his pocket and wiped the blood from his face. In the glow from a street light he could see the man who had spoken. It was one of Spanish John's men, a tall, muscular man, a tattoo of a ship on his arm, not that it was easy to see as the man was black.

'You're—'

'Best not to say anything, copper, not if you know what's good for you.'

It wasn't the first beating for Larry, although on a previous occasion he had nearly died, which had been the intention of his attackers. But this was different. Apart from the beating, they had now sat him down, a sign he was there for a reason.

If only he could stand, Larry thought, he could deal with one of them, maybe two, and the pub wasn't far away, and inside was Spanish John.

'We're here to help,' the lead man said.

'A funny way to help,' Larry said, emboldened, his breath returning, able to stand again.

'It comes with conditions.'

'It depends on what they are.'

'The choice isn't yours to make.'

'And if I don't agree to whatever it is?'

'You'll not be going home tonight.'

It seemed to make no sense to Larry. After all, he was in a busy part of London, apart from the alley which smelt of stale urine and beer, a stopping-off spot for the drunks as they wound their way home after the pubs had closed for the night.

Larry said no more. If the men were acting on instructions, then wiser minds than theirs had thought it through, weighed up the pros and cons. The killing of a police officer always created the maximum response from the police force, something no self-respecting gang leader, criminal or hooligan wanted.

'What's the condition?'

'Stop asking questions about Julius Rios.'

'You could have told me that without beating me up.'

'The beating was our idea; payback for putting me behind bars, and as for my colleagues here, they don't like nosey policemen any more than I do.'

'Are you saying that whoever put you up to this told you not to hit me?'

'His instructions were clear; rough the man up, don't hurt him, and don't kill him. I would have, but then, I don't like you.'

'The feeling's mutual,' Larry said.

One of the three moved forward, a clenched fist. The leader grabbed the man's arm. 'Don't, not now.'

'You're members of a gang, Spanish John's. Are you working on instructions from him?'

'We aren't.'

Larry knew they were, but it didn't make sense. In all the time that Larry had known the man, he had never threatened violence. And if it wasn't Spanish John, Larry knew his enquiries were rattling chains, getting someone nervous. And that meant he was on the right track, and that given time, he would find out who had killed Rios.

Crime-fighting at the cutting edge, on the front line; it was how he liked his policing, although his body, now that he relaxed, hurt and he was sore.

'And if I don't pursue Rios's death?'

'We'll give you a name.'

'Whose name? And why?'

'You want the name of the two men who shot Joe Foster, don't you?'

'We do.'

'One of the men goes by the name of Basil Dixon.'

'Never heard of him.'

'You wouldn't. He's in Liverpool, not that we've met him.'

'What's to stop me reporting this assault?'

'Nothing at all. After all, you're a police officer, a man with a family. But it wouldn't make sense to cause trouble, and besides, information comes at a cost, and our cost was the satisfaction of beating you up. As I said, I would have killed you, but not this night; maybe the next, who knows. It's up to you.'

The three gang members melted away, each going in a different direction after leaving Larry. Across the street, another man watched, careful to ensure he wasn't seen.

He was pleased with his men, up until he saw Larry hobbling out of the alley. The message had been given, but those who had disobeyed his instructions would pay for their crime.

***

Larry arrived home, his wife distraught. 'You need to go to the hospital,' she said.

In the time before he reached his home, Larry had managed to clean off most of the evidence of his beating and had had time to reflect on what had happened.

Of the three assailants, two he could name, the other one he had seen in the area. They were marked men now, but that was as far as it went.

It was a warning to lay off one investigation, and then, as a reward, the name of a person in another. It proved two things to him, not doubting for a minute that Spanish John was behind it. Firstly, Spanish John was involved in the death of Julius Rios, and secondly, and more importantly, he was innocent in the death of Joe Foster.

Proof, hard-won and painful, had moved the case forward. Spanish John was no dummy; he knew how Larry would react. And he was right.

'No questions, not now,' Larry said to his wife, as she pulled the clothes from his body and helped him into a warm bath.

'They could have killed you.'

'Whatever you do, don't mention this to DCI Cook, not now. Promise?'

'But you should. It's a crime, assaulting a police officer. They could go to jail for what they did.'

'One's already been, the other two will eventually if they live that long.'

'What does that mean?'

'They disobeyed orders. They were meant to jostle me, not to beat me up. They're answerable to a higher court than ours.'

'Up above?' Larry's wife said, not understanding the significance of what he was saying.

'Down below, on the street. The code of the gangs.'

'Oh,' the response. Larry knew she still did not understand, which was fine by him. It was best if she didn't know the full truth of the people that he met with occasionally.

After thirty minutes in the bath, Larry, calm again, made a phone call.

'We need to find and question a Basil Dixon, a Jamaican, living in Liverpool. He's implicated in the shooting of Joe Foster,' he said.

'Are you sure?' Isaac said.

'I guarantee the information is accurate. Don't ask me how I know.' Larry moved his left arm, walked on the spot. He was sore; he was beyond further policing that night.

Isaac, however, was not. A name from Larry was to be acted on. He phoned Bridget, even though it was late, asked her to search the various databases. He then contacted a counterpart in Liverpool, let her know the seriousness of the matter.

It was way past midnight, but people in London and Liverpool were following through.

Bridget phoned back. 'Basil Edwin Dixon, thirty-nine years of age, born in Ocho Rios, Jamaica, arrived in England at the age of eleven. There are several crimes against him, a conviction for grievous bodily harm, suspended sentence due to his age at the time. Apart from that, minor convictions: theft, stealing a car, driving with a suspended licence.'

'An address?' Isaac asked.

'It's four years old, probably not of much use.'

'Thanks anyway. Once he's in custody, I'll need to go up to wherever he is, Liverpool probably. Larry's certain of his source. He can come with me, give him a chance to grab the glory, get the doubters off his back.'

'You're sure of him?' Bridget said.

'He's played it close to the line, but yes.'

'Good. We were worried, Wendy and I.'

'Goodnight,' Isaac said. He could have said more, but it was best not to. After all, he had instigated the internal investigation into his inspector. It was vital for him to remain impartial and not to interject his personal views.

***

Six in the morning, the team met in Isaac's office. Bridget was yawning after having had only two hours' sleep, whereas Wendy had slept through from eleven in the evening, until five o'clock. Isaac was elated, and Larry was bright and alert, after his wife had provided a good breakfast, not the usual muesli and a cup of tea, but bacon and eggs. For once, an exception had been warranted.

'They picked up Basil Dixon at five this morning,' Isaac said. 'A good team effort.'

'Liverpool?' Larry said. He had not taken a seat, preferring to stand. The fist to the stomach was still painful. He had strolled into the office, attempting not to show the results of the previous night's beating. It had worked with Wendy and Bridget, not with Isaac.

'Hard-won?' Isaac said.

'It was,' Larry replied.

'We'll talk about it later.'

'Off the record. An overnighter?'

'If you've packed your bag.'

'I have every confidence in my source. Yes, I'm ready.'

'From the look of you, I'd better drive.'

'Hard-won, as you say. But worth it.'

'You're convinced this is one of the men?' Wendy asked.

'My source is infallible,' Larry replied.

'Proving it is another matter,' Isaac said.

'I'm not too keen on approaching my source for further proof.'

'And this source, still someone you can talk to?'

'He's made his point, but yes.'

It was eleven twenty in the morning when Isaac and Larry arrived in Liverpool and drove out to St Anne Street Police Station.

Detective Inspector Sally Thompson, a seasoned police officer in her fifties, was waiting for them on their arrival. 'He's a cool customer,' she said. 'Came as meekly as a lamb, which considering his history was as a surprise.'

'Easy to find?'

'Easy enough. It's part of their creed: a bravado, a sense of their worth, our stupidity, not to hide.'

'He judged wrongly this time,' Isaac said.

'We'll bring him up when you're ready, but first, you must be hungry,' DI Thompson said.

'We are.'

'My treat. There's a good Italian restaurant not far from here. We can walk.'

Larry, stiffened from sitting in the car for so long, would have preferred to have not walked, but politeness decreed that he would not say so. 'That's fine,' he said.

On their return, Basil Dixon was brought into the interview room. As it was DI Thompson's arrest, she would sit in with Isaac, while Larry would watch from an adjoining room on a monitor, a video camera in the interview room recording and relaying the video and sound.

Dixon leant back on his chair, a look of nonchalance. He was, Isaac could tell, a cocky individual, disdaining of authority, assured of his worth.

Isaac, whose parents had come from Kingston, looked across the table at the man who had been born in

Ocho Rios, the haunt of cruise ships and western tourists aiming to get the flavour of the Caribbean but preferring to stay in western hotels. Although some of the tourists would venture further afield, some even climbing Dunn River Falls, others visiting Firefly, Noel Coward's house, not far from Oracabessa.

It was unlikely, however, that Dixon, if he had revisited Jamaica as an adult, would have been interested in the history or the sights of his birth country. The man, by reputation and his criminal record and his demeanour, was a Yardie, the uniquely peculiar term for a Jamaican gangster.

'Sold out, have you?' Dixon said to Isaac after the formalities had been dealt with.

'We have proof that you were in Basing Street, Notting Hill, London on the night of the sixteenth of July, last month,' Isaac said, not rising to the bait.

'If the carnival was on, I might have been.'

'It wasn't.'

'Then I wasn't there.'

'We can bring forward a witness that will testify that you were.'

Isaac looked across at DI Thompson. 'Do you have any more on Mr Dixon's movements?' A question for which he already had the answer.

'Mr Dixon's movements are well known. On the fourteenth of last month, he was involved in a brawl. He gave a statement at the time; no charges laid.'

'A minor disagreement,' Dixon said. 'No need for the police to be involved, but then, you've not got much to do other than hassle people you disapprove of. Racism, that's what it is.'

'It wasn't, and you know it,' Isaac said. 'You are a man used to violence; a person who finds it too easy to inflict pain, probably enjoys it as well.'

Isaac looked at a message on his phone, and across at Sally Thompson. She understood.

'Mr Dixon,' Isaac said, leaning forward on his chair, 'we have very sophisticated equipment at our disposal in London.'

'So?'

'You drive a blue BMW 320i?'

'What if I do?'

'Yes or no?'

'Yes.'

'Registration plate, SM58 HKM?'

'So what? It's paid for.'

'We can prove that the car was parked outside a house no more than a five-minute walk from where a murder was committed on the sixteenth of July.'

A nervous shuffling from Dixon, a look of concern. 'I lent it to a friend, or maybe I was down there. I can't remember which.'

'I suggest you do, or it's you who will be charged with murder. Is that what you want?'

'If this friend of mine killed someone, that's what he deserves.'

'A fair-minded citizen, that's what we like to see,' Isaac said. 'A man who believes in upholding the law.'

'I don't agree with murder if that's what you mean.'

'It is, and unfortunately for you, it wasn't only the car that was picked up on a surveillance camera. You were also picked up.'

'I wasn't there.'

'We can prove it. You're going to go down for a long time for the murder of Joe Foster. How do you plead?'

'I never killed anyone.'

For another hour, Dixon stonewalled.

In the end, Isaac formally charged the man with the murder of Joe Foster.

Outside, once Larry had joined Isaac and Sally Thompson, the DI asked the obvious question. 'Can you prove that he shot Foster?'

'No,' Isaac's one-word reply, looking over at Larry. 'Can you take any more questioning of your contacts in Notting Hill?'

'Painfully, but yes. Just take a note of what I'm willing to do for the cause of justice.'

'I am,' Isaac said. It had been a long day, and neither Isaac nor Larry wanted to drive back that day. And besides, Basil Dixon was a Liverpudlian villain. Any additional insights into the man, his colleagues, persons who may have accompanied him on the trip to London and to the murder were in Liverpool. If they were known and revealed before Isaac and Larry left the next morning, they could be given to Bridget, who would check the surveillance cameras, to Wendy, who would organise a team of uniforms to knock on doors, to waylay people walking on the street, and Larry to risk once again the hostility of Spanish John.

Larry knew his was the most dangerous.

Chapter 24

Jacob Morgan, the man who had pulled the wool over Joe Foster's eyes, woke to find himself restrained. It was clear as his eyes started to focus that he wasn't in the plush hotel suite where he had been staying, and neither of the two sitting on chairs was the woman he had taken to his room.

'We've got a few questions for you,' a small toothless man said. He was, from what Morgan could tell, in his fifties, dressed in a white shirt and a pair of navy shorts; he was barefoot and very black.

Life in the sun didn't seem as appealing to Morgan as it had before. His situation was parlous. He had read the warnings, the attacks on westerners with more money than sense. He had taken the necessary precautions, carrying only enough money for his immediate needs, not wearing a watch or carrying a wallet.

'Is it money you want?' Morgan asked, aware that he had wet himself; not out of fear, but because of the copious amount of alcohol the previous night, and then a woman in his bed. He was also hungry.

'Not from us,' the small man said. 'We're only looking after you for someone else.'

It made no sense, and for someone who had led a life of caution, he wasn't sure how to react. He had wanted adventure, but not with a capital 'A', just a jolt to the system, to shake him out of apathy, and then Joe had died.

Morgan realised that alive he was worth money, dead he was not. After all, the passwords to his bank accounts were on his laptop, and they were encrypted. No one was going to break them, and if they tried more than three times, the bank would block the accounts. Although the men who sat nearby might have been after the cash at the hotel: two thousand dollars, as well as six hundred euros in his room safe. They were welcome to that, he thought.

Morgan shuddered, more conscious than before. Whatever it was, it had the hallmarks of an intelligent mind. But whose, he wondered. Could it be the Fosters? He soon discounted them as an option. Astute as Samantha was, the only one capable of knowing or being able to estimate the extent of Morgan's deception, she wouldn't have had the connections overseas to set this up. Or the two men could be working for a local crime syndicate, preying on the gullible and naïve tourists, of which he had been one. He remembered that apart from the drinks and the food he had plied her with, the previous night's woman had not once asked for money. He had thought her to be a prostitute, out to make a financial killing with an older man, but she had denied it, only said that she enjoyed his company.

He mentally gave himself a kick for his stupidity.

'I need some food,' Morgan said, confident his life was not in danger.

The two men took no notice and continued to play cards, using an upturned barrel as a table.

Morgan moved, tried to position himself more comfortably. His legs weren't restrained, only his hands behind his back, the ropes too tight. Able to raise himself, he moved over to a chair nearby and sat down, aware that a rope around his waist was tied to a metal support.

A door opened, and a man walked in, a white man. Morgan looked up and studied him. It wasn't any of the Foster family; it wasn't someone he knew. In his hand, he carried a sports bag, Nike emblazoned across the side.

'Hungry?' he said to Morgan as he removed the rope from his wrists.

'What's this all about?' Morgan said, feeling calmer with the man present.

'Taking other people's money, that's a crime. You know that.'

Morgan took hold of the burger he had been given, taking large mouthfuls, almost choking on it. The two men who had been playing cards left. It was just two white men: one, the captive; the other, a man in his forties, casually dressed in an open-necked shirt and a pair of light-coloured trousers.

'A drink?' the man said.

'I could do with a visit to the toilet.'

'Of course.'

Morgan felt the final restraint being removed. He stood up and left the building, conscious that he needed to get as far away as he could. Relieved, he looked around. The two card-playing men were no longer on the island, but in a dinghy heading out to sea. They waved at him; he waved back.

'We're on an island, nowhere to go,' the other man said as he joined him on the small beach. 'It's just the two of us.'

'But why? I don't understand.'

'It's simple. You stole from my client; he wants his money back, no questions asked, no damage done.'

'The Fosters couldn't have pulled this off; too stupid for that.'

'Who said it was them?'

'Then whom?'

'It's not important. All I know is that there are eight million pounds that belong to someone else. You left England with more than that. Give back what my client wants, and you're free.'

'And if I don't?'

'Ah, well, then you will experience great pain. It's best to give me the account details, and then we'll shake hands. I'll even give you a lift to the airport.'

'To where?'

'Wherever you want; stay here if you like, but those two who just left know who you are and where to find you, and their method of extracting money won't be as civilized.'

'We could do a deal?'

'We could, but I have a reputation to uphold. If I get the eight million pounds from you, I'll receive two hundred thousand, enough for me.'

Morgan looked at the contents of the sports bag, the instruments the man had brought.

'Don't underestimate my resolve,' the would-be torturer said. 'You will hand over the money. He only wants what is owing to him. Give me that, and you're free, no unpleasantness, no crying out in pain, and we're far enough away that no one would hear you. What do you say?'

'The exact amount?'

'Exact to the penny, plus my commission,' the man said as he gave Morgan the itemised amount.

Even after paying the money, Morgan knew he had enough to live well, but not in a sunny clime, where pickpockets and thugs lurked around every corner.

'Very well. How do you want to do this?' Morgan said.

'On my boat, not far from here, I've got your laptop and a satellite internet connection. Make the transfer. Once it's confirmed, we'll leave the island, head back to your hotel. From then, it's up to you.'

'And you?'

'That woman you sampled last night. I'm meeting up with her.'

'A whore?'

'Who isn't, and besides, she got five hundred pounds for her efforts, and from what I heard, she didn't have to do much.'

Behind the urbane and agreeable façade, Morgan could see an amoral man, a man capable of violence, a sociopath.

He suddenly felt afraid. 'Your boat, let's get this over with.' He knew whose money it was.

***

Eileen Cavendish refused to go back to the office where she worked for Joe, preferring to stay in her flat. Samantha arranged for whatever she needed to be sent to her. After all, Samantha had always been agreeable, if distant, not indulging in idle conversation, which had suited her fine.

Eileen knew that she was a good person that bad happened to, and as long as her inner worth remained intact, the world could take what it wanted. She would stay impervious, not tainted by crimes committed by her or by others.

Even during her time in university her part-time activities as a prostitute had never affected her, and apart from Joe, she hadn't slept with another man since she had graduated. Her feelings were confused, unsure whether she should hate or love the man; after all, both of them had been oblivious as to their incestuous relationship. Her mother should have warned her, but hadn't. But then that was her mother, attractive when young, pleasant to look at when older, but a propensity for men of little worth, marrying one, losing him in an accident. Apart from Joe when younger, and then a brief affair later, her mother had chosen poorly.

The dilemma weighed heavily on her. She was glad of the distraction of work, even though Samantha's presence could irritate at times, and Ben Foster's inevitable daily visits, pleasant at first, had soon soured.

For eight days she laboured, going through all the accounts, checking the cash flow, compiling a list of what money should be in the bank accounts she knew of and the money there actually was. The discrepancy was large, in the order of twenty-four million pounds, enough to live like a king or a queen, enough to kill for.

During that time, communication between Eileen and Terry Foster had been minimal, only a few phone calls, when she had wanted the records for the strip clubs and the brothels which masqueraded as massage parlours, and with which he had complied.

At the end of nine days, she had completed her analysis, and a report was ready for the family. One condition elicited by Gladys at Emily's house was that Eileen would present the report to the entire family, including Terry, to which Eileen had initially objected, but afterwards agreed.

Wendy would not be present, not because of the monies involved, but because it was a family matter and specific confidential details would be spoken about, such as where the money had come from, who had been cheated.

221

However, Samantha Foster had phoned Wendy to tell her that she would be given a ballpark figure of how much Jacob Morgan had stolen. Which, as it turned out, wasn't needed, as a sunburnt man walked into Challis Street Police Station.

'I need immunity from prosecution,' Morgan said as he took a seat in Homicide.

'I'm not certain we can give you that,' Isaac said. 'After all, people have died.'

'Consider the situation,' Morgan continued. 'I have not committed a crime in this country, other than taking money from people who didn't deserve it, people who obtained it by deceit and dishonesty. The scum of the earth, not worthy of any of the common decencies. I am here to return all their money, to tell you what I know, and to go back to the life I had.'

'Not so good, overseas?'

'I'm a creature of habit. What others find exciting doesn't interest me.'

Morgan's confident, almost dismissive attitude was gone, replaced by a shell of a man, his shoulders more hunched than before.

'If we agree, how does that advantage you?'

'My conscience will be clear. If fate decrees that I am a threat to certain people, then so be it. If I am to die, then I'm ready. But I know this; you will know as much as I do.'

'Have you been back to your flat?'

'Not yet. I arrived this morning, came straight here. I have the information with me, and subject to agreement, I will transfer what I have.'

'And what do you have?'

'As an accountant and financial adviser, I committed no crime. Let us be clear about that.'

'But you knew or suspected?'

'I did. As to his legal affairs, you will need to talk to Gerald Braxton.'

'Another person who claims innocence. Frankly, Mr Morgan, I find all of this hard to swallow. If, as we believe, and so do the Fosters, you had access to numerous offshore accounts, criminal money a lot of it, that makes you culpable.'

'Do I have immunity?'

Isaac picked up his phone, made a phone call, explained the situation. After five minutes, he put his phone back in his pocket. 'You've got a deal. Not for murder, though.'

'I killed no one, nor did I commit a crime other than moving money around the world.'

'Avoiding tax?'

'The prerogative of the wealthy and astute. Nobody needs to pay more tax than they should, or would you disagree?'

'I wouldn't, but crime is another issue. This was dirty money.'

'Dirty, clean, what's the difference? You may believe in a sanitised world, but it's rough out there. Joe Foster did it better than most; I admired the man, still do. He rose to the top, not that I saw the violence, but I heard about it. And now, with an agreement from you, I will transfer all the documentation over to your people.'

Isaac called out for Bridget to come in.

'Mr Morgan wants to transfer some documents to you.'

'Dropbox or OneDrive?' Bridget said.

'Dropbox will do.'

Morgan opened his laptop, logged onto the internet through a connection that Bridget had given him.

He then opened a folder on his laptop, right-clicked and sent it to Bridget.

'Got it,' Bridget said after twenty seconds.

'My work is done. If you will excuse me, I will go home and rest. It was a long flight, an even longer day.'

'And if we need to talk to you again?' Isaac asked.

'You will not need to. What your colleague has is comprehensive. It details all activities that the money came from, although some are vague. Also, all the accounts and the passwords.'

'You are placing a lot of trust in us,' Bridget said. 'It could be a lot of money.'

'You're the police; you're accountable. The majority of the money belongs to the Fosters, assuming they can account for it, able to prove to your Fraud Squad that it was obtained legitimately, and no doubt Inland Revenue will get involved.'

'Is there any more we should know?'

'There was a transfer of just over eight million pounds made to another party one day ago. Dealing with that person will be more difficult than the Foster family. How you deal with Tony Rafter is your issue, not mine.'

'Why are you doing this?' Isaac asked.

'I would have died if I hadn't paid the money back to the man. I will gain satisfaction when Rafter is arrested.'

'Bridget, work overnight if you have to. We need to know everything by tomorrow morning,' Isaac said.

'Yes, of course.'

'As for you, Mr Morgan, we will speak again at some time.'

'Maybe, but no more, not now. I wish you a good day,' Morgan's parting words as he picked up his suitcase.

Chapter 25

Basil Dixon sat calmly in his cell, maintaining passive defiance, not once shouting out
his innocence, only making himself comfortable, asking for some magazines to be sent to him, and an extra pillow.

It was a display of arrogance, and even though he remained in Liverpool, those in London were working hard to gather the evidence that would turn suspicion into fact. And for that, there was only one place to go, to the man who had painfully given Dixon's name to Larry.

Larry did not relish meeting with Spanish John, the beating not only confirming Dixon as one of the two men who had killed Joe Foster, but also that the gangster had been behind the murder of Julius Rios.

Wendy maintained a healthy scepticism about Eileen Cavendish. Association with a gangster, access to his finances, were clear indicators that the woman had seen wrong but had not walked away from it, and the story about her mother never telling the truth about Foster was flawed.

As Wendy saw it, why was the mother asking Joe Foster to give her daughter a job? It irked Wendy, the reason why a caring mother, and that was what she appeared to be when Wendy had phoned her, would allow Eileen to work for a previous lover of hers, an unfaithful husband and a scoundrel, and then, above all else, not to tell her that he was her father.

It was the reason why, after a less than a satisfactory phone call, Wendy decided to confront the mother face-to-face.

The modest semi-detached house in a modest part of a small town, a two-hour drive north of London, wasn't as downmarket as it had been described by Eileen, nor did the mother fit Eileen's description. The youthful beauty that had attracted Joe Foster in his younger years had been replaced by a woman who had seen more than her fair share of life, her clothes clean and tidy but dowdy and worn, a cigarette in her mouth.

The two women sat in the kitchen, a dog outside barking, a cat sitting on a window sill, the noise of a washing machine in the laundry to one side of the kitchen.

'You asked Joe Foster for a favour, is that correct?' Wendy said.

'We had kept in touch over the years.'

One cigarette finished and thrown in the kitchen sink, another placed in the mouth. Even though Wendy had forsaken cigarettes for a healthier lifestyle, the smell still drew her. She could have accepted the cigarette offered, but she refused. The visit was not social but interrogative. Now was not the time to break her resolve.

There was something seductive about how Eileen Cavendish's mother lived, something Wendy could identify with. At her worst addiction to nicotine, she had become as slovenly but still maintained a good house, ensuring her children were neatly turned out for school and friends, that her husband had a clean shirt for work. Yet, on the days when she wasn't policing, and no one was in the house, she would be in the kitchen, a cigarette in hand, a cup of tea to one side, just savouring the moment, not caring if the world came to an end, not even if the house crumbled around her.

But the mother of a pregnant woman, the unborn child the result of an incestuous relationship, did not have moments, she had an eternity.

'Your husband?' Wendy asked.

'There is no husband, only a dog outside, a cat that only comes near when it wants food.'

'Eileen said that you were a good person. I can't see it myself.'

'Not that good, not after I asked Joe to give her a job, and now she's pregnant.'

'She's told you?'

'She has.'

'And the father?'

'She told me.'

'If it were me, I would be horrified. Yet you sit there calmly, taking it in your stride. What kind of mother are you?'

A vacant expression came over the mother's face, not a sound, just a sucking of the cigarette. Wendy wanted to grab her and shake her. Eileen Cavendish's description of her mother was wrong; she had lied. And if she could lie about her mother, what else could she have lied about, Wendy thought.

'Why would Joe do that? With my daughter?'

'He knew?'

'I told him before she started work with him.'

'But why would a mother want her daughter to be involved with such a man? He might have been charismatic, willing to pay her well, but he was a gangster.'

'Did all that matter? You know about university?'

'I do. How do you know?'

'Eileen told me, said it was a bit of a lark.'

'Your reaction?'

'I didn't give much thought to it; after all, it's a new world, they're all at it.'

'In your world, not in mine.'

As Wendy looked at the woman, melancholy settling over her, a man walked in the door, took one look and left. He returned thirty seconds later, picked up his wife and carried her into another room, laying her down on a sofa. 'She's having one of her turns,' he said. 'And you are?'

'Constable Wendy Gladstone, Challis Street Police Station, London.'

'Pleased to meet you. I'm Bob Grant. This is about Eileen.'

'How did you know?'

'She's my stepdaughter. We don't get on that well, but I was always cordial with her. My wife, telling stories again?'

'She is. What's the problem with her?'

'A pathological tendency to exaggerate or tell lies. It's called mythomania. Some days she's worse than others. She means no harm by it; doesn't even know she's doing it.'

'Drug-induced?'

'Apart from the cigarettes, no. It could be a trauma or a head injury, even the central nervous system, but there's no definite medical reason, no cure, other than to let her rest for a while. Disarming if you're not prepared for it.'

'You mentioned Eileen?'

'Eileen doesn't have her mother's condition, although she learnt to lie from her mother. Told you she prostituted at university?'

'Yes.'

'She might have, but I'm not certain. I used to send her money regularly.'

'But she's not your child?'

'No, but she isn't Joe Foster's either.'

'You know about that?'

'I do. My wife has a past, not always good, and she's had this condition for a long time. It's got her into trouble on more than a few occasions, and caused her to sleep around, Joe Foster, for instance.'

'Your wife told her daughter that Joe Foster is her father.'

'The sort of thing she might do.'

'Eileen should have realised that.'

'She may have, but Eileen has picked up traits from her mother. She may be lying to herself and you.'

'Working for Joe Foster, that doesn't make sense.'

'Joe knew of my wife's condition. He had loved her once; he felt for her, and I knew that Eileen couldn't return to the family home after university, and if she wasn't watched, she could have got into trouble. It was me that asked Joe to look after Eileen. He was, as you say, a gangster, as violent as any, but he was also a good family man. With him, she was safe; with others, who knows, and maybe my wife's condition is hereditary. Medical science isn't sure, and if Eileen's lying to you, you'd better check it out. But please, be careful. To me, she's my daughter, even if biologically she isn't. And please don't judge my wife harshly; she doesn't deserve that.'

'I won't,' Wendy said.

***

'Why?' Larry said.

'Why, what?' Spanish John replied.

Larry didn't pursue the question, aware that a warning had been given, painful as it was.

'Let's not talk about it,' Larry said.

'Good idea. Life's too short for disagreements and misunderstandings between friends.'

Friendship, given freely before by Larry, no longer applied. To him, Spanish John no longer had any redeeming features; he was a marked man, and with time, he would see once again the inside of a prison cell. But for now, it was information that was required.

'We went to Liverpool, interviewed Basil Dixon.'

'Who?'

Larry picked up his pint of beer, took one mouthful of it and put it down on the table; Spanish John downed his pint in one go.

It was early afternoon, and there was a meeting at Challis Street later, an end-of-day debriefing. Larry cast his eyes around the pub, noticed that one of Spanish John's men, one of those that had beaten him up, wasn't present. The man had been a foot soldier, cannon fodder and expendable. If he never appeared again, he would not be missed.

'We received a tip-off that Basil Dixon was one of the men who gunned down Joe Foster.'

'I've heard of him.'

The conversation was to be cat and mouse, with Spanish John admitting nothing, saying a lot.

'We met him in Liverpool. He denies it, of course, but we can place his car in the area at the time of the shooting.'

'Proof enough?'

'For us, but not for a judge and jury. As long as the man holds to his story that a friend had borrowed it, or it was stolen, or he was down visiting friends, we won't get a conviction.'

'Foster's dead. Why should I care?'

'I don't expect you to, but if our investigation continues, questions will be asked, extra people will be seconded, and then you know what will happen.'

'Idle minds, false suspicions, intrusion into places they shouldn't go, innocent people harassed.'

'I'd agree with the first three. If we can get a conviction for Foster's killers, then the man's other crimes are not our concern. Life will return to normal; you and I won't meet as often for a quiet drink, peace will reign.'

'You make it sound idyllic, a scene out of a children's fairy tale.'

'It'll never be that.'

'Ah, yes, now I remember. Basil Dixon, not long from the homeland.'

'Over fifteen years,' Larry said. 'As English as you and me.'

'Short man, on the chubby side?'

'Tall and slim,' Larry replied; cat and mouse, it was.

'I met him once, not sure where. He was friends with someone I knew. A decent sort, give you the shirt off his back.'

Spanish John didn't know anyone that generous; steal the shirt from someone else, more likely.

'His name?'

'Lyron something. I can't remember his surname.'
'Lyron Sealy?'

'That's it. Do you know him?'

'We do,' Larry said. 'Are you suggesting we have a chat with him?'

'I'm suggesting nothing. I only know the man was a friend of Dixon.'

The second man involved in the murder of Joe Foster had a name.

***

Bridget had not spent all night going through all the documentation that Morgan had handed over. However, she had worked until two thirty in the morning, until totally exhausted and unable to progress further. Wendy had stayed with her until one o'clock, having ensured that the two of them were fed with a pizza early on, then KFC, the family pack, and, to finish, a cheeseburger with French fries each from McDonald's.

The two women had overeaten, and the next morning neither had needed breakfast, only a cup of tea.

Morgan had been comprehensive in his documentation, and although Bridget understood the majority of it, there were still some questions to be asked. Certain points still needed clarification, in particular the eight million pounds.

Larry, alert and relieved that his meeting with Spanish John had proved not to be as fractious as expected, that a name of someone known to the police had been given, and that the investigation against him had been shelved, after Larry had proved that his wife's mother had given her fifty thousand pounds to help with the new house's purchase, took responsibility for bringing Morgan back to Challis Street.

Arriving at Morgan's office, Larry, along with a uniformed constable, found the place locked, the lights off inside.

Not lingering at the office, Larry drove the short distance to Morgan's flat. The uniform got out of the patrol car that had been following him. The two men climbed the stairs to Morgan's flat, knocked on the door and waited.

Two minutes, then five, and finally, after eight, Larry, tiring of shouting the man's name and banging on the door, looked at the constable. 'You or me?' he said.

'It might be better if you do it, Inspector.'

Larry, still sore from his ordeal at the hands of Spanish John's three henchmen, put his shoulder to the door and pushed. It gave easily.

Inside, Larry called out again. The constable waited outside.

'You can come in,' Larry said. 'Make sure you don't touch anything. Have you any crime scene tape in the car?'

'We have.'

'Good. Phone your offsider, tell him to bring it up. It could be a crime scene.'

The constable looked into one of the bedrooms. 'He looks peaceful, as though he's asleep,' he said.

'The CSIs can tell us, pathology can confirm, but you're right. It looks as though he just lay down and died. Even so, we need to know if that's the case. The man was important. He knew he had signed his death warrant when he came back to England, willing to accept his fate.'

'You knew him?'

'More money than Croesus, miserly as Scrooge.'

'Croesus?' the constable said.

'More money than you and I will ever see in a lifetime,' Larry said.

'And he lived here?'

'Scrooge, every Christmas on the television?'

233

'I don't think he was killed. Maybe a visitation from the ghost of Christmas Past gave him a shock,' the constable said.

Regardless of how the man had died, Larry left it to the CSIs. He returned to Challis Street.

Chapter 26

Lyron Sealy had not been difficult to find. However, Larry was still troubled as to why Spanish John had firstly had him beaten and then given him a name, only to provide another name over a pint of beer.

'The man's got an ulterior motive,' Isaac said.

'That doesn't make sense,' Larry said. 'Those who roughed me up are nowhere around, except for one of them.'

'They hadn't followed orders, made it personal.'

'To Spanish John, we're irritants, tolerated if needed, helped if we're treading on his toes, eliminated if he has no option.'

'He thinks it through.'

'A worthy successor to Joe Foster.'

'Each man is as bad as the other, but you're right; Spanish John has the discipline and the intelligence that Joe had, but Terry doesn't.'

'Is he trying to tell us something, not wanting to raise the ire of an opponent without laying the groundwork?'

'Are you saying that Terry Foster's behind his father's death? Isaac said.

'We get Terry Foster out of the way, and then Spanish John walks in unchallenged.'

'Or else he's setting him up. Not so difficult if we give it some thought. Terry's got a reputation as a hard man. Circumstantial evidence would point to him, but Basil Dixon's not talking, and we can't prove he was in Basing Street at the time. Now, Lyron Sealy, a part-time bouncer and enforcer, is offered up as a scapegoat. Either or both could be innocent.'

'They're not,' Larry said.

Isaac was willing to concede to his inspector. Spanish John had been at school with Isaac, but back then the gangster had just been a tearaway, fights in the school playground, once with Isaac until Isaac had grabbed him around the neck with one arm and punched him. It was one of the few times when Isaac had been disciplined at school for his actions. Although, after that, Spanish John, known as John back then, the nickname given when he joined his first gang, a reference to his coming from Spanish Town in Jamaica, had kept his distance.

'What makes you so sure?' Isaac asked.

'Spanish John wouldn't play us for fools, not at this juncture. There's too much riding on this for him, assuming he's trying to expand his influence.'

Isaac had to admit his inspector was showing more wisdom than previously. He hoped it was as a result of his reduced alcohol intake, a chance for the brain cells to regroup, although he doubted it.

'Framing Terry Foster isn't a bad way to go about it, but Dixon and Sealy aren't likely to admit to their guilt, not if they've any sense, not even if Spanish John is giving them money.'

'For now, we go with what we've got, try to place Dixon in the area of the murder,' Larry said. 'Basing Street if we can.'

'The police in Liverpool are checking out his alibis. His car was in London, and the friend he said had borrowed his car can't be found, although there's a woman adamant that Dixon spent that night with her. And considering the time to drive from London to

Liverpool, either her watch was faulty or Dixon drove like a madman to get back.'

'The power of love can't be beaten.'

Isaac smiled; the humour wasn't lost on him. However, Sealy was ready and waiting in the interview room.

Isaac went through the formalities, told Sealy his rights, that he could have legal representation if he required. Sealy declined, which was duly noted and recorded.

'What's this all about?' Sealy, an unpleasant man with a crooked nose, an amateur boxer in his youth, asked. Apart from his physical appearance, he was a snappy dresser, although out of vogue for the year, more akin to the seventies: a gold necklace, the top three buttons of his shirt undone and his fingers adorned with rings of various types.

'Joe Foster's murder in Basing Street.'

'Notting Hill?'

'Is there another?' Isaac said.

'Just checking, can't say I know it.'

'Strange, seeing we can prove that you spend time in the Castle pub in Notting Hill, park your car in Basing Street.'

'I don't check the address where I park the car, only for how long I can leave it before one of your friends gives me a ticket.'

'Okay, we'll give you that. You have, however, been implicated in the murder of Joe Foster. What do you say?'

'Not much, never met the man.'

'You've heard of him?'

'Who hasn't? Something of a reputation, a man not to cross.'

'And you, a law-abiding citizen, wouldn't,' Larry said.

'I go to the Castle from time to time, meet a few friends, have a few drinks, some laughs. Nothing wrong with that.'

'You've done time for violence.'

'A man's allowed to make a mistake. You would have made a few.'

'I'm not a suspect. I haven't shot down a man in cold blood.'

'Nor have I, and besides, this Joe Foster, not someone the police would shed a tear about.'

'It's still a homicide. The law applies to the meek and mild, the humble and innocent, as well as to the malignant. Justice needs to be done.'

'An eye for an eye, is that what you mean?'

'Gentleman,' Isaac interjected, 'we're not here for a philosophical discussion on right and wrong. Yes, we all agree, Joe Foster is not up for sainthood, but you, Lyron Sealy, have been named as one of the two men who killed him. The question is, were you the shooter or the driver of the car? Which one were you?'

'Neither. And you can't prove it either way.'

'Maybe we don't have to. Basil Dixon's on ice up in Liverpool. All we need to do is play one off against the other. One of you will go down for murder; the other might get off with manslaughter, possibly mitigating circumstances, not certain that the man was to be killed, thought it was only a warning. After all, Joe Foster was nobody's fool, and if someone's heavying in on his territory, they would be willing to let you and Dixon take the blame.'

'I've nothing to say. You think you're so smart, the two of you. What do you know about what goes on out there? The people involved, the deals made, the people who die. I admit I'm not a good man, but I'm not a murderer.'

'As you say,' Isaac said.

Larry looked bewildered, not sure what to make of Isaac's tactics.

'As I say,' Sealy said. 'And if you're finished with this nonsense, I've got someone to meet.'

'A hot date?'

'As always.'

'The only date you've got is a cell. And the most you'll get there are a blanket and a few fleas. Not much of an exchange, but I'm charging you with the murder of Joe Foster.'

'You can't prove it,' Sealy said.

'I don't need to, not now, but I can keep you for twenty-four hours, up to seventy-two if I have to, long enough to let Terry Foster know we've got his father's killer in Challis Street and that we're about to release him without sufficient evidence.'

'You can't do that. Foster's a madman.'

'We can and we will. If we can't convict you and Dixon, the least we can do is see that justice is done. Poetic, I'd say.'

'Our source is reliable,' Larry said. 'He gave us your names; no doubt he could identify both of you. He doesn't want scum like you on the street any more than we do.'

'Foster won't be looking for evidence. Anyway, you're bluffing. The police don't work like that,' Sealy said.

'Don't they? Can you be so sure?' Isaac said. 'After all, we're not about to let a murderer out on the streets, no more than Foster would. Inspector Hill and myself, we live local, families to consider. It's our civic duty that's more important. What if you'd killed a bystander in Basing Street? Did you look around, check it was clear, no witnesses? Of course you didn't.'

'I'm innocent.'

'So's Dixon; innocent of thinking this through. Why Basing Street? Why in daylight? You must have known that was the worst time to choose or was it that someone smarter than you knew Foster would be vulnerable.'

Larry nodded to Isaac and then left the room, his place in the interview taken by Wendy.

Outside of the interview room, Larry made a phone call, DI Sally Thompson answering up in Liverpool. 'Get Dixon,' he said. 'Are you ready?'

'We are.'

Before Isaac called a break from the interview, he phoned a legal aid lawyer. 'You need legal representation,' he said to Sealy.

'For what?'

'For when Dixon admits your part in Joe Foster's murder.'

'He won't. He wasn't there.'

'Who was?'

'I wasn't. How would I know?'

'How indeed?' Isaac said as he noted the time and paused the interview.

'Pizza?' Wendy said.

'Hawaiian,' Sealy said. 'A cappuccino, as well.'

'The same for me,' Isaac said. He called out; a uniform came into the room. 'Make sure Mr Sealy's comfortable. He's got a long night ahead of him.'

'One of your people from the Caribbean,' Sealy said. 'You've sold out.'

'Dixon said the same. The two of you must have been comparing notes. I'm English. These are my people, not scum like you.'

***

In Liverpool, DI Thompson and a sergeant sat with Basil Dixon; in London, Isaac and Wendy sat opposite Lyron Sealy.

Two hours had passed since the interview had paused in London. Enough time for Sealy to have eaten his pizza, drunk his coffee and met with his legal aid.

If the ruse went according to plan, Sealy would need a lawyer, and circumventing the rights of the suspect, even if Sealy maintained his innocence, could prove prejudicial at a subsequent trial.

Basil Dixon said little as Sally Thompson explained the situation.

'Lyron Sealy's in an interview room at Challis Street Police Station in London. My colleagues down there tell me that he's implicating you as the shooter; him as no more than a man who thought you were just going to rough up Joe Foster.'

The sergeant sitting alongside Sally Thompson looked at his inspector, wondered where she was going with the fabrication. A plump, plodding police officer in his forties, Sergeant Clough was regarded in Liverpool as decent and honest, but devoid of ambition and initiative, and most of his peers saw him as a joke. Sally Thompson didn't, not as much as the others. Clough, not a man to rock the boat, or to stand up and be counted, or to do anything contrary to proper police procedures, failed to see that playing off two men, separated by over two hundred miles, when the evidence was flimsy was just that.

Sally Thompson hoped her DCI, outside in another room, wouldn't intervene. He was a man of few accomplishments, a poor record of arrest, a sycophant who would make sure he was there for the glory, not for work. If Challis Street's ruse worked, then he would be there to take the acclaim, but if it didn't… Sally Thompson knew what would happen; it would be her head on the chopping block.

She and her chief inspector had been an item six years back, when they were both sergeants and before she found out that he was a spineless wimp, and even though they had been sleeping together, it hadn't stopped him from pushing her to one side when it came time for promotion. It had been the end of a budding romance, the start of a starchy, discordant relationship. It still gave Sally some satisfaction that on the rebound she had married a decent and solid man whom she loved and who loved her back. In contrast, the DCI had married another woman in the station who bore him two snotty-nosed children and then walked out of the marital home, leaving him with the alimony payments and not much else.

At Challis Street, a scenario similar to Liverpool's was in play. Lyron Sealy was now with a legal aid lawyer, although he had been adamant that he didn't want one, only withdrawing his opposition to the world-weary man in his fifties after the situation had been explained in detail.

'One of you is going to be charged with murder. Whichever of you gives us the name as to who set it up, paid you both to kill Foster, it will go in his favour,' Isaac said.

'I didn't kill anyone; no one can prove it.'

The team in Homicide knew the legal aid lawyer, and whereas he wasn't the person you'd want on your side in a court, he was experienced and articulate and determined that whoever he represented at the police station would be treated fairly.

He had confided to Isaac a couple of times outside the police station that he was well aware of the vermin he sometimes represented.

Basil Dixon's legal aid knew her client. She'd defended him on three occasions previously, getting the charges against him dismissed on two of them and passing the third charge for the savage beating of a man over to a more experienced lawyer. Dixon had been found innocent of that charge.

The legal aid knew what and who she was representing, and although not as experienced as Sealy's legal aid, she would be watching every trick the police tried. To her, the law would be upheld, but as her mother had been mugged three days earlier by a dissolute youth who thought the world owed him a living, she regarded Dixon as probably guilty. After all, the evidence against him, circumstantial but condemnatory in its detail, placed her client in the area at the right time on the right day.

'Mr Sealy,' Isaac said, 'Basil Dixon has admitted to his presence at the murder, stating that you killed Foster and he was duped, his words not mine.'

'Innocent? Dixon? I don't think so,' Sealy said.

'You're guilty of murder. Dixon's testimony could be enough to convict you.'

'Detective Inspector, you're indulging in speculation, aiming to intimidate my client,' the legal aid said.

'Dixon's a bad man, mean as they come,' Sealy said.

It wasn't an admission, but it was a welcome step forward, an acknowledgement that the two men knew each other.

Up in Liverpool, after Larry had phoned her, Sally Thompson put a similar set of questions to Dixon. His responses were more guarded.

'Are you saying that you don't know Lyron Sealy?'

'Never heard of him.'

'That's strange,' Sally Thompson said.

'Why? I can't know everyone, and yes, I was in London the other week, but that doesn't mean I would have met someone, forgotten his name already.'

'Denial might work for now, but Chief Inspector Cook believes that you and Sealy are guilty of murder, and your record does you no credit. A smart prosecution will ensure a prejudiced jury who'll take one look at you and condemn you out of hand.'

'Bullying tactics won't work,' the legal aid said.

'Not bullying, factual,' Sally Thompson said. 'Lyron Sealy states that he knows your client and is willing to draft a statement admitting to his involvement. After all, Sealy's more charismatic, known to be less violent. His chance of acquittal or a short custodial sentence is a lot better than Mr Dixon's.'

Dixon looked over at the police, fiddled with the lapel of his jacket, rubbed one of his hands over his head, a perplexed look on his face.

Not a lot of brainpower, there, Sally Thompson thought, about the same as my sergeant, a lump of lard.

'Okay, I know Sealy, not that I killed anyone, nor did I have anything to do with a man's death,' Dixon said.

'Progress of sorts,' Sally Thompson said.

'That's it. I can't tell you anymore.'

'You can and you will. Sealy's not going down for a murder he says he didn't commit, and I believe him more than you. After all, you're one of our home-grown villains. I know you, so do most of the police in Liverpool. You're a nasty piece of work with a bad reputation and an even worse attitude.'

'You can't insult my client,' the legal aid said.

Sally Thompson knew she could and would continue to do so.

'It's not insults that should concern your client, but the fact that he's facing a lengthy prison sentence for murder, even if he manages to live that long.'

'What does that mean?' Dixon asked.

'Joe Foster, what do you know about him?'

'I didn't kill him.'

'But you've heard of him?'

'I read the papers, keep up to date with what's happening.'

'Foster's death might not have featured high in Liverpool's newspapers, although it would have been on the internet, and seeing that you're a great friend of Sealy's, he would have told you.'

'I knew him, nothing more.'

'Why were you in London?'

'Sightseeing, meeting up with old friends.'

'You don't look like the sort of person who'd queue to see the crown jewels, attempt to get a glimpse of royalty at Buckingham Palace.'

'I don't have to visit those places to sightsee, do I?'

'Maybe you don't, or is your taste in sights more suburban? For instance, a strip joint, time with one of Foster's girls, and yes, he had prostitutes working for him.'

'And if it was?'

'No concern to me as to how you live your life, depraved as it is. And if you did meet up with some women, take in a show or two, then you can tell me who they were, the name of the women, your friends.'

'This is a farce,' the legal aid said. 'Even if my client had spent time with prostitutes, that's hardly a matter for the police. You're not arbiters of morality, just servants of the law, and unless you've got anything more substantial, I suggest you end this and let my client leave.'

At Challis Street, a similar situation. Lyron Sealy in the hot seat, feeling more uncomfortable by the minute as the events in Liverpool were relayed by another inspector up there who was listening in on Dixon's interview.

'Dixon's admitted that he knows you,' Isaac said.

'So?' Sealy's response. The man had adopted a laidback, disinterested manner. It didn't suit him well, made him look shiftier than he was; more guilty, as though he was sneering at the police.

'I intend to charge you both with premeditated murder, and given the severity of the crime, you and Dixon should have plenty of time to cement your friendship, twenty years at least.'

'On what proof?' the legal aid asked.

'The evidence is overwhelming,' Isaac said.

'It's circumstantial. Dixon was in London; the two men admit to knowing each other. Where's the proof in that?'

'If one admits to their guilt, or states he was an innocent dupe and that it was the other one who shot Joe Foster, then maybe one of them might get off with a five-year sentence, or thereabouts. Otherwise, our investigations will continue, and remember, the murder area is inundated with surveillance cameras. We'll find further proof.'

Sealy leant over to his legal aid, whispered in his ear. The legal aid shook his head.

'It was Dixon, he shot the man,' Sealy blurted out. 'Sure, I was there in the car, but I thought it was just a warning, to get the man to ease off, a punch in the stomach, a fist to the face. How was I to know he intended to shoot him. I'm innocent, I tell you. You can't lock me up for a crime I didn't commit, no way. Innocent, don't you hear me?'

'We hear you. If you would put this down in writing, from the time you met with Dixon up to when you parted from him, it will go in your favour.'

'My client has acted against advice,' the legal aid said. 'However, I will ensure that the statement he presents to you is correct and confirms what he has just said.'

Up in Liverpool, Dixon was told what had happened in London. He chose to make no comment. He was, as it turned out, a smarter man than Sealy.

After all, as Isaac admitted to Sally Thompson later that day, the evidence was circumstantial. No one had placed either of the two men in Basing Street. But for now, a sense of relief that two men, undoubtedly guilty, had been charged with murder.

The pressure on Challis Street Homicide to find additional evidence was overwhelming.

Chapter 27

Jacob Morgan's death, inopportune as it had been, came with no suspicion of foul play. The CSIs had checked his flat, and the pathologist had conducted an autopsy. High blood pressure, a possibly stressful time overseas in a hot climate, and then Morgan's return to England, his willingness to cooperate with the police, had all combined to cause a massive stroke and he had died in his sleep.

Thankfully, Homicide had a lot of documentation from him, and his laptop, as well as his office and his flat, were in the control of the police. Bridget had received a set of keys to his office, and she was already there, to spend time searching through the contents of his laptop – the password easily cracked – and to add information to what she already had, filling in what she would have asked Morgan if he had been alive.

The eight million pounds transferred while he had been in the Caribbean was the first consideration. The account that it had been sent to was an offshore account, and there was no way that the account holder's name would ever be known, even if attempts were made to find out. The only indicator was that the amount appeared to correlate to some invoices and a couple of business analysis statements that Morgan had handed over. Other than that, the majority of Morgan's documentation was easy enough to understand, the financial deceptions he had committed against the Fosters clearly detailed.

Isaac, who had been given updates by Bridget, could only believe that Morgan had had a death wish and that his death, premature as it had been, was to the man's benefit. And even if the majority of the money he had stolen had come from the Fosters, the eight million clearly hadn't.

Homicide had their suspicions, Morgan had even mentioned the name, but proving it was one thing, but knowing it was one thing, and even if proven, doing something was another.

'One law for the rich and another law for the poor' Isaac knew, paraphrasing the line from Frederick Marryat's book *The King's Own*. And in this case, the rich were very rich, and Rafter's influence stretched far and wide. Homicide had been there before. Rafter would be hidden behind an impenetrable veil of power and a gaggle of lawyers – not using the correct collective noun, superimposing another more reflective of the legal men Rafter used – and a team of obstructionist lackeys.

Isaac refocussed on Dixon and Sealy. Two men, neither of them with a reason to kill Joe Foster in the style of a Chicago thirties-era shooting, led Homicide to reconsider who had been behind the slaying of Joe Foster.

With both men charged and their legal teams strengthened, although Dixon had engaged a lawyer at his own expense, they had both clammed up. The initial admission of guilt by Sealy, even if in writing and signed, did not stop the legal teams claiming that police badgering and inaccurate facts presented to Dixon and Sealy, together with their low intellects, meant that they were not able to understand the full implication of the charges against them. The last claim, Isaac knew, was not correct, although acting dumb would be a lot easier than pretending to be smart.

Sally Thompson in Liverpool had met with Dixon before, knew him to be an articulate man with a ready wit, a colourful turn of phrase and capable of finding alibis out of thin air, attributes not within reach of a man who claimed to be of substandard intellect, unable to hold down anything other than a menial, repetitive job. Sealy was even smarter, able to write unaided a statement admitting to driving the car in Basing Street that had no more than two grammatical errors.

The statements would be put forward as evidence at a trial, a psychologist in the witness stand debating the validity of IQ tests, the possible errors, and that an examination of intelligence is invalid and discriminatory, and that the results, dependent on which instrument was used, can vary widely.

Regardless of intelligence, it was clear that collusion between the two legal teams had occurred, and neither man was willing to say more. Isaac knew that bringing them into the interview room again would be a waste of time and that apart from stating their names, there would be no other utterances.

It was a strategy that was going to work, as long as there was no further proof.

***

This time, openly and with his DCI's blessing, Larry met with Spanish John.

The mood was downcast; Spanish John was not only angry but verging on the uncontrollable. Larry was not feeling comfortable with the situation.

'Hill,' Spanish John said, 'I've given you two names. You don't need me anymore.'

Outside the room in the gangster's house, a three-storey terrace close to Regent's Canal in Little Venice, an upmarket district to the north of Notting Hill, two men stood.

Larry recognised one of them as the man who had given him Basil Dixon's name, told him to lay off investigating Julius Rios's murder.

If the master gangster wouldn't talk, Larry thought, then one of his subordinates might.

'Dixon's no fool, and Sealy's smart enough, but you could have extracted more from them,' Spanish John said. 'Thumbscrews, take them around the back of the police station and rough them up.'

'That's not how we work,' Larry said.

'It's you that want law and order, not me. If you want to be pussy cats, then that's what you get.'

'You'd rather have anarchy.'

'Why not? The law of the jungle, the strong in control, the weak underfoot.'

'And you on top, stronger than ever. Joe Foster out of the way. Who next? Terry Foster?'

'Joe Foster was a nuisance, riding roughshod over everyone, crooked or otherwise.'

'And which one are you?'

'More legitimate than you credit me.'

'But not totally.'

'Inspector,' Spanish John said, a little calmer now, 'there's a fine line between illegal and legal, as you well know. Those who say that crime doesn't pay have their heads in the sand, but there's also a lot of money to be made legally: property development, for instance.'

'For that, you need deep pockets.'

'Foster had deep pockets, and mine are not shallow. Joe Foster was moving out of crime, no longer peddling drugs.'

'You make it sound as though he was selling uppers and downers in a school playground.'

'You're trying to be smart doesn't help.'

'It doesn't, but Foster was a major force in illicit drugs.'

'He was, but he was pulling back. Too dangerous, the risk not worth the reward, and Foster had stashed a fortune. The man would have been legit within five years.'

'And why should that frighten someone?'

'Legit, buying up businesses, selling them, property development, purchasing swathes of land and buildings. What do you reckon? The man was experienced, an intimidating character, smart. And rough-arm tactics, a bully boy approach, and he would have made others nervous.'

'He wasn't about to become kind and friendly.'

'He wouldn't have stepped over the line, but he would have used the law to his advantage, rammed through deals, suing if someone got in his way, driving others to bankruptcy. Nothing wrong in that if you've got the skill, and he did.'

'And his criminal empire? Still valuable.'

'Others would have taken it over.'

'And by others, you.'

'Foster wasn't killed by criminals, not that I'm certain on that, but by others who feared him more as an honest man.'

'Murder is a harsh way to deal with a competitor, especially if you're an honest person.'

'It's not the way the gangs would operate. People disappearing is more their style, or found dead down a dark alley.'

'Or a headless torso in the canal, not fifty yards from here,' Larry said, remembering back to a previous murder case.

Larry thought the conversation was going nowhere. As to how Spanish John knew so much, that was clear. He was intricately involved, playing one group off against another, attempting to come out on top. It was a game he might not win.

Homicide had seen these upstarts before. Full of arrogance and self-belief, quick to rise to the top by intimidation, violence and crime, equally fast to fall into a chasm.

Joe Foster had been on top for a long time, and he had succumbed. And a previous contact of Larry's, Rasta Joe, another gang leader, a more charismatic man than Spanish John, a person who had embraced Rastafarianism, apart from abstaining from alcohol, had ended up dead.

Spanish John was a man who had played it too hard, too fast. He was a man on the edge of a precipice.

A knock on the door; one of Spanish John's men rushed in. 'Terry Foster's been shot,' he said.

Larry picked up his phone, checked with Isaac. It was confirmed; Foster was at St Mary's Hospital in Paddington.

The conversation with Spanish John would have to be put on hold for now.

'This changes the dynamics,' the gangster said.

'Maybe,' Larry said. 'It depends on who shot him.'

'Not me.'

It was a good alibi. In his house, a detective inspector from Homicide able to verify it. Whatever the truth, Spanish John had more talking to do, if he lived that long.

At the hospital, the Foster clan: the mother, Gladys, the sister, Samantha. Ben, the youngest, had walked in with Larry. On one side of the door leading to the operating theatre stood Isaac and Wendy. On the other, the Fosters.

It reminded Larry of a Mexican standoff: each side eying up the other, not sure who was going to speak first.

Billy had not yet arrived at the hospital.

Emily Foster's arrival had been unexpected. After all, the man in intensive care, a surgeon removing three bullets, had attempted to rape her, almost certainly would have succeeded if not for Emily's son intervening. She rushed over to Gladys and threw her arms around the woman.

'It'll be alright,' Emily said, not that she knew any more than the others.

'Thanks for coming,' Gladys said.

It was a touching scene, Wendy thought. Joe's two wives united in tragedy.

Emily, once she had detached herself from Gladys, crossed the separating doorway, effectively bridging the gap between the law and the criminal. 'What have you found out?' she said.

'I believe the question should be directed at you,' Isaac said.

'Not now,' Wendy said. 'There's a man inside fighting for his life.'

'Yes, you're right,' Isaac conceded. 'It was your house, Emily.'

'It was a coffee shop, three doors down, not my house.'

'Had he been waiting for you?'

'I don't think so. He hasn't bothered me since.'

Gladys Foster came over. She had been crying, but for now she was composed. 'Can't this wait?'

A surgeon came through the door. 'Mrs Foster,' he said.

The two wives replied in unison: 'Yes.'

'Terry's my son,' Gladys said.

The surgeon, a man in his fifties, hair greying at the temples, took Gladys into a small room adjacent to where everyone had been standing. The remainder of Joe Foster's first family, apart from Tom who hadn't been found, filed in soon after. Billy, the last to arrive, was present as well.

Isaac observed that he was the least concerned of the Fosters as to Terry's condition, and had continued to talk on his phone after briefly embracing his mother, a kiss on the cheek.

The three police officers stood outside the room with Emily, who was attempting to hear the conversation, but the door was closed and only snippets could be garnered.

'Gordon Windsor?' Isaac said.

'They're on their way,' Larry said. 'The coffee shop's been taped off; the uniforms are there.'

'How did you know, Emily?' Wendy asked.

'I saw the ambulance outside the place. Curious, I suppose. I took a look, could see it was Terry. That's when I phoned Gladys, and let you know.'

'And you don't think he was looking for you?'

'Gladys gave me her word that he wouldn't bother me again. I trusted her, and she was the only person he'd listen to. No, I don't think it was me. Besides, it wasn't the first time he'd been in the coffee shop; the reason I don't walk down past it these days.'

Larry and Isaac left. Wendy, the more compassionate of the three, stayed. Isaac, if he was honest, had little sympathy for the shot man.

Having grown up in the area, at school with Spanish John and Rasta Joe, and then as a police officer, he felt he had a unique view as to why those from the Caribbean had gravitated to crime: hunger and slum landlords, blatant discrimination at one time, substandard education, indoctrination from possibly well-meaning but naïve persons. But Joe Foster wasn't the result of a broken home or prejudice; he was a criminal by choice, and Terry Foster, his eldest son, was a violent man due to his temper and arrogance.

Wendy and Emily waited for the Fosters to come out of the room. Gladys came first, Samantha's arm around her shoulders. 'He'll be alright, Mum. Don't you worry,' she said.

Emily grabbed hold of Ben's arm, pulled him off to one side. 'What did the surgeon say?' she asked.

'Terry will live, although he took two bullets to the stomach, another to the head. There's bleeding in the brain; they're not sure if he'll be okay afterwards.'

'Possible brain damage?' Wendy asked.

'The surgeon was noncommittal, but that was for our mother's benefit. Terry's not coming back, not the way he was.'

'Any idea who shot him?'

'None at all. Whoever it is, we'll find out soon enough.'

Wendy could see that Ben was speaking out of anger, not being rational.

Even though their father's murderers were in custody, the evidence wasn't cast iron, and now, with

Terry, there was another person on the loose who had attempted to kill.

Wendy couldn't feel sorry for the man, although she felt a mother's grief. To Gladys, as to any mother, the child was still hers, still loved, a remembrance of a happy baby bouncing on a knee, his first steps, his first words, and then taking the child to school. And now, as an adult, brain-damaged.

Wendy went over to Gladys, put a hand on the woman's arm. 'I'm sorry,' she said.

***

At just after four in the afternoon, Wendy left the hospital and drove to Basing Street. Eileen Cavendish opened the door to her, welcomed her in.

'Emily's coming over later,' she said.

'You two are friends?' In one corner of the room, a baby's cot. It was, Wendy thought, not a time for joy. 'I met your mother,' she continued. 'Your stepfather, as well.'

'How is she?' Eileen said.

'You've not seen her?'

'Not since she said those terrible things.'

'Your mother has a medical condition. Do you know about it?'

'Pathological lying. Yes, I know.'

'And you believed your mother when she said that Joe was your father?'

'She wouldn't lie about that.'

Wendy knew the mother could have, but why Eileen believed it was unclear. Regardless of the child's parentage, and the initial concerns that the young woman

257

had had, it was clear that she had moved on and was embracing impending motherhood.

From one tragedy to another, Wendy thought. She couldn't feel any emotion for Terry, but she could for Eileen. The woman needed help, possibly medical, undoubtedly mental. Eileen's abrogation of fact, an inability to acknowledge the seriousness of the situation caused Wendy profound concern, not only for the mother but also for the child.

'Would you consent to a DNA check?' Wendy asked.

'It's Joe's. I know it is.'

Wendy, not willing to allow the situation to continue, took command. At St Mary's Hospital, another wing of the building, a nurse took a sample of saliva, some blood and urine from Eileen. Wendy intended to be thorough.

While they waited, the two women went to the cafeteria, Wendy helping herself to a slice of cheesecake, Eileen ordering two. 'Two mouths to feed,' she said.

'Jacob Morgan is dead,' Wendy said.

'I didn't like him much, although Joe did.'

'He stole a lot of money from your father, a lot from someone else. Did you know?'

Eileen decided not to elaborate on what she had found out for the Foster family. 'Not really. I only did Joe's accounts. Jacob dealt with Joe's property portfolio, his stocks and shares,' she said.

'These accounts? What were they? For what?'

'His clubs, the people he employed. Not everyone filled out their timesheets correctly, nor their expenses.'

'There were a couple of strip clubs, some massage parlours. You're aware of them?'

'Terry used to look after them, deal with staff turnover. He was good at that.'

'And he didn't bother you?'

'Terry was frightened of his father, respectful too.'

'But you were having an affair with Joe. I just saw Gladys at this hospital, in tears over Terry. Why didn't he tell his mother about you and Joe?'

'Why would he? Gladys wasn't married to Joe when I was with him, Emily was.'

'A friend now?'

'Emily understands. After all, she was worse than me. My relationship with Joe was incidental, just two people together in a small flat, late at night, a couple of glasses of wine.'

'Who made the first move?'

'I'm not sure. Both of us, I suppose. Emily had been calculating when she grabbed him.'

'A good and loyal wife afterwards.'

'She had what she wanted, so did I.'

'You didn't want Joe to marry you?'

'No. Only to support and love me, nothing more. I saw my mother, what she had gone through. That wasn't for me, not a chance.'

The two women walked back to where Eileen had given the samples. The nurse from before took the women into a side room, handed over a sheet of paper to Eileen.

Eileen studied the paper, read it a couple of times, before looking over at the nurse. 'This can't be right,' she said.

'Unfortunately, it is. You're not pregnant.'

Wendy hadn't expected that result. To her, tragic as it might be to Eileen Cavendish, it simplified the situation. Whether the mother had been correct or not about Eileen's parentage was moot. Having an affair with her father still brought into consideration moral questions, although a child was another issue.

Eileen burst into tears, buried her face in Wendy's shoulder. 'Poor Joe, not a father,' she said.

As they left, Wendy cast an eye back at the nurse. The nurse shook her head; Wendy understood what it meant. DNA sampling took longer to give a result that the hospital would sign off on, although preliminary tests, based on the DNA from Eileen and a copy of the DNA from Joe Foster, indicated another fact – Eileen was not Joe's daughter.

Back at Basing Street, Wendy phoned Emily, who said she would be over in twenty minutes to stay with Eileen. She also called Eileen's stepfather; the mother deemed unreliable.

'Three hours. I'll be there,' he said. 'She would be better off with us.'

'Your wife?'

'It's still better for Eileen to be with her.'

Chapter 28

'I was out the back, and apart from Terry Foster at a table, there wasn't much for me to do,' Harry Farnham, a middle-aged man, his greying strands of hair combed over an otherwise bald head, said.

It was a lame excuse, more worthy of someone younger and more irresponsible, not of a retired police officer who Isaac remembered as being a curmudgeon.

'You knew him?' Larry asked.

'Terry Foster, local hooligan made good.'

'Good?'

'A rich father. Terry was a bit stupid, but he came in occasionally, sometimes on his own, sometimes with others.'

'Today?'

'On his own. He might have been waiting for someone, but I wasn't going to ask.'

'Frightened of the man?'

'Me? Frightened? You must be joking. It's a café, pay your money, drink your coffee and leave. His business wasn't mine, and if he wasn't angry, he was decent enough.'

'Had you ever seen him angry?'

'Not personally, but I still keep in contact with a few down at Challis Street. They told me about him, even came in themselves for coffee, went so far as to shake Foster's hand if he was here at the same time.'

'Harry,' Isaac said, 'you heard about Joe Foster's death?'

'Who hasn't?'

'I'll take that as a yes. Doesn't it strike you as suspicious that Terry was on his own? Joe always had protection, apart from the day he died, so did Terry, a couple of heavies, neither of them charming or polite.'

'Not the sort of thing I think about these days. I might have been a police officer, but I took early retirement, bought this place.'

Isaac thought back seven years ago. Harry Farnham had been shot in the leg when he had entered a supermarket where two individuals were helping themselves to the contents of a cash register.

'You're not limping.'

'Not now. That's why I was around the back. I've learnt to walk without it showing, but the knee still gets sore. I take every opportunity to get the weight off of it. Not something to do in front of the customers.'

'You, as a seasoned police inspector, with as many years as the two of us combined,' Larry said, 'what's your take on this? Why in here?'

'It's overkill, more of a statement,' Farnham said.

'Statement for whom?'

'Just a supposition. No idea, not really.'

Isaac remembered more about Farnham as they spoke. A slow-witted man, the subject of an internal investigation about possible bribe-taking, similar to what Larry had just been subjected to. His dismissal four months after he had been exonerated had the makings of a cover-up, an unwillingness for the police force to admit to wrongdoing by one of their own, a concern that public trust would be undermined. And then, the week he was due to leave, a bullet to the leg.

Farnham was not trustworthy, and his being out in the back of the café at the time of Terry Foster's shooting gave Isaac concern, although allowing an assassination in your place of business, somewhere you had a financial stake, wouldn't have been just slow-witted, it would have been financial suicide.

Gordon Windsor came over, acknowledged Farnham, spoke to him briefly before turning to Isaac.

'One man, three shots, but then you know that much already. Bridget Halloran's got the van that was used on CCTV; she's attempting to trace it.'

'Fingerprints?'

'Too many in here to be certain. The shooter would probably have worn gloves, or if he didn't, then he would have pushed open the door to enter, jammed a chair to stop it closing, shot the man and left. Ten, twelve seconds at most.'

'He didn't wear gloves,' Farnham said.

'You saw him?'

'You never asked.' Farnham was looking at a computer monitor. 'I only put it in to keep the insurance cost down, never expected to use it. How much can anyone steal in a café? Apart from the furnishings, there's only the coffee beans and sugar, some milk in a refrigerator.'

'You've kept us waiting this long?' Isaac said.

'Not intentionally. I'm a Luddite when it comes to computers, never learnt to make much sense of them. It's taken me until now to get the video to work.'

'You're not the only one,' Isaac said by way of an apology. 'We've got people in our department who have the same trouble.'

'Is that on a disk?' Larry asked.

'It's stored somewhere, not sure, though.'

Isaac phoned Bridget, asked her to get down to the café and download the video. Until then, he told

Farnham to leave well alone. Luddites, intentional or otherwise, were capable of erasing the evidence.

'You had a look,' Isaac said to Larry. 'Any idea?'

'The man kept his head down, a scarf around his face, but I know who it is.'

'How?'

'The way he walked, a distinctive swagger. I've seen it before, too close on one occasion.'

***

Eileen Cavendish's character was of concern, not only for the woman herself but for the investigation in particular. Initially an assistant in Joe Foster's legitimate side of his business, she had gone from there to admitting that she had sold herself at university, then to being Joe's lover, to her pregnancy and then saying that her mother had told her that Joe was her father. And now all of that was open to speculation, wide open as to the truth. The university and selling herself was true, but what else? Wendy didn't know.

At Eileen's flat, the mother and Wendy sat with the young woman.

'It was true, all true,' Eileen said.

'Whether it was or wasn't, isn't the police's concern now,' Wendy said. She could feel sympathy for the woman: it was clear that the mother had issues and the stepfather, in another room, wasn't the gentleman he had previously portrayed. His entry into the flat had been aggressive, accusing Eileen of upsetting her mother, humiliating the family. Wendy was sure that if she hadn't been there, he would have slapped Eileen across the face.

An attractive and outwardly middle-class family, thwart with issues. The mother, with her lying, probably mentally ill, but as stated before, not significant; a stepfather who alternated between charming and aggressive; and Eileen, the victim of their flawed characters, forced to leave home at an early age and find her way in the world. The stepfather's assertion that he had helped with the expenses of university was now taken with a pinch of salt.

Wendy's two sons had worried her in their youth, but that had just been youthful high spirits until their late teens, and then after that, getting drunk, sneaking girls into the house, and one of the sons coming home with a tattoo. On reflection, although she had been upset at the time, none of their misdemeanours was vindictive or deluded, and they certainly didn't lie to her; quite the opposite. Sometimes they were too honest, telling her things she'd rather not hear.

'We'll take her home with us,' the mother said.

'I'm fine here,' Eileen said.

Wendy had to agree. A dysfunctional household was not what the woman needed. She needed counselling, something that was possible in London, not at her home.

'It would be best if Eileen stays here,' Wendy said. That hadn't been her opinion at the hospital, but the situation had changed. Out in the kitchen, a kettle was boiling, the stepfather pacing around, making a noise.

Wendy phoned Larry, asked him to come over to talk to the stepfather and to get him out of the house. Larry declined. He had bigger fish to fry, an individual by the name of Jerome Hadley, a smart-arsed individual who had beaten him in an alley on Spanish John's authority.

Larry tried the man's bedsit, spoke to the landlady, received a scowl and not much else. The pubs hadn't seen him, nor had Spanish John, a man playing it too close to the limit.

With no Larry, Wendy excused herself from the two women and went out into the kitchen. 'Could you leave us alone, go for a walk, grab a pint in the pub?' she said.

'I thought you might need me,' the stepfather said.

Not a chance, Wendy thought but said, 'No, we're fine. Women's talk, I'm sure you understand.'

Whether he did or did not, he left soon after.

In the other room, Eileen stared out of the window; her mother had her face in a magazine. Neither wanted to speak to the other.

Wendy would have preferred the mother not to be present, but there was no alternative.

'Eileen, we need the truth. You know that Terry's been shot?' Wendy said.

'You told me,' the reply.

'The person who shot him and those who shot Joe are not the same.'

'Why tell me about Terry? You know I didn't like him.'

'It's not true, is it? You and Joe?'

'Please, is this necessary?' the mother asked.

'It might be best if you join your husband,' Wendy said.

'My place is with Eileen.'

'I would have had his child,' Eileen said.

'Even if he had been your father?' Wendy asked.

'Even. God's will.'

'That's the first time you've mentioned religion.'

'Joe believed.'

'That's the first we've heard.'

'He didn't talk about it much. It was only recently, the belief that he had led an evil life.'

266

'Is this to do with his attempt to divest himself of his criminal ventures, embrace respectability?'

'I don't know. I just know that he would speak about religion sometimes; how he found solace in the bible.'

'What do you want to do?' Wendy asked. 'Stay here or go home with your mother?'

'I'll stay here.'

Wendy phoned Emily, explained the situation, the truth of the pregnancy. Emily, who had become fond of the woman, regardless of whether Joe and Eileen had been lovers, said she would stay with her for a few days.

Wendy had doubts about the affair, but for now, it wasn't important.

Larry had phoned. He needed assistance.

***

'Not too smart, our man inside,' Larry said when Wendy arrived at the squat in Camden Town. Outside on the street, a wrecked car. A couple of dogs lolled in the afternoon sun.

Derelict buildings and their occupation by the homeless, the drug-addicted and now Jerome Hadley were few and far between. It was an old factory, pre-war, built in the thirties when manufacturing and England were synonymous, but since then it had been a backpacker's hostel, a brothel, and then an arts and crafts market for over ten years.

Its future, a heavily-graffitied sign showed, was as an eighteen-storey block of executive apartments, yet another in the relentless march of the gentrification of the area. The previous low-cost rented accommodation and its working-class inhabitants pushed further away from the centre of London.

'How did you find him?' Wendy asked.

'Spanish John. Reticent at first to talk, but later a phone call told me where to look.'

'Not too smart of him.'

'He's distancing himself, and I don't think he's involved. Not sure why someone would use the man inside; hardly the smartest person there is. I heard his name mentioned by one of the others in the alley, and I'd seen him since.'

'A café, point-blank range. How could he miss?'

'The question is, why use him?'

'Jerome Hadley,' Larry spoke into a megaphone. 'The place is surrounded.'

'You could have phoned him,' Wendy said. 'Anyone else in there?'

'I phoned before you came.'

'Why here? Why did he think he could get away with it?'

'Hadley's just a foot soldier; does what he's told.'

'Attempted murder, surely he was wise enough to know we would find him.'

'Don't try to attribute wisdom to these people. If everyone who committed a crime were smart, we'd never catch anyone.'

'He thought covering his face would keep his identity secret.'

'It was only me who knew who he was; I've dealt with him before.'

'Painful dealings,' Wendy said.

She had to admit to a sense of excitement. The road on either side of the building was blocked off; a police helicopter was hovering above, a television crew recording the unfolding drama.

Larry's phone rang. 'I didn't do it,' Hadley said.

'If you're innocent, why are you holed up in there? You'll get hungry soon enough, and there's no electricity. Dark and cold at night, although you've got company. Keep you warm, will she?'

Larry shook his head, put his hand over the phone's mic. 'Probably a girlfriend, or a woman he knows. It's unlikely she's there by choice, but not a hostage.'

'You know her?'

'Femi Galton.'

'Her! Drug addict, prostitute, strips at one of Foster's clubs.'

'If she's a hostage, too spaced out to know it, Hadley will soon be cold and hungry, and she'll be desperate for a fix. Either we go in, but he could be armed, or we wait it out.'

'The chief inspector's looking to wrap this up soon,' Wendy said.

'That's what I thought. An armed response can flush out the man. You can talk to the woman, find out her angle. After all, she hasn't done anything wrong, other than her unusual lifestyle.'

'Maybe she's in love with Hadley.'

'Takes all sorts. If she gives you any nonsense, make her sweat. Hadley's close to Spanish John and I only got help from him if I laid off pursuing Julius Rios's murder.'

'It still doesn't help with Joe Foster's murder, or does it?'

'I don't know. None of us does, but people are getting nervous, making mistakes. Shooting Terry seems foolish; trusting it to Hadley was idiotic, and Spanish John's no fool, or I thought he wasn't.'

'Hadley, what's the point of this charade?' Larry said, returning to the phone call.

'I need immunity from prosecution,' Hadley replied.

'You shot Terry Foster. Do you deny it?'

'It wasn't me. It was someone impersonating me, trying to shift the blame.'

'I've seen the video. How could it be someone else and what's the point?'

'I was there in that alley. It was me who gave you Dixon's name.'

'Not that we can prove it was. Are you going to give us something else?'

'I saw them shoot him. It was Dixon who shot him, Sealy in the car. I'll stand up and give evidence if you give me immunity.'

'Give me five minutes,' Larry said. He turned to Wendy. 'You heard?'

'He shot Terry Foster. You can't offer him what he wants. Is it important what he's saying about Dixon and Sealy?'

'It is. Not that his testimony in a court will hold much weight. A known criminal, on trial for attempted murder, giving evidence in another murder trial. The defence would be laughed out of the place if they tried it.'

'Not if it was corroborated.'

'By whom?'

'Sealy or Dixon, one blaming the other, giving up hitherto unknown information. And then there's Spanish John, squeezed into a corner, revealing his sources as to how he knows so much about Foster's death, and Hadley is one of his men. Although if those behind the shootings get to Hadley, make sure he can't testify, then we've no case against Dixon and Sealy.'

'Hadley's only protection is us,' Larry said.

The armed response team were enlarging the exclusion zone and conducting a check of the building, all its possible exits, including the windows. On the roof of a building across the road, one of the team down on his belly, a rifle on a tripod trained at where Jerome Hadley was thought to be.

Larry picked up the phone, called Hadley. The man answered on the second ring.

'The woman, let her go,' Larry said.

'She's staying with me.'

'Her choice?'

'She's my woman.'

And everyone else's, Larry thought.

'You're safe as long as she's with you. Look out of the window, across the road, down in the street. The place is surrounded by armed response, and they don't miss, not like you. You've not a chance of getting out of there in one piece.'

'Then I'll die here.'

'You and your woman? What does she say about it?'

'She's with me.'

'Unlikely, unless she's got a death wish,' Wendy whispered.

One of the armed response team came over to where Larry and Wendy were standing. 'We've got a sight on him.'

'The woman?' Larry asked.

'She's nearby. Separate her, get her out of the room, and we'll make sure she's safe.'

'We need him alive,' Wendy said.

'Too much paperwork if we kill him,' the armed sergeant said.

'Let the woman go, put down your gun,' Larry said, returning to his conversation with Hadley.'

'My woman?'

'She's not committed any crime, other than her poor choice in men.'

'I had no option.'

'Spanish John put you up to it?'

'Not him.'

'Who then?'

'Femi, she knows the truth. She'll tell you.'

'Let her come out and tell us. We've got nothing against her.'

'It's our child,' Hadley said.

'We didn't know about a child. What about it?'

'Someone phoned me, told me if I didn't shoot Terry Foster, they would kill the child.'

'And you believed them?'

'They sent a photo, showed a gun not more than ten yards away, sighted in on her. She's at school; she was in the playground. I had no option.'

'A name?'

'I don't know.'

'You have the photo?'

'On my phone.'

'Mitigating circumstances. It will go in your favour, especially if you help us with Joe Foster's death.'

For seven minutes, not a sound from inside the building. The armed response busied themselves, went through the plan once more, waiting for the go-ahead from Larry.

A door opened on the ground floor; a gun was thrown out. 'Inspector, Femi's coming first, and then me. Our child?'

Larry said to Wendy, 'Go with the woman, pick up the child, make sure the two of them are safe.'

'It's a sadistic bastard who uses the life of a child as leverage,' Wendy said.

'It's a sick world. Sometimes I think we see too much of it, makes us blasé, unsentimental, uncaring,' Larry said.

Two of the armed response team moved forward after Femi Galton and Jerome Hadley were ordered to lie face down on the street, arms stretched out, legs splayed. One took hold of Femi Galton, frisked her, before handing her over to Wendy.

Hadley's frisking was not as gentle, his captor placing his boot into the small of the man's back and holding a rifle to his head. Another team member came over, knelt and ran his hands around Hadley's body, making sure to ram a clenched fist hard between the man's legs, making him squirm and squeal.

With his hands cuffed behind his back, Hadley was put into a police van – his next location, a cell at Challis Street. The man had a busy night ahead of him, a lot of talking to do.

Chapter 29

'Hadley claims that his child was threatened,' Larry said. 'I've seen the photo on his phone, and it appears genuine. Wendy's with the mother and the child. Femi Galton, regardless of her record and her lifestyle, has done right by the child, a five-year-old girl, neatly dressed and polite.'

'Easy enough to fake a photo on a phone,' Isaac said.

'Agreed, but Hadley's adamant that it wasn't Spanish John who sent the photo and that he doesn't know who it was.'

'Have you checked the man's bank account?'

'Bridget has. A deposit of five thousand pounds from an overseas account in the last three hours.'

'And you remain convinced that your gangster friend isn't involved?'

'Why send one of his men, knowing that Hadley isn't the smartest and that we would have found him in due course?'

'A mistake?'

'Not with Spanish John. What if it was a setup; kill two birds with one stone?'

'Get rid of Terry Foster, blame Spanish John, leave it free for a third party to carve up Foster's empire.'

'Carve up or keep; it doesn't matter which. Terry Foster should be dead, and there's no natural successor, other than Samantha, and she might not be keen on getting herself killed.'

'If what you say is true,' Isaac said, 'how did whoever it is, intend to level the blame at Spanish John? An assumption by us is hardly proof.'

'Not unless we get assistance from some quarter.'

'But whom?'

'I don't know, but, so far, every death points back to Spanish John. If he had wanted to kill Joe Foster, not that I'm convinced he did, why on Basing Street, why in daylight, and not far from where he was having a beer? According to Hadley, he saw the two men shoot Joe, fingered Dixon as the gunman.'

'He told you to save his skin. He could be lying through his teeth.'

'He could, but I doubt it.'

Eventually, Hadley, his head down, a look of remorse, arrived in the interview room. His legal aid, a smart middle-aged woman, her hair short, cut almost like a man's, sat next to her client. She was sharp, all business, and as good as any lawyer that cost money.

'My client is willing to talk,' the legal aid said.

'We still have Camden Town, the hostage you were holding,' Larry addressed his remarks to Hadley.

'What hostage?' the legal aid said.

'Femi Galton.'

'If I understand the situation, my client at no time said he had a hostage. Am I correct on this point?'

Larry had to reply in the affirmative.

'And that the woman, Femi Galton, is the mother of my client's child?'

'That is correct.'

'Then it needs to be noted on the record that my client committed no offence in Camden Town and that the armed response was an overreaction.'

'You're arguing a point of law,' Isaac said. 'Mr Hadley did refuse to exit the building as ordered, attempted to make a deal.'

'And, DCI Cook, if you were cornered, a child under threat, an armed response team outside, armed to the teeth, what would your reaction have been?'

Well played, Isaac thought.

'Let it be placed on record that Jerome Hadley did not resist arrest, nor did he make a direct threat against the police,' Isaac said. 'Now, can we get on?'

'Thank you,' the legal aid said.

'There's still the matter of the attempted murder of Terry Foster,' Larry said, 'not forgetting that Mr Hadley was the leader when I received a beating.'

'At which you were given the name of one murderer. I would have thought the name was more important than pursuing a man who had followed orders.'

'We're conceding too much,' Isaac said.

'My client is a man who has been on the receiving end of violence, as well as the instigator of it. He is willing to concede that he is a dangerous man, although in his defence, you, Detective Inspector Hill, walked out of that alley bruised and battered, but alive.'

'I can agree with you on that point. However, it was never explained as to where he had got the name.'

'You were asking questions, sticking your nose in where it wasn't wanted.'

'I was doing my job.'

'The upholding of the law is not so simple. My client is willing to tell you more.'

'Which he could have done before,' Isaac said.

'Indeed, he could. But now we are here, and my client has some conditions.'

'We're not here to make deals. Your client shot Terry Foster.'

'He was protecting his child. If what he did is a crime, which clearly it is, then there is mitigation.'

'Leniency in the sentence, not an acquittal.'

'My client is aware of what he's done. He regrets his actions.'

It was a good speech by legal aid; it just wasn't true. Jerome Hadley had lived with violence all his life, almost certainly killed as a gang member. The only regret that a reprobate such as Hadley had was his capture.

'I suggest your client tells us what he knows, what he saw on the day Joe Foster died,' Larry said.

Hadley cleared his throat, looked over at his legal aid; she gave him a nod of her head. 'I knew Lyron Sealy from way back; not so much Basil Dixon, but I met him once with Lyron. The two of them were friends, grew up together or something like that, not sure though.'

Vague, Isaac thought. He hoped the man wasn't about to waste their time, and that he hadn't blatantly lied about the promise of a breakthrough in the homicide to get out of the now-discarded hostage situation. Although, if he had, the leniency that might have been forthcoming wouldn't eventuate.

'I gave you the one name because I was told to,' Hadley said.

'It was because of Spanish John,' Larry said. 'What about the other two who were there?'

'I don't know. One day, they were in the area; the next they were gone. I saw Dixon and Sealy drive up the road. I had been nearby, buying cigarettes. They didn't see me, but I knew Joe Foster by sight. And then they pulled up the car sharp, Dixon got out, shot Foster, got back in the car and drove off.'

'How come nobody else saw anything?'

'Nobody was looking, and Dixon and Sealy didn't come to Notting Hill, not that often, and if Sealy came, it was to the Castle down in Portobello Road, not Basing Street.'

'Can this be proved?' Larry said.

'You've got my phone?'

'We do, as evidence.'

'Give it to me, or scroll through the photos. You'll find thousands there; I enjoy taking them, post them on Instagram, got myself a following.'

'What of? Villains I've known,' Larry said sarcastically.

'If you would give my client the phone and stop accusing him of crimes he hasn't committed, we will all be the better for it,' the legal aid said.

Isaac made a call; one of his people brought the phone down in a sealed evidence bag. He opened it, checked with Bridget that all data on the phone had been downloaded – it had – and passed it over to Hadley.

The man scrolled through the photos, handed it over to Isaac. 'That one, it's got a date as well.'

Isaac looked at it, and then Larry. Both smiled. Jerome Hadley, gangster, murderer, thug and the father of a child with a drug-addicted prostitute, had an interest in social media and photography. Clearly shown on six photos and a twelve-second video was the time when Basil Dixon got out of the car, shot Joe Foster and departed, the final photo showing the dead man on the ground.

'Why didn't you hand this over before?' Larry asked.

'I didn't want to get myself killed. The gangs don't like people who snitch.'

'You're snitching now.'

'I'm about to be charged with attempted murder. I need something and someone on my side.'

'This implicates Spanish John.'

'How? He knew Sealy, but not Dixon. It was me that gave him the names.'

'And beating me up was the only way to get those names to me?' Larry said.

'A beating isn't murder, and my shooting Terry Foster wasn't either; it was the preservation of the life of a child. You would have done the same.'

Larry knew he wouldn't have, but then, he would never be placed in the position that Hadley had found himself in.

Whatever the reason, no matter how long and tortuous the route, on the man's iPhone was the proof positive that Dixon and Sealy had murdered Joe Foster.

***

Terry Foster, his life not in danger, returned to his mother's home. The prognosis was not good, and the chance of a full recovery was less than twenty per cent. A nurse hovered nearby, his mother attempting to feed him. Gladys Foster was pleased that her son still lived, and even if he was in a vegetative state, she was willing to commit to the sacrifice of years of recovery and speech training and visits to a rehabilitation clinic for those who had suffered a brain injury.

Visitors regularly came to sit with the one-time hooligan and street fighter, the man who would be king. Even Emily had visited, not for the son, but the mother. Emily had kissed the man who had attempted to rape her on the cheek. From now on, she would have no fear of him.

'He'll get better,' Gladys said.

Emily could see it was unlikely. The man's countenance was vague, although she had sensed a twitching as she came close to him, a recollection. She hoped he would improve for the mother, not for the man.

Hatred was a strong emotion, and Emily Foster knew that she had plenty of it. After all, wasn't it Terry who had paid Dixon and Sealy to kill her husband?

Ben visited the house to see Terry, to console his mother, and to announce that he intended to marry Margareta, his long-time girlfriend. He hadn't put a hand on Terry, only looked at him briefly before turning away and to his mother.

'He's still alive,' Ben said. 'We must be thankful for small mercies.'

Samantha, who had been nearby, pulled Ben to one side. 'Did you mean that?' she said.

'It would have done us all a favour if Hadley had finished the job,' Ben said, winking at his sister.

'And now?' Samantha's reply.

'We'll see. With no Terry, there's the leadership to consider.'

Ben walked away, a smile on his face.

Wendy had also visited the Foster home to update Gladys on developments but had not felt the need to spend time with Terry, only to glance at him.

***

Basil Dixon's reaction had been explosive, and as expected, a virulent denial of his involvement in Joe Foster's death, a denouncement of the photographic proof from a man who had shot another, a passionate defence of his good character.

Dixon had stood up in the interview room, swearing and sweating, unable to comprehend what was happening, until eventually he calmed down and took his seat. Dixon's lawyer had questioned the validity of a photo on the phone, attempting to minimise its importance and whether it would be admissible evidence. Sally Thompson knew it would be; the location verified by the telephone company.

Dixon was guilty, Sally Thompson knew that, and the charge of murder came with proof.

Lyron Sealy's reaction had been more restrained for two reasons. The first was that his legal aid was competent and diligent; the second was that he would be able to continue to use his lame excuse that he had been an unwilling partner, believing that Dixon had wanted to talk to Joe Foster.

It would, Isaac knew, require persuasive arguments to get a cynical judge and a disbelieving jury to believe it. Even so, Sealy would see a time when he would be released from prison; Dixon might not. Moreover, the vengeance of the Foster family remained; people died in jail and not always of old age.

Effectively, the murder of Joe Foster and the attempted murder of Terry Foster had both been solved. However, there was to Isaac a troubling aspect, something that Chief Superintendent Goddard regarded as important, but not critical. For him, it was the acclamation of Homicide for bringing to justice those who had committed murder, letting his seniors know that their faith in him was justified and that the promotion to commander was warranted.

The team sat in Isaac's office. It was the end of a long day, the christening of his and Jenny's first-born the next day, the promise of a break from the relentless pressure of the last few weeks.

'Eight million pounds?' Isaac asked. 'Any further updates?'

'The transaction was made overseas,' Bridget said. 'Whether the money was transferred by Jacob Morgan to a third party due to intimidation or torture or the threat of violence is not the issue. As far as the police in that country are concerned, no complaint has been registered, no crime committed. And the bank he transferred it from will not give us more details, and the bank the money was transferred to won't help either.'

Isaac had his suspicion – Tony Rafter, a name mentioned by Morgan. The man dealt in the millions, most of it legal, some of it suspect. However, fraud and dubious money transactions, under duress or otherwise, weren't murder. And it was still the person or persons behind the two shootings that concerned him.

'Spanish John?' Isaac said.

'He could have been behind Terry Foster's attempted murder,' Larry said, 'but I don't believe it.'

'Jerome Hadley, the incompetent marksman, is or was one of his men.'

'That's why Spanish John is not the murderer. He told us where to find Hadley, that's proof enough for me. Hadley had been one of his men, but someone else had forced him. If Spanish John had been behind it, we would never have found Hadley alive, not even dead.'

'He wouldn't have thrown his man to the wolves, to us.'

'Someone might have thought it was a way to rein in Spanish John; guilt by association. But why a café? The gangs don't operate in the open, and Hadley's two offsiders in that alley disappeared without a trace.'

'Propping up a bridge somewhere, in with the concrete.'

'Or feeding the fish. Anyway, Spanish John's not guilty of the attempted murder of Terry Foster. Not even of Joe Foster. Too close to home, too visible, and Hadley, who luckily for us had seen the killing, no doubt told Spanish John who kept it concealed from me, drip-feeding me snippets.'

'And if Hadley hadn't told us?' Isaac said.

'Or deleted the pictures from his phone, we would never have known.'

'Shouldn't we leave it there?' Wendy asked.

Isaac put his hands behind his head, looked up at the ceiling. To him, the investigation had finished on a low. Those who had committed the crimes were only minor players. Somewhere, hidden behind a veil of respectability or in plain sight, someone was sitting down with a glass of wine, a cigar in hand, savouring their success.

He wasn't happy, but for now he had other things to distract him: his wife, his child.

It was a time for celebration, not for worry. 'Yes, you're right, not today, that is. Next week, we'll focus on whoever it was,' Isaac said as he got up from his chair and left the office.

***

Larry stayed late in the office that night. Not because he wanted to, but because it was necessary.

His defence of Spanish John had been concise; the man was innocent of both crimes. However, as a police officer who had been subjected to the possibility of an internal investigation into his collaboration with criminals, in particular his friendship with Spanish John, there was unfinished business – Julius Rios.

Notwithstanding that Rios's death was a cold case, filed away and not an active crime for Homicide, Larry still smarted from the treatment he had received from the police force, and the pain he had felt after the beating by Hadley and two others.

And why had he been beaten? Why had he been given the names of Dixon and Sealy? Larry knew the truth. Spanish John, not guilty of current crimes, had murdered Julius Rios; the most likely motive, Spanish John's former girlfriend.

Larry did not intend to let the murder rest, and even if it took him a long time, even if he had to sit in a pub downing pints of beer with Spanish John and other gangsters, he would be looking and asking and listening. And when the time was right, Spanish John would find himself in a cell at Challis Street.

Larry read once again the case file on Rios, a man who contributed as much to society in death as he had in life. It was vengeance on Larry's part, justified vengeance, and in that he would succeed.

***

Tony Rafter looked out over the skyline of Canary Wharf and of central London in the distance. The next day he and his wife had a function to attend. It was to be outside, a restaurant beside the River Thames, a chance for him to tell those assembled about his latest construction project, a forty-five-storey building in Canary Wharf, the bottom ten for offices, the top thirty-five for residential. It was something that he was proud of. And then, in the afternoon, a charity function at a children's home for the disadvantaged, to which he gave his time and a great deal of money. After all, knighthoods came as a result of achievement in the arts and in business, and for charitable deeds.

He knew that the award was a certainty purely on the weight of his business achievements, although he could admit to a sense of fulfilment in helping the less advantaged.

And besides, as he said to his wife, lifting a glass of brandy to his lips, 'We've got another eight million pounds that we thought had gone to the grave with Joe Foster. A few thousand as a gift to the home won't cause us anguish.'

His wife lifted her glass and clinked it against his. 'So right, Tony,' she said as she admired the latest Gucci handbag she had bought, the cost of no relevance.

***

Two weeks after Rafter had presented a cheque to the children's home, and Isaac and Jenny had christened their first-born, a procession moved slowly along Ladbroke Grove heading towards Kensal Green Cemetery.

As befitted a man of Foster's stature, a long line of vehicles followed the hearse. In the first of the Rolls Royces, Emily and Gladys Foster in a spirit of unity, in the second, the children of both marriages, and in the third, Eileen Cavendish and her mother. After that, those who had known the man in life, including Spanish John, suitably attired in a black suit and a black tie. Unemotional when the man had been alive, he had cried.

At the cemetery, an air of sad reflection as the coffin passed through a door and disappeared.

Outside, those present mingled and spoke endearingly of the dear departed, reflected on a life well spent, on his legacy.

Two people walked away, glancing at the headstones of people long dead.

'Have you dealt with it?' one of them said to the other.

'I have. From this week, the Fosters are no longer involved in crime.'

'Spanish John will take over the drug trade, pay us for the privilege?'

'A one-time payment, yes. Your plan to get him arrested for our father's murder didn't work,' Samantha said.

'Nor for Terry's attempted murder. I never knew about the photos on Hadley's phone.'

'It could have gone wrong. You never wanted a part of the business when our father was alive.'

'I never wanted to be involved in crime. I did what I had to.'

'Murder?'

'Was it? Or was it the protection of our family? My conscience is clear. Exceptional circumstances demand exceptional actions.'

'And exceptional people to lead. Terry was never cut out for leadership, but you are.'

'As you are, sister, to be my faithful lieutenant. Between us, the Fosters will rise higher than before.'

'Emily? Do you still want her?'

The two looked over at the others. Gladys was talking to Emily and Eileen, three women united.

'Yes, Samantha, to the victor goes the spoils,' Ben Foster said.

The End

ALSO BY THE AUTHOR

DI Tremayne Thriller Series

Death Unholy – A DI Tremayne Thriller – Book 1

All that remained were the man's two legs and a chair full of greasy and fetid ash. Little did DI Keith Tremayne know that it was the beginning of a journey into the murky world of paganism and its ancient rituals. And it was going to get very dangerous.

'Do you believe in spontaneous human combustion?' Detective Inspector Keith Tremayne asked.

'Not me. I've read about it. Who hasn't?' Sergeant Clare Yarwood answered.

'I haven't,' Tremayne replied, which did not surprise his young sergeant. In the months they had been working together, she had come to realise that he was a man who had little interest in the world. When he had a cigarette in his mouth, a beer in his hand, and a murder to solve he was about the happiest she ever saw him, but even then he could hardly be regarded as one of life's most sociable people. And as for reading? The most he managed was an occasional police report, an early-morning newspaper, turning first to the back pages for the racing results.

Death and the Assassin's Blade – A DI Tremayne Thriller – Book 2

It was meant to be high drama, not murder, but someone's switched the daggers. The man's death took place in plain view of two serving police officers.

He was not meant to die; the daggers were only theatrical props, plastic and harmless. A summer's night, a production of Julius Caesar amongst the ruins of an Anglo-Saxon fort. Detective Inspector Tremayne is there with his sergeant, Clare Yarwood. In the assassination scene, Caesar collapses to the ground. Brutus defends his actions; Mark Antony rebukes him.

They're a disparate group, the amateur actors. One's an estate agent, another an accountant. And then there is the teenage school student, the gay man, the funeral director. And what about the women? They could be involved.

They've each got a secret, but which of those on the stage wanted Gordon Mason, the actor who had portrayed Caesar, dead?

Death and the Lucky Man – A DI Tremayne Thriller – Book 3

Sixty-eight million pounds and dead. Hardly the outcome expected for the luckiest man in England the day his lottery ticket was drawn out of the barrel. But then, Alan Winters' rags-to-riches story had never been conventional, and some had benefited, but others hadn't.

Death at Coombe Farm – A DI Tremayne Thriller – Book 4

A warring family. A disputed inheritance. A recipe for death.

If it hadn't been for the circumstances, Detective Inspector Keith Tremayne would have said the view was outstanding. Up high, overlooking the farmhouse in the valley below, the panoramic vista of Salisbury Plain stretching out beyond. The only problem was that near where he stood with his sergeant, Clare Yarwood, there was a body, and it wasn't a pleasant sight.

Death by a Dead Man's Hand – A DI Tremayne Thriller – Book 5

A flawed heist of forty gold bars from a security van late at night. One of the perpetrators is killed by his brother as they argue over what they have stolen.

Eighteen years later, the murderer, released after serving his sentence for his brother's murder, waits in a church for a man purporting to be the brother he killed. And then he too is killed.

The threads stretch back a long way, and now more people are dying in the search for the missing gold bars.

Detective Inspector Tremayne, his health causing him concern, and Sergeant Clare Yarwood, still seeking romance, are pushed to the limit solving the murder, attempting to prevent any more.

Death in the Village – A DI Tremayne Thriller – Book 6

Nobody liked Gloria Wiggins, a woman who regarded anyone who did not acquiesce to her jaundiced view of the world with disdain. James Baxter, the previous vicar, had been one of those, and her scurrilous outburst in the church one Sunday had hastened his death.

And now, years later, the woman was dead, hanging from a beam in her garage. Detective Inspector Tremayne and Sergeant Clare Yarwood had seen the body, interviewed the woman's acquaintances, and those who had hated her.

Burial Mound – A DI Tremayne Thriller – Book 7

A Bronze-Age burial mound close to Stonehenge. An archaeological excavation. What they were looking for was an ancient body and historical artefacts. They found the ancient body, but then they found a modern-day body too. And then the police became interested.

It's another case for Detective Inspector Tremayne and Sergeant Yarwood. The more recent body was the brother of the mayor of Salisbury.

Everything seems to point to the victim's brother, the mayor, the upright and serious-minded Clive Grantley. Tremayne's sure that it's him, but Clare Yarwood's not so sure.

But is her belief based on evidence or personal hope?

The Body in the Ditch – A DI Tremayne Thriller – Book 8

A group of children play. Not far away, in the ditch on the other side of the farmyard, the body of a troubled young woman.

The nearby village hides as many secrets as the community at the farm, a disparate group of people looking for an alternative to their previous torturous lives. Their leader, idealistic and benevolent, espouses love and kindness, and clearly, somebody's not following his dictate.

The second death, an old woman, seems unrelated to the first, but is it? Is it part of the tangled web that connects the farm to the village?

The village, Detective Inspector Tremayne and Sergeant Clare Yarwood find out soon enough, is anything, but charming and picturesque. It's an incestuous hotbed of intrigue and wrongdoing, and what of the farm and those who live there. None of them can be ruled out, not yet.

The Horse's Mouth – A DI Tremayne Thriller – Book 9

A day at the races for Detective Inspector Tremayne, idyllic at the outset, soon changes. A horse is dead, and then the owner's daughter is found murdered, and Tremayne's there when the body is discovered.

The question is, was Tremayne set up, in the wrong place at the right time? He's the cast-iron alibi for one of the suspects, and he knows that one murder leads to two, and more often than not, to three.

The dead woman had a chequered history, not as much as her father, and then a man commits suicide. Is he the murderer, or was he the unfortunate consequence of a tragic love affair? And who was it in the stable with the woman just before she died? There is more than one person who could have killed her, and all of them have secrets they would rather not be known.

Tremayne's health is troubling him. Is what they are saying correct? Is it time for him to retire, to take it easy and to put his feet up? But that's not his style, and he'll not give up on solving the murder.

DCI Isaac Cook Thriller Series

Murder is a Tricky Business – A DCI Cook Thriller – Book 1

A television actress is missing, and DCI Isaac Cook, the Senior Investigation Officer of the Murder Investigation Team at Challis Street Police Station in London, is searching for her.

Why has he been taken away from more important crimes to search for the woman? It's not the first time she's gone missing, so why does everyone assume she's been murdered?

There's a secret, that much is certain, but who knows it? The missing woman? The executive producer? His eavesdropping assistant? Or the actor who portrayed her fictional brother in the TV soap opera?

Murder House – A DCI Cook Thriller – Book 2

A corpse in the fireplace of an old house. It's been there for thirty years, but who is it?

It's murder, but who is the victim and what connection does the body have to the previous owners of the house. What is the motive? And why is the body in a fireplace? It was bound to be discovered eventually but was that what the murderer wanted? The main suspects are all old and dying, or already dead.

Isaac Cook and his team have their work cut out, trying to put the pieces together. Those who know are not talking because of an old-fashioned belief that a family's dirty laundry should not be aired in public, and never to a policeman – even if that means the murderer is never brought to justice!

Murder is Only a Number – A DCI Cook Thriller – Book 3

Before she left, she carved a number in blood on his chest. But why the number 2, if this was her first murder?

The woman prowls the streets of London. Her targets are men who have wronged her. Or have they? And why is she keeping count?

DCI Cook and his team finally know who she is, but not before she's murdered four men. The whole team are looking for her, but the woman keeps disappearing in plain sight. The pressure's on to stop her, but she's always one step ahead.

And this time, DCS Goddard can't protect his protégé, Isaac Cook, from the wrath of the new commissioner at the Met.

Murder in Little Venice – A DCI Cook Thriller – Book 4

A dismembered corpse floats in the canal in Little Venice, an upmarket tourist haven in London. Its identity is unknown, but what is its significance?

DCI Isaac Cook is baffled about why it's there. Is it gang-related, or is it something more?

Whatever the reason, it's clearly a warning, and Isaac and his team are sure it's not the last body that they'll have to deal with.

Murder is the Only Option – A DCI Cook Thriller – Book 5

A man thought to be long dead returns to exact revenge against those who had blighted his life. His only concern is to protect his wife and daughter. He will stop at nothing to achieve his aim.

'Big Greg, I never expected to see you around here at this time of night.'

'I've told you enough times.'

'I've no idea what you're talking about,' Robertson replied. He looked up at the man, only to see a metal pole coming down at him. Robertson fell down, cracking his head against a concrete kerb.

Two vagrants, no more than twenty feet away, did not stir and did not even look in the direction of the noise. If they had, they would have seen a dead body, another man walking away.

Murder in Notting Hill – A DCI Cook Thriller – Book 6

One murderer, two bodies, two locations, and the murders have been committed within an hour of each other.

They're separated by a couple of miles, and neither woman has anything in common with the other. One is young and wealthy, the daughter of a famous man; the other is poor, hardworking and unknown.

Isaac Cook and his team at Challis Street Police Station are baffled about why they've been killed. There must be a connection, but what is it?

Murder in Room 346 – A DCI Cook Thriller – Book 7

'Coitus interruptus, that's what it is,' Detective Chief Inspector Isaac Cook said. On the bed, in a downmarket hotel in Bayswater, lay the naked bodies of a man and a woman.

'Bullet in the head's not the way to go,' Larry Hill, Isaac Cook's detective inspector, said. He had not expected such a flippant comment from his senior, not when they were standing near to two people who had, apparently in the final throes of passion, succumbed to what appeared to be a professional assassination.

'You know this will be all over the media within the hour,' Isaac said.

'James Holden, moral crusader, a proponent of the sanctity of the marital bed, man and wife. It's bound to be.'

Murder of a Silent Man – A DCI Cook Thriller – Book 8

A murdered recluse. A property empire. A disinherited family. All the ingredients for murder.

No one gave much credence to the man when he was alive. In fact, most people never knew who he was, although those who had lived in the area for many years recognised the tired-looking and shabbily-dressed man as he shuffled along, regular as clockwork on a Thursday afternoon at seven in the evening to the local off-licence.

It was always the same: a bottle of whisky, premium brand, and a packet of cigarettes. He paid his money over the counter, took hold of his plastic bag containing his purchases, and then walked back down the road with the same rhythmic shuffle. He said not one word to anyone on the street or in the shop.

Murder has no Guilt – A DCI Cook Thriller – Book 9

No one knows who the target was or why, but there are eight dead. The men seem the most likely perpetrators, or could have it been one of the two women, the attractive Gillian Dickenson, or even the celebrity-obsessed Sal Maynard?

There's a gang war brewing, and if there are deaths, it doesn't matter to them as long as it's not their death. But to Detective Chief Inspector Isaac Cook, it's his area of London, and it does matter.

It's dirty and unpredictable. Initially it had been the West Indian gangs, but then a more vicious Romanian gangster had usurped them. And now he's being marginalised by the Russians. And the leader of the most vicious Russian mafia organisation is in London, and he's got money and influence, the ear of those in power.

Murder in Hyde Park – A DCI Cook Thriller – Book 10

An early morning jogger is murdered in Hyde Park. It's the centre of London, but no one saw him enter the park, no one saw him die.

He carries no identification, only a water-logged phone. As the pieces unravel, it's clear that the dead man had a history of deception.

Is the murderer one of those that loved him? Or was it someone with a vengeance?

It's proving difficult for DCI Isaac Cook and his team at Challis Street Homicide to find the guilty person – not that they'll cease to search for the truth, not even after one suspect confesses.

Six Years Too Late – A DCI Cook Thriller – Book 11

Always the same questions for Detective Chief Inspector Isaac Cook — Why was Marcus Matthews in that room? And why did he share a bottle of wine with his killer?

It wasn't as if the man had amounted to much in life, apart from the fact that he was the son-in-law of a notorious gangster, the father of the man's grandchildren. Yet, one thing that Hamish McIntyre, feared in London for his violence, rated above anything else, it was his family, especially Samantha, his daughter; although he had never cared for Marcus, her husband.

And then Marcus disappears, only for his body to be found six years later by a couple of young boys who decide that exploring an abandoned house is preferable to school.

Grave Passion – A DCI Cook Thriller – Book 12

Two young lovers out for a night of romance. A short cut through a cemetery. They witness a murder, but there has been no struggle, only a knife to the heart.

It has all the hallmarks of an assassination, but who is the woman? And why was she alongside a grave at night? Did she know the person who killed her?

Soon after, other deaths, seemingly unconnected, but tied to the family of one of the young lovers.

It's a case for Detective Chief Inspector Cook and his team, and they're baffled on this one.

The Slaying of Joe Foster – A DCI Cook Thriller – Book 13

No one challenged Joe Foster in life, not if they valued theirs. And then, the gangster is slain, his criminal empire up for grabs.

A power vacuum; the Foster family is fighting for control, the other gangs in the area aiming to poach the trade in illegal drugs, to carve up the empire that the father had created.

It has all the makings of a war on the streets, something nobody wants, not even the other gangs.

Terry Foster, the eldest son of Joe, the man who should take control, doesn't have the temperament of his father, nor the wisdom. His solution is slash and burn, and it's not going to work, and people are going to get hurt, some of them are going to die.

Murder Without Reason – A DCI Cook Thriller – Book 14

DCI Cook faces his greatest challenge. The Islamic State is waging war in England, and they are winning.

Not only does Isaac Cook have to contend with finding the perpetrators, but he is also being forced to commit actions contrary to his mandate as a police officer.

And then there is Anne Argento, the prime minister's deputy. The prime minister has shown himself to be a pacifist and is not up to the task. She needs to take his job if the country is to fight back against the Islamists.

Vane and Martin have provided the solution. Will DCI Cook and Anne Argento be willing to follow it through? Are they able to act for the good of England, knowing that a criminal and murderous action is about to take place? Do they have an option?

Standalone Novels

The Haberman Virus

A remote and isolated village in the Hindu Kush mountain range in North Eastern Afghanistan is wiped out by a virus unlike any seen before.

A mysterious visitor clad in a spacesuit checks his handiwork, a female American doctor succumbs to the disease, and the woman sent to trap the person responsible falls in love with him – the man who would cause the deaths of millions.

Hostage of Islam

Three are to die at the Mission in Nigeria: the pastor and his wife in a blazing chapel; another gunned down while trying to defend them from the Islamist fighters.

Kate McDonald, an American, grieving over her boyfriend's death and Helen Campbell, whose life had been troubled by drugs and prostitution, are taken by the attackers.

Kate is sold to a slave trader who intends to sell her virginity to an Arab Prince. Helen, to ensure their survival, gives herself to the murderer of her friends.

Malika's Revenge

Malika, a drug-addicted prostitute, waits in a smugglers' village for the next Afghan tribesman or Tajik gangster to pay her price, a few scraps of heroin.

Yusup Baroyev, a drug lord, enjoys a lifestyle many would envy. An Afghan warlord sees the resurgence of the Taliban. A Russian white-collar criminal portrays himself as a good and honest citizen in Moscow.

All of them are linked to an audacious plan to increase the quantity of heroin shipped out of Afghanistan and into Russia and ultimately the West.

Some will succeed, some will die, some will be rescued from their plight and others will rue the day they became involved.

Prelude to War

Russia and America face each other across the northern border of Afghanistan. World War 3 is about to break out and no one is backing off.

And all because a team of academics in New York postulated how to extract the vast untapped mineral wealth of Afghanistan.

Steve Case is in the middle of it, and his position is looking very precarious. Will the Taliban find him before the Americans get him out? Or is he doomed, as is the rest of the world?

ABOUT THE AUTHOR

Phillip Strang was born in England in the late forties. He was an avid reader of science fiction in his teenage years: Isaac Asimov, Frank Herbert, the masters of the genre. Still an avid reader, the author now mainly reads thrillers.

In his early twenties, the author, with a degree in electronics engineering and a desire to see the world, left England for Sydney, Australia. Now, forty years later, he still resides in Australia, although many intervening years were spent in a myriad of countries, some calm and safe, others no more than war zones.

Printed in Great Britain
by Amazon